CHERISH AND THE DUKE

The Silver Dukes
Book 1

by
Meara Platt

ARE YOU SIGNED UP FOR DRAGONBLADE'S BLOG?

You'll get the latest news and information on exclusive giveaways, exclusive excerpts, coming releases, sales, free books, cover reveals and more.

Check out our complete list of authors, too!

No spam, no junk. That's a promise!

Sign Up Here

www.dragonbladepublishing.com

Dearest Reader;

Thank you for your support of a small press. At Dragonblade Publishing, we strive to bring you the highest quality Historical Romance from some of the best authors in the business. Without your support, there is no 'us', so we sincerely hope you adore these stories and find some new favorite authors along the way.

Happy Reading!

CEO, Dragonblade Publishing

The Dance of Love
The Miracle of Love
The Remembrance of Love (Novella)

Dark Gardens Series
Garden of Shadows
Garden of Light
Garden of Dragons
Garden of Destiny
Garden of Angels

The Farthingale Series
If You Wished For Me (Novella)

The Lyon's Den Series
Kiss of the Lyon
The Lyon's Surprise
Lyon in the Rough

Pirates of Britannia Series
Pearls of Fire

De Wolfe Pack: The Series
Nobody's Angel
Kiss an Angel
Bhrodi's Angel

Also from Meara Platt
Aislin
All I Want for Christmas

CHAPTER ONE

Shoreham Manor
Brighton, England
August 1817

*D*EAR HEAVEN, HE *is gorgeous.*

Lady Cherish Northam stared at Gawain, Duke of Bromleigh, who had just arrived at Shoreham Manor, the Brighton estate of her dearest friend and neighbor, Lady Shoreham. He strode into the parlor with his two friends, also dukes, and all three of them graying at the temples. These men were known throughout the *ton* as the Silver Dukes, and Cherish now understood what all the fuss surrounding them was about. They weren't so much silver as *silverish*, for there were only hints of gray shot through their hair and none of them looked at all feeble.

A buzz of excitement filled the air as others noticed them.

They had arrived fashionably late to Lady Shoreham's week-long house party, striding into the room with all the arrogance of warriors just returned from battle. Lady Shoreham, who stood beside Cherish, now frowned. "So typical of those beasts to purposely make a grand entrance. Now all the ladies are going to fuss and flutter over them because they are dukes and too handsome to ignore."

"Is that so terrible, Fiona?" Cherish asked. "Was this not the point of your house party, to match unmarried young ladies to

1

eligible gentlemen?"

"Yes, but these three are confirmed bachelors, and it will take more than a week to wear them down." She tapped a finger to her lips as she stared at them. "But wouldn't it be fun if we managed it?"

"We? Oh, no." Cherish's eyes rounded in surprise. "Fiona, do not get any silly ideas into your head, especially about me."

"You are my dearest friend," Fiona said with a little sniff. "I would never do anything to hurt you."

Cherish trusted Fiona. In fact, she adored her. But she could also tell that her friend was plotting something.

Dear heaven.

She hoped Fiona was not thinking to match her to one of those *ton* gods.

"Oh, drat," Fiona said with a huff. "The ladies are already fluttering around them. What a nuisance. And just look at how those rascals are eating up the attention. They will ruin my party because no lady will pay attention to the other gentlemen while busy swooning over those old dogs. What gall, showing up late. They did this on purpose to rile me, I'm sure. I ought to toss them out on their vaunted backsides."

Cherish laughed. "Why did you invite them if they were only going to rile you? And especially if they are not of a mind to marry."

"I had to. Bromleigh is a cousin of mine, and we are on a mission."

Cherish wanted to ask what sort of mission, but they were interrupted as the three dukes now marched toward them with smiles on their faces. She meant to ease away, but Fiona grabbed her hand. "Stay right here, Cherish. I have need of you."

"What for? Surely you do not need me to—"

"Gawain!" Fiona cried with abundant cheer, giving her cousin, the stunning, dark-haired one with a hint of silver at his temples and striking green eyes, a kiss on the cheek as he reached their side.

"Sorry we're late, Fiona." He bussed her cheek in return. "Camborne's horse threw a shoe and it took us forever to find a farrier to repair it."

"I suppose there were serving maids to comfort you while you waited at the nearest tavern," Fiona muttered. "You had better be on your best behavior here, or I will never forgive you."

The other two dukes now joined them in time to hear her grumbling.

"Och, no lassies for us," Malcolm, Duke of Camborne, assured her. "We've sworn off them. Well, I have for now. It'll be off to Scotland and fishing next for me. Alone, I assure ye. I'll be having no theatrics from a fish."

Cherish had read in the gossip rags about this duke's latest fiasco with some actress, but she kept her expression blank. It was not her place to approve or disapprove of his behavior. She disapproved, of course.

Connor, Duke of Lynton, nodded as he stepped forward to give Lady Shoreham a kiss on the cheek. "I have my own theatrics to attend to," he said with a light groan. "My children are acting up again. I fear I will have to cut short my visit and return to Lynton Grange to see what they have done to their latest nanny. I hope to still find her alive."

Fiona appeared genuinely concerned. "Oh dear. When will you go, Connor? But yes, you must go to your children. They are most important and you mustn't neglect them."

The Duke of Lynton laughed. "Neglect them? I cannot be away from them for more than a week or two before they act out. I suppose it is their way of telling me to come home, which I will do tomorrow. But I wanted to see you first. It has been too long since…well, since you lost your Albert. I'm sorry I did not visit sooner."

"You've had your own troubles," she said with genuine sincerity. "How are you managing on the whole?"

"Apparently quite badly, if you ask my children. However, I think I am doing well. And you?"

"I am managing, mostly because of the kindness of good friends." She now turned to Cherish, who had remained beside her despite her wish to run away from these daunting men. "Lady Cherish Northam is my neighbor and dearest friend. You might have known her late father, the Earl of Northam? He was a lovely man and not to be mistaken for his toad of a brother, who recently inherited the title. Well, he is a half-brother who can only be described as despicable."

"*Fiona,*" Cherish said in an urgent whisper, wishing her friend was not so vocal in her opinions.

She tried not to blush as each duke in turn bowed over her hand, the Duke of Bromleigh being the last to greet her and somehow neglecting to let go of her. "Lady Cherish, it is an honor," he said in a husky rumble that shot tingles through her. "None of us were well acquainted with your father, but he was reputed to be an excellent man. Seems you are cut from the same cloth. My cousin speaks very highly of you."

Dear heaven, this Silver Duke was devastatingly handsome and quite dangerous. What had Fiona told him about her? Why had she told him *anything*?

"Thank you, Your Grace." She held her smile, waiting for him to release her hand. When he did not, she finally slipped it out of his grasp. "I ought to leave you to catch up with each other. I am only in the way."

"Stay, Lady Cherish," the Duke of Bromleigh said, his gaze lingering on her with enough heat to melt her insides. Was this duke eyeing her for a meal? Well, she had no intention of becoming the latest gullible lady to satisfy his appetite. "My cousin is obviously busy, so why don't you take me around to make introductions?"

She swallowed hard. "Me? You must forgive me, Your Grace. I do not know most of these guests. You see, I have not been to London in quite a while. Not since I was a little girl."

He frowned. "Were you never presented at St. James?"

"No."

Fiona took it upon herself to embellish Cherish's response. "Lady Cherish had her hands full managing her father's estate when she ought to have been making her debut. My dear Albert and I offered to sponsor her at the time, since her parents were not in good health and could not manage the London whirl."

His frown deepened. "Did they refuse?"

Cherish cleared her throat. "No, *I* refused. I am an only child and all they had. They were my heart and my life. I could not leave them in their time of need."

His expression softened. "I see. And what of now? Will the new Earl of Northam sponsor you?"

"No," Fiona cut in, her tone incensed. "He is an ogre, Gawain. Utterly detestable. Why he—"

"Fiona," Cherish whispered once more. "*Please.*"

She did not need her dirty linen exposed to these strangers. Besides, she was too old now to make a debut. Standing among all the fresh young partridges would only make her look ridiculous.

"Lady Cherish, I see your throat is parched. So is mine." The Duke of Bromleigh held out his arm to her. "Come onto the terrace with me and we shall have a lemonade." He gave her no chance to protest, wrapping her arm in his and then placing a hand over hers to make certain she did not dart away. "My friends will not be here long, and I am sure they would prefer to chat with Lady Shoreham without us."

Cherish thought his excuse was utter nonsense, but did not protest, since others were on the terrace and there was a refreshing breeze off the sea. She had to admit, the odor of sweating bodies and stale perfume was a bit overpowering in the parlor. Even though the doors and windows had been thrown open, there were too many guests packed in here to allow the breeze to properly circulate.

As for this duke, despite his having just arrived after a long ride, his scent was divine. A mix of bay spices and male heat. A bead of sweat trailed down his neck. Cherish blushed as she watched it slowly slide along his skin.

She wanted to put a finger to it. Perhaps take out her handkerchief and gently dab it dry.

Or put her lips to it and taste it.

Dear heaven. What would he think of that?

Probably nothing at all, since he must be used to women fawning over him. He had to know how the fairer sex responded to him. He was tall and powerfully built, somehow managing to look exquisite despite his long journey and the heat of the day.

She groaned inwardly, hating to think she was no better than the mob of silly ladies who simpered over him. But she could not blame them, for there was a ruggedness to this man she found irresistible.

Everyone turned to watch them as he escorted her onto the terrace. What did he want with her? The other ladies surely were wondering the same.

He motioned for one of the footmen to bring them lemonade and then led her to a bench under a shade tree just beyond the terrace. They were now in Fiona's garden surrounded by a soft breeze that carried the lemony scent of roses from a nearby arbor.

There was nothing improper about their sitting together, since others were strolling on the grounds and they were in full view of the parlor, yet it all felt exceedingly improper because she was with *him*. "Tell me more about yourself, Lady Cherish."

She pursed her lips, not liking this one bit. "Your Grace, I am sure this will sound impertinent, but why do you wish to know anything about me?"

He arched an eyebrow and laughed. "You do not like that I am paying you attention?"

"Not at all, to be truthful." Honestly, would a hen be pleased to find a fox licking his lips while staring down at her in the henhouse? It was no different for her to be caught under the assessing gaze of this handsome fox.

"Why not? I expect every young lady here is wishing at this moment to exchange places with you."

"Modest fellow, aren't you?" Oh, she ought to have kept her mouth shut. He would now take insult, and Fiona would be irritated with her for offending him within minutes of his arrival. She rose, muttering something about the need to excuse herself.

He rose along with her, his eyes agleam as he caught her wrist gently and held her back. "Stay, Lady Cherish."

"I'm afraid I cannot. Will you let me go?"

"No." His laughter was deep and rich, as divinely husky as his voice. "Forgive me if I am too forward. You are right to rebuke me. It is easy to be full of myself when all I receive is adulation. But I am glad you are not like the others. It is refreshing to chat with someone as sensible as you."

Cherish shook her head. "No, actually, quite the opposite is true. If I were sensible, I would have grabbed the chance for a Season or two and found myself a biddable husband."

"Biddable?"

"Yes, someone who would have allowed me to stay with my parents to nurse them and not made a fuss about it. Someone who…" She sighed. "Well, it did not happen."

"And now you are in a coil because your father has broken your heart by leaving everything to the new earl, including a trust fund reportedly set up for you that he controls."

She stared at him in surprise. "How did you know? Oh, of course. Lady Shoreham wrote to you about my circumstances. How much did she tell you?"

He arched an eyebrow.

By his expression, Cherish gathered he had been told everything. "And now that I am utterly humiliated, I hope you will excuse me."

He would not let her go. "No, I am not of a mind to excuse you. In fact, I would like you to sit with me and tell me more about yourself."

His hold remained gentle but firm.

"Why in heaven's name do you care? Well, I don't suppose you really do. But if you think I am now some sad spinster who will be an easy mark for you, then think again."

His smile was devastatingly appealing. "I was not considering that at all. How old are you? Twenty? Well, probably older than that, although you do not look it. Twenty-two? Twenty-three?"

"I turn twenty-five next month." She was now blushing furiously and wishing he would just walk away and leave her alone.

"And your trust fund will not be released to you until you turn thirty, or is it thirty-five? Or unless you marry?"

Cherish felt completely stripped of her dignity by this man. Why was he asking her these questions? The conversation was completely inappropriate. More important, why was she fool enough to stand here and listen?

Well, she had to admit that despite his roguish reputation and impossibly good looks, there was something quite trustworthy about him. She did not know why she should think so. Perhaps because there was no hint of condescension in his voice.

In fact, his deep rumble was quite soothing. He also had a broad and lovely shoulder to cry on. She feared to succumb to his comforting manner.

No, she would never dare get that close to him.

"You seem to know all there is to know about me," she said, no doubt sounding a little snappish. "Now, you really must let me go, Your Grace. I doubt we have anything more to say to each other, unless you wish to save me from my desperate straits by offering to marry me. Do you?"

She was certain that comment would chase him off.

Why was the wretch still smiling at her?

He appeared quite relaxed and certainly amused as he said, "In truth, I am almost tempted."

She laughed at the sheer impossibility of it. "Dear heaven, you are a haughty fellow."

His expression turned serious. "I am not going to offer to marry you, but I know someone who will. I am speaking of my nephew, Lord Reginald Burton. He is my sister's only son and my heir. Have you met him?"

Cherish swallowed hard as she nodded. "The one who laughs like a woodpecker?"

Bromleigh winced. "Only when he is drunk."

"Which he has been since arriving at Lady Shoreham's two days ago. I'm sure you'll find him off in the study with some of the younger reprobates digging into her stock of brandy."

"Ah, then you have met him." He raked a hand through his hair. "He is nice looking, isn't he?"

Cherish was either going to hit this arrogant man or choose to go along with the humor in the absurd situation. She chose the humor because she was not a violent person and would never strike anyone. "Did you plan this ambush of me with Lady Shoreham?"

"I wouldn't call it an ambush," he replied.

"Oh, then what would you call whatever it is that you are doing?"

"Matchmaking," he said in all seriousness. "Fiona is my cousin and sort of a godmother to Reginald. We are worried about him. He is a good lad, but perhaps immature for his age. At the age of six and twenty, he ought to be thinking like a man and building a respectable future for himself. We were hoping that marriage to a beautiful, sensible young lady like you might appeal to him and mold him into the good man he has it in him to be."

She curtsied, bowing low and keeping her gaze on him as she said, "Well done, Your Grace. You have thoroughly humiliated me, completely demolished my pride and self-respect. I thank you for considering me as the sacrificial lamb, but I must decline." She straightened and glowered at him. "Do me the courtesy of *never* speaking to me again."

His mouth gaped open.

Was this man serious? Had he believed she would leap at the chance to marry his wastrel nephew just because her life was utterly abysmal at the moment?

Well, perhaps she was the idiot. But she could not bring herself to sell her soul to some dolt who would never love her.

She strode back into the parlor and sought out Fiona, hoping to draw her aside for a serious conversation. Fortunately, she happened to find her in the hallway with her housekeeper, the very able Mrs. Harris, discussing room arrangements. Cherish approached as soon as the housekeeper hurried off. "Fiona, how could you do this to me? I thought we were friends."

"Do what, Cherish?" She appeared genuinely confused.

"Foist me on your nephew, Reginald Burton. Will you deny this was your scheme all along?"

Fiona's eyes widened in surprise. "Bromleigh told you that? Lord, he is such an ass."

"For telling me the truth about your intentions? Yes, he is a supreme ass and impossibly arrogant, but at least he is honest about your schemes."

Fiona emitted a trill of laughter. "*His* scheme."

Cherish eyed her warily. "Only his?"

"Good heavens, you don't think I would ever consider matching you with Reggie. You are completely unsuited to each other. However, Bromleigh is determined for the lad to marry someone strong of heart, reliable, intelligent, and honest. Good looking, too, since Reggie has an eye for the ladies and would not look twice at someone he did not deem beautiful. I immediately thought of you. Apparently, Bromleigh believes you have all these qualifications. It certainly did not take him long to approve. One glance at you and he knew."

"But—"

"I knew it as well, but that is because we have been friends for quite some time now. And before you berate me, just be aware that I quickly dismissed you as a possibility for Reggie."

"Thank goodness for that," Cherish muttered.

"Indeed, you are far too educated for him. Oh, I love him dearly. But he can be a bit of a clot at times, don't you agree? I put your name forward and am only pretending to go along with Bromleigh's scheme because...well, because my scheme is something altogether different."

"Yours?" Cherish clasped her hands, now worried about what Fiona had in mind.

"Do you really think I would burden you with Reggie? Oh, he is a good-hearted boy, but I fear this is all he may ever be. Sweet, fun loving, and not nearly as sharp as Bromleigh."

"How do you know? Has Bromleigh ever given Reggie a task that would test his mettle?" Although she did not know the duke or his nephew, Cherish understood how it felt to be living under another's control and how daunting it could be.

Perhaps Reggie was behaving like a schoolboy because he had never been given the chance to be anything more.

Or was she giving him too much credit because she felt so trapped under the weight of her own uncle's control?

Fiona sighed. "I know Bromleigh will see him set up well and leave him in the capable hands of his best advisors when the time comes. But that will not be for quite a while yet. My cousin may be a Silver Duke, but he has a lot of life still in him. Don't you think? Goodness, he is only forty."

"And your point?"

"I do not want you matched with Reggie. Good gracious, you are far too smart for him. But it is imperative that you agree to gaining Reggie's affections."

"Fiona, you are making no sense. Why should I agree to your cousin's scheme? First of all, I am not Reggie's type at all and do not stand a prayer of gaining his affections."

"You are very pretty, Cherish. I'm sure every man thinks so. But as I've said, you and Reggie would not suit."

Cherish nodded. "Second of all, I would not even know how to go about gaining any man's affections. Yes, it is my fault for never taking lessons in such matters. But the fact remains, I do not know how to flirt."

"Which is why you are so perfect." Fiona glanced around furtively and then cast Cherish a beaming smile. "This is what you will say to Bromleigh when you approach him to tell him you have reconsidered and will accept the challenge."

"I am to admit that I do not know how to flirt?" Cherish burst out laughing. "And why would I tell him that?"

"Because he will never be able to resist the challenge. More important, he will never be able to resist you. Do you not see where I am going yet? I want you for Bromleigh. Is it not obvious? I mean to make you *his* wife."

CHAPTER TWO

"LADY CHERISH IS perfect," Gawain said, smiling as Fiona approached him later that evening shortly before supper was announced. He stood toward the rear of the parlor, nursing a brandy and hoping to avoid the throng of guests now gathered for a welcome reception to start off his cousin's week-long house party.

Well, the party had started two days ago and the reception was to celebrate his arrival and that of his two friends. In truth, nobody really cared what reason was given for this party so long as there was ample libation and an orchestra to provide music for a night of dancing after supper was served.

The large glass doors leading onto the terrace were open to allow in a gentle breeze off the sea, and Gawain had moved closer to those doors in order to inhale the bracing sea air. It was a hot day and the sun had been shining with no reprieve until now.

"Did I not tell you she would be just the one?" Fiona replied with a smirk.

"Yes, but I dared not suppose you would come up with the right girl so easily." He refused to expound on just how perfect he thought Lady Cherish was, for Fiona might make too much of it.

Lady Cherish had certainly caught his attention.

She was physically beautiful in a quiet way that wrapped around a man's soul, a point in her favor and undeniable. Her hair was the color of molten honey and her eyes were a dark, brandy brown. Deep, rich, and intelligent. Indeed, he could go down the list of her attributes and find them all to his liking. Soft lips. Creamy complexion. Generous bosom and a slender frame.

She was also sharp witted, sensible, and could stand up for herself.

Yet despite that streak of independence, there was something fragile and lovely about her. Perhaps it was because he knew her situation and understood how frustrated a competent woman like Cherish must be feeling while under the thumb of an oaf like the new Earl of Northam.

She was a trapped bird, a lovely nightingale in a cage, unable to escape due to circumstances partly of her own making. But he could never fault her for choosing loyalty to her parents over her own Society debut. That her father had not trusted her to manage her own funds after his demise must have stung deeply, especially since she had shown herself worthy by running the Northam estate when he was no longer up to the task. Why had he left her to the mercy of an obviously uncaring uncle?

Well, her father's failing was now serving Gawain's purpose. Reggie would flourish in the hands of a woman like Lady Cherish.

"Speaking of Cherish, where is she?" Fiona craned her neck to search the gathering. "I thought she had come down ahead of me, but I don't see her here."

"She slipped past a cluster of guests a few minutes ago and is hiding out on the terrace," Gawain said. "I've been watching her."

Fiona's eyes widened. "You have?"

Gawain chuckled. "Surprised?"

"Yes, I thought her earlier rejection might have put you off."

"Actually, it had quite the opposite effect. I like that she knows how to stand her ground. She was honest with me and I admire her for it. She is a bit sensitive and feels things a bit too much, but is this not better than hiding her intentions behind a false smile?" He glanced across the room. "Would any of these young ladies have been so forthright with me?"

Fiona graced him with a knowing smile. "No, they would have fussed and fluttered over you, indulged you if they thought there was profit in it for them." She looked around and then eyed him curiously. "I am surprised to see you standing alone."

He shrugged. "I might have been scowling and chased everyone away."

Fiona laughed. "It must have been some scowl."

"I suppose I could have been more polite, but I do not wish to get caught up in this marriage business."

"It is a business," Fiona agreed. "But a husband is a husband. If those young ladies cannot have you, then any one of them would be amenable to settling for Reggie as the next best thing."

"Which is why they are unacceptable for Reggie. Lady Cherish is not so mercenary. I think I will have to get to know her better if I am to warm her up to the idea of Reggie. She does not come across as grasping."

"She is kind and generous. In truth, I wish she would be a little tougher and think more about her own interests. How else is she to escape her uncle's clutches?"

Gawain looked toward the terrace again, his heart unexpectedly tugging as he noticed Cherish standing alone, her slender form illuminated by the golden light of the setting sun. She was incredibly pretty, and he found it difficult to tear his gaze away. Her hair gleamed as rich and beautiful as a flame-gold sunburst. "I am going to try again."

Fiona's eyes rounded in surprise. "But she refused you the first time. What makes you think she will reconsider?"

Gawain grinned. "I can be persuasive."

Fiona sighed and shook her head. "She is my dearest friend and I will never forgive you if you hurt her, Gawain. She isn't merely a mission. She may seem resilient, but she's quite soft on the inside. Tread carefully with her heart."

He arched an eyebrow. "Reggie's the one who needs to appreciate her. I'll keep an eye on him to make certain he does not take advantage."

He left the parlor and strode out onto the terrace in time to see Lady Cherish skitter away into the garden. No doubt she had noticed his approach and chose to run off rather than face him.

Well, he would deal with her as gently as he might any skittish filly.

He ambled slowly toward her, but she wasn't having any of it. Instead, she frowned at him and started toward the beach. Shoreham Manor was on the water and had its own private sand beach within a sheltered cove.

In truth, this was a lovely estate and quite a pleasant reprieve from London's summer heat. He would enjoy spending more than a mere week here. An entire summer would do him nicely, swimming or riding in the mornings, and hiking in the afternoons.

But first, he needed to deal with Cherish and gain her cooperation.

Gawain folded his arms across his chest as he continued to watch the girl scurry away. He knew she could escape no farther than the beach. He would follow her into the water if had to, assuming she were so foolish as to take her escape that far.

But he knew she was no fool and was not going to leap into the water.

She came to a halt at the top of the stairs leading down to the beach, seemingly lost in thought as she stared across the crystal-blue waters. However, he had no doubt she was acutely aware of his approach.

The wind was dying down, so there was hardly a ripple upon the water. Waves gently washed to shore with the softest *whoosh*. Several birds flew overhead, occasionally breaking the silence with their caws as they soared and dove against a deep blue sky.

He stopped beside her, ignoring her frown when she turned to acknowledge his presence. "Lady Cherish, we started off badly. I did not mean to embarrass you. Why do we not take a step backward and simply start again? You might find me less of an ogre as we get acquainted."

She fumbled with her hands, first clasping them in front of her, and then setting them at her sides.

Well, Fiona had said she was shy, so perhaps the girl found his attention more disconcerting than he realized. Had he been rude to put his cards on the table within minutes of meeting her? He merely wanted to be honest, certainly did not wish to lie to her. He also did not want her thinking he was interested in her. Was this not considerate of him?

"Yes, let's get acquainted," she agreed, surprising him. "The sooner we get to know each other, the sooner you'll realize how foolish your venture is. Might I suggest you stop meddling in the lives of others and simply look out for yourself?"

He laughed. "Is your tongue always this sharp, or have you honed it just for me?"

"I do not mean to speak harshly, but you are a man used to getting your way in all things. Is this not so? I suppose it is because you are always fawned over by the ladies and sought out by those who want something from you. You plow ahead like a determined bull and will not listen unless someone stops you by hitting you over the head... Verbally, I mean. I would never actually hit you."

Gawain used this remark as an opening to tell her a little about himself, hoping it might soften her. "Walk down to the beach with me and we'll talk. Did Fiona not tell you about my upbringing?"

"No."

"So this is why you assume my life has always been pampered and soft."

She glanced at him, obviously assessing his looks. "You are not soft, that much is apparent. I also know you served in the military, so your life could not have been easy for you while in service to the Crown, even if you were supplied with all the luxuries appropriate for your noble rank."

"There are few luxuries supplied on a battlefield. As for my noble rank... Yes, I was born the son of a duke, but I was never expected to step into the title. I am the youngest of four children."

"Youngest?"

He nodded. "I had two older brothers and a sister who was Reggie's mother."

She turned to him in surprise. "I did not realize…"

He gestured toward his face. "I did not gain these scars or the wear lines on my brow from living an easy life. I've spent most of my years in military service, not just a few pampered moments, as you seem to think. It was never my wish nor my expectation to become the Duke of Bromleigh. But with the deaths of my father and brothers all in short succession, I suddenly found myself in this position. When my sister passed, I also took on the responsibility of seeing to Reggie's care."

She cast him a pained look. "Oh, I see."

"Unfortunately, Reggie's character was mostly formed by the time I stepped in. But there is much good in him that can still be salvaged." He shook his head and hastened to press on when he saw her tense at the mention of his nephew. "Do not be so quick to judge any of us. I would not be bothering with Reggie if I did not think he had significant merit."

"You are right." She nodded. "Forgive me."

"I did not take offense. The men in your life have disappointed you, so you have reason to be wary. As for me, I spent most of my life as the ignored third son until suddenly coming into the title and overnight becoming everyone's darling. I was in my early thirties by then. It is the insincerity of it all that galls me. I do not think I shall ever grow used to it."

"But are you not perpetuating that insincerity by trying to match me to your nephew? How does this help anyone?" She cleared her throat. "Why do you not marry and sire heirs? Then your nephew will not be a concern for you."

They had walked down the stairs and were now about to step onto the sand. "No, I have no desire to be a sixty-year-old father to a son about to enter university. My time has come and gone."

She shook her head. "I beg to disagree. Facing an empty future is no way to live one's life. Well, I am one to talk, since I have done nothing to help myself. But there is nothing stopping you. With your present wealth and title, you have only to crook your finger to have any woman you want for a wife. The most beautiful. The wealthiest. The most charming. Even a royal princess, if that is your aspiration."

She paused and stared at her slippers. "Do you mind if I walk barefoot? It is shockingly forward of me, but I cannot abide the thought of those grains of sand getting into my slippers."

He grinned. "Go right ahead. I am hardly one easily shocked."

She sat on the bottom step and daintily took her slippers off. She then left them neatly on the bottom step and stood by his side. A sense of warmth flowed through him, an odd feeling of... He wasn't certain what it was, only that he liked having Cherish beside him.

He thought she would start hurling questions at him, but was surprised when they merely walked along the beach in companionable silence. She darted close to the waves, and then darted back as they swept to shore, her smile enchanting as she indulged in the simple pleasure.

He enjoyed watching her, but kept to the sand, since he was not about to take off his boots or allow them to get wet. To his own surprise, he found himself smiling at her in return, liking her ability to take genuine delight in a mere stroll along the beach.

Sunlight caressed her face, and he could not seem to take his gaze off her.

In truth, she was such a pretty thing.

His own tension receded, for walking beside her was quite pleasant. However, he was never going to accomplish his purpose if they did not talk.

He cleared his throat, seeing that he would have to take the laboring oar in this conversation. "Have you and Fiona been neighbors long?"

She darted close in order to avoid a wave that came in suddenly and nipped at her toes. "Yes."

He lifted her slightly as he drew her back to avoid the hem of her gown getting soaked. "How long?"

She smiled in gratitude as she looked up at him with those big brandy eyes of hers. "Very long."

He sighed. "Lady Cherish…"

Bollocks.

He was going to kiss her if she did not turn away.

To his relief, she resumed walking along the sand. "I suppose merely bobbing my head in response to your questions will not do."

He chuckled. "It is hard to hold a conversation when only one party is forthcoming."

"Which leaves me a little confused. I know this will sound impertinent, Your Grace, but why are you still bothering with me when I told you I will not agree to your scheme for Reggie?"

The wind blew her curls loose so that a few fluttered about her ears. On instinct, he reached out and tucked a strand or two behind her ear. "I think the question to ask is, why are you so reluctant to better your circumstances? Marriage to Reggie would offer you a way out of your situation. Or has Fiona exaggerated the problem between you and your uncle?"

She sighed. "No, she hasn't exaggerated it. With each passing day, I am further reduced in the household. My clothes are several years old now and would be out of style if not for the alterations Fiona had her seamstress make for me. As for this week, I am here because my uncle and his family happen to be visiting his wife's brother. They left me behind, of course."

Gawain tamped down his irritation over her treatment. It would not do to allow his feelings to become entangled. "I think you are going to haul off and hit me as I ask this next question," he said. "But it must be asked."

He was a big man, and she looked quite little standing beside him, but there was also a lovely strength to her that made them more than equals. She frowned at him. "Are you going to insult me by bribing me now?"

Yes, he was.

But dealing with Cherish required battle strategy, so he was never going to admit he intended to do just that. "I wish you would not look upon my attempt to help your situation as a bribe. Shouldn't you be more concerned for yourself? Fiona suggested to me that you needed to think more about yourself. What is so wrong with that?"

She nodded, looking not at all angry. "You are right. I should. It is something that has become increasingly hard for me to ignore. Perhaps it is foolish of me to hold on to the dream of love. My parents were a love match. I wish for the same. Did you ever hold out such hope for yourself?"

He shook his head. "No. As the third son, I was destined for the military and just assumed I would be shot on a battlefield someday. Once I moved beyond my foolish youth, I never gave much consideration to falling in love. It is an impediment in battle because it makes you think of what you might lose and distracts you as you rush forward in the face of cannon fire. A moment's hesitation can be the difference between life and death. I found it was easier never to burden myself with such fancies."

"But it has all changed for you now." She looked straight at him as she spoke, their gazes meeting, and neither of them seemed capable of turning away. "Has there never been anyone who filled your heart? Who took your breath away and made you want to spend the rest of your life with that person?"

Gawain felt as though she were reaching into his soul. He did not like this feeling of opening himself up. Everything had been denied to him before, all possibilities for happiness. Now it was too late for him. He did not like her jarring him out of the comfortable independence he had settled on for the remainder of his life.

"No," he repeated, knowing it was a lie. "Nothing has changed for me, Lady Cherish. The years have taken their toll.

There is nothing of the hopeful boy left in me. In truth, I never had the luxury of idle, poetic thoughts or falling into raptures over a woman. That I am now a duke does not change the man I am inside. Who I am is now set in stone."

"No one is suggesting that you change the essence of yourself. In truth, it probably enhances your appeal to women."

He laughed and shook his head.

She frowned at him again. "Why are you so determined to keep yourself cut off?"

The question troubled him more than he would let on. "This conversation is not about me. I have no need to be saved, but you do. What would it take for you to consider marrying Reggie? And don't punch me. This is just as important a question for you as it is for me."

"I wasn't going to punch you," she muttered, pursing her lips. "You are asking me to be mercenary, and it is completely against my nature."

"I am asking you to tell me what you wish. I am not agreeing to grant you any of it. I just want to hear what is important to you."

"You answer first," she said. "If you were of a mind to marry, what would you wish for in a wife?"

Her curls had blown out of place again, so he reached out once more and tucked a few stray ones behind her ear. But touching her was not a good idea, especially since he was not as unaffected by the girl as he'd expected himself to be. "I never allowed myself to wish for something that I thought was out of my reach."

"But you are now the Duke of Bromleigh and nothing is out of your reach. Nor has it been out of reach for you these past several years. You can make those wishes come true for yourself. If you could have one wish granted, what would it be?"

To kiss you.

Well, that would be a disaster. Cherish was the one girl he could not touch. Not even Reggie, as much of a clot as that boy was at times, would have her then.

"I don't know," he said more harshly than intended. "To be left alone, I suppose. That would be my wish."

She shook her head and cast him an admonishing look. But her expression was soft, so he knew she was not trying to criticize him. "We are a woeful pair, aren't we? Your choice is almost as bad as mine. Yours is a terrible and sad state of affairs."

"Not at all. Terrible and sad is making the wrong selection in a wife and having to live with the mistake for the rest of my existence."

"So it is easier for you to make no choice at all?" She was still frowning at him, in a delightfully tender way, if such a thing were possible. "I will make a deal with you. I think we must both give this question some thought. I shall sleep on it tonight and let you know what I would wish for, assuming I agreed to consider Reggie as a husband."

"That is fair enough." He was not going to push her by suggesting she and Reggie could be a love match. Even he knew it was not possible. Cherish would be good for his nephew, but those two were never going to fall into raptures over each other. "We had better head back to the others," he said. "The dinner bell will sound shortly, and there will be talk if we show up late."

She shook her head and laughed, her impish grin charming as she regarded him. "Ha, that would be a scandal broth. The two of us caught together on the day of your arrival. That would shoot your plans for Reggie to bits."

"It would not be funny at all," he said quite soberly. "I have no intention of seeing you ruined by gossip."

"Especially since you would not do the honorable thing and marry me." She cast him that look again, the one that seemed to reach into his soul. "Yet I think it would prey upon your sense of honor if you were not to step up. I wonder what you would do if it ever came to that?"

"Do not put it to the test."

"I would never trick you into a compromising situation. You

are the one who followed me down here. I was trying to escape you. Even so, I would not demand you marry me. But I suppose that is me being foolish again, for that scandal would give my uncle all the excuse he needed to further demote me in the family's standing."

"All the more reason why you must seriously consider Reggie and not dally over your decision. We have only the week to make this happen. Reggie and I return to London once the party is over." He held her lightly by the elbow and walked her back to the beach steps.

The girl looked as though she wanted to cry.

Well, she wasn't really a girl. Cherish was a woman and had the luscious curves to prove it. But it was time she stepped up to the realities of her spinster future and made those hard decisions for herself.

"My father was inconsolable," she said, taking a seat on the step and dusting the sand off her feet, "already grieving the loss of my mother before she passed on. Having seen this bond develop between two people, it is very hard for me to give up on the hope of finding it for myself."

"Eternal love?"

She nodded. "The sort that silly girls like me wish desperately for themselves. I cannot even consider myself a girl anymore. I am too old now."

"You are still young enough, and beautiful. Even if we could not come to an agreement on Reggie, there are other bachelors here. You will never find one to look at you if you continue to hide yourself away."

"Hiding? You think I am hiding?" She shook her head and gave a mirthful laugh. "I know you will not believe me, but this *is* me making an effort to be seen. I suppose I am rather bad at it."

"Yes, you are," he said with a chuckle, and shook his head. "Granted, I have not been here very long. But I have yet to see you chatting among a circle of friends. Mingling requires you not to be standing alone."

She cast him an impertinent smile. "But I am not alone now. You are here with me."

He laughed again. "I do not count. First of all, I am old enough to be your father... Well, not quite that old, but almost. No, I am a confirmed bachelor. But my nephew—"

"Oh, please. Give me at least the night to mull over the possibility of Reggie. Never once in all my years have I considered marrying someone who laughs like a woodpecker."

This was progress. She hadn't hit him or outright said no.

The dinner bell sounded as they approached the house. In the next moment, a shrill woodpecker laugh emanated from the parlor and carried on the wind to Gawain's ears.

Cherish shot him a look.

He winced. "I know. Do not say it. I know."

The peahens surrounding his nephew thought his antics were hilarious.

Gawain sighed, for Reggie attaching himself to one of those little dimwits would be a disaster. As they strode in, he counted six young ladies clapping their hands and squealing with glee around the boy.

Gad, could they be more foolish? Or had he become that much of an ogre to frown on every bit of enjoyment? It was a summer house party, after all.

"Uncle! You made it!" The lad came over and gave him a drunken hug.

Gawain hugged his nephew back because, after all, he did love the boy.

Bloody blazes.

He turned to include Cherish in their conversation, but she had quietly slipped away. This was going to be more difficult than he imagined.

Cherish was perfect, of course. But why did Reggie have to be such a clot?

A most amiable one, of course. But still a clot.

Where was Cherish?

CHAPTER THREE

"LORD HELP US, is he to be the next Duke of Bromleigh?" Gawain shook his head and sighed as he, Lynton, and Camborne returned from their early morning ride the following day in time to find Reggie already in the study with several of his bachelor friends, about to break open another bottle of brandy. "What is this country coming to?"

Gawain strode over to his nephew and grabbed the bottle out of his hand. "We haven't even been called to breakfast yet, Reggie. If I catch you tippling before five o'clock this evening, I am going to give you the hiding of your life."

"Uncle! That is unfair. This is a house party. Are we not permitted to misbehave?" Reggie glanced at his indolent friends, who did not look happy with Gawain but were too afraid to complain to his face.

Good, because he was not about to indulge these wastrels.

"I do not care what your friends do. They are not my responsibility, but you are, and I say you are not to misbehave." He raked a hand through his hair in consternation. "Men do not act in this reckless way. Certainly not men who will be expected to shoulder responsibilities. You are to be my heir, so it is time you took your role seriously."

His nephew frowned at him. "Aren't you being harsh?"

"In truth, I have been far too lax with you." Gawain glanced at Lynton and Camborne, both of whom were grinning at him instead of supporting him. He grunted at his two friends before returning his attention to Reggie. "You will destroy all that I and my predecessors have built within a year of your inheriting the dukedom if you continue down this dissolute path."

"I am hardly dissolute. It is just a party and I am enjoying myself. Aren't the ladies lovely? You ought to choose a tempting morsel for yourself and—"

"I am not interested in any of the ladies here."

"But I am, so why are you determined to spoil my fun? What do you propose I do?"

Gawain began to feel exactly like the cantankerous ogre he feared he might become. He met his nephew's gaze and noted his dismayed expression, but refused to soften toward the lad. "Start getting your life in order."

"Here and now? Just how am I supposed to accomplish that? You might have given me fair warning about your purpose. Is it not cruel of you to spring this on me unaware? And unwarranted, in my opinion."

"Fair or not, this is what I am doing, and I will hear no more argument about it from you or any of your friends." He shot Reggie's companions a warning scowl that had them all clamping their mouths shut. "In the short time I have been here, all I've seen you do is behave like a nitwit, drinking too much and ogling every girl you see."

"But they are all so pretty," his nephew said with a pout.

His comment was quickly approved by his companions, who were afraid to speak but did not hesitate to nod. One or two muttered under their breath, quick to point out their favorites among the young ladies.

Gawain was not surprised when not even one mumbled Cherish's name. All these lads were young and foolish.

To his mind, Cherish was easily the standout among all the young ladies present at this party. "Looks fade over time, Reggie. The right wife must offer you more than just a pretty smile. You have to be careful about this, for the woman you marry will be a duchess someday. She will represent the Bromleigh family as much as you will. You cannot marry a peabrain or a wanton."

"Is this why you never married?" his nephew asked, sounding not at all insolent.

This was the thing about Reggie—he was so likeable and did take things to heart. This was why Gawain wanted to ensure he found the right woman to guide his nephew. "My situation was different from yours. I was off fighting battles and never expected to be settled in one place long enough to set up a family. Nor did I ever expect to become a duke. It seems ridiculous for me to go on the hunt now. I am too old. You are to take up the mantle in continuing the family line."

Reggie regarded him with affection and perhaps a touch of pity, something Gawain hated but could not fault the lad when even he looked upon his lost time with regret. "Uncle, you are too hard on yourself. There is not a woman here who would deny you."

"I am not marrying someone young enough to be my daughter. Put it out of your head." What genteel young lady would have him now, with these scars on his face or the gray in his hair? He had no desire to see the cringe in her eyes when she looked at him in the intimacy of their bedchamber. Oh, any sweet young thing would gladly accept his offer of marriage because she wanted to be a duchess. But none of them would want the man he truly was at heart. He had no doubt that bedroom door would slam shut against him as soon as he bred heirs off his chosen wife.

No, that humiliation was not for him.

He set the bottle of brandy back in the cabinet and herded the young bucks out of the study. "Go have your breakfast. I'm sure there are some lovely ladies already there by now enjoying their morning cup of tea. Reggie, try not to make an ass of yourself."

"Thank you, Uncle. Your faith in me warms my heart." Reggie marched out with his friends, leaving Gawain alone in the study with his own companions.

Camborne slapped him on the back. "Was that insolence I

detected in Reggie's last remark? Good for him. It is time he showed a little spine."

Lynton laughed. "I would say something, too. But my children are going to rake me over the fire as soon as I get home, so I am hardly one to comment. Losing a nanny just now is the worst possible thing to happen. My hellions are going to burn down the house if this latest one walks out and I am not back in time to stop them. To add to my misery, my mother has invited a circle of her friends and their lovely daughters to Lynton Grange, no doubt in furtherance of her relentless efforts to marry me off. I will politely endure, but I stand with you, Bromleigh. No wife for me."

"Aye," Camborne said with a shake of his head. "I canno' even choose my mistresses right. No, there'll be no permanent commitments for me, either."

As more guests began to make their way downstairs, Gawain and his friends joined them in the dining room for a quick bite. He was casually dressed, having just come back from that early morning ride with his friends. But house parties were generally relaxed affairs, so he did not feel as though any of them stuck out inappropriately. He would retire upstairs to properly wash and dress for the day's activities after he ate. The early morning air and exercise had left him famished.

Gawain noticed Cherish was not down yet.

Frowning, he served himself from the salvers lined up along the buffet, piling on the eggs and sausages, then requested a footman to bring him a cup of coffee. "At once, Your Grace."

He settled beside Fiona and was not surprised when one of the silly geese with flaxen hair and big blue eyes took the seat on the other side of him. "Good morning, Your Grace," she said with a giggle.

"Good morning." He forgot her name, blast it. But these young girls all looked the same to him with their baby faces and flirtatious manner.

She batted her eyelashes at him. "It is a lovely day for a picnic,

29

is it not?"

"Yes, just perfect." Dear heaven, what was her name?

He must have looked perplexed, because Fiona shot him a knowing smirk before leaning over and joining in the conversation. "Lady Margaret, each lady shall have a basket with the name of a gentleman written in it. That gentleman is to be your partner for the picnic."

Ah, Lady Margaret.

Right.

He hoped Fiona had not assigned him to her.

What was he going to say to this girl who would have been in leading strings when the Peninsular War started and not even a glimmer in the eye of her parents when hostilities arose in the American colonies? Perhaps he was being too harsh, but she did not appear to have anything but air between her ears.

However, that did not stop her from talking at him...incessantly. Drat, she was all giggles and effervescent chirpiness. How did a man survive this onslaught every morning?

No one was more relieved than he when Cherish finally walked in.

She was dressed in a fairly plain gown, but the rose color suited her complexion, as did the hint of lace at the collar and sleeves. Her hair was done up in a loose bun that flattered the fullness of her hair. She had little hoop earrings in her ears, but no other adornment.

She looked beautiful.

He came to his feet to offer his chair, since the table was crowded and most of the seats were already taken. "Please, have mine."

She smiled at him. "I do not wish to kick you out."

"Not at all. I am finished." He glanced down at himself. "Besides, my friends and I only returned a short while ago from our morning ride and are hardly presentable. I understand we are to have a picnic later this morning."

Fiona rose as well. "Yes, and as I've told Lady Margaret, each lady will have the name of a gentleman written in her basket."

Margaret giggled and batted her eyelashes at him again.

Fiona, smirking once more, leaned over and whispered something in Cherish's ear. Cherish blushed as she glanced at him.

He hoped this meant Fiona had placed his name in Cherish's basket. The two of them needed to talk. Now that he had lectured Reggie and hopefully gained the lad's cooperation, he wanted to waste no time in putting Cherish forward as a prospect for wife. But he had to be sure she would agree.

He excused himself, and then strode back to his room to wash and dress for the picnic.

Lynton and Camborne had mentioned they were leaving after breakfast, so he made certain to seek them out as soon as he returned downstairs. He caught them moments after they had said their farewells to Fiona. "Safe journey," he said, giving each a brotherly pat on the back.

"Take care of yourself," Camborne said. "You know the ladies all want you. Watch out for their traps."

Lynton nodded. "These wretched house parties ought to be outlawed."

Gawain grinned. "Aren't we a dour threesome? Yes, I'll be careful. In truth, there isn't much danger. These *ton* diamonds are little more than children, and their mothers are too old. I think I will be safe enough."

Camborne arched an eyebrow. "And what of Lady Cherish? Ye spent quite a bit of time in her company yesterday."

"For the sake of Reggie. She's a good choice for him, don't you think?"

Lynton patted him on the back. "Just remember she is for Reggie."

Gawain frowned. "I am hardly likely to forget."

He watched his friends ride off and waited for them to disappear beyond the entry gates before he rejoined the gathering in Fiona's parlor. Wicker baskets had been set up on long tables along the walls, each having the name of a young lady pinned to the outside.

He paused beside Cherish, who was the only one not giggling, cooing, or squealing in delight. She arched an eyebrow in greeting as he approached. "Are you ready for the battle, Your Grace?" she said. "Every lady in the room hopes your name will be the one in her basket."

"I am not concerned. Knowing Fiona, she has placed my name in hers or yours. Either way, I shall be spared the tedium of having to make conversation with a little goose."

Cherish laughed. "You are a curmudgeon, aren't you?"

He shot her a pained grin. "I suppose I am. Reggie thinks I am a complete ogre."

"Why? Oh, no. What did you say to him?"

"Nothing," he assured her, raising his hands in mock surrender.

"Oh, really? Then why is he frowning at you from across the room?"

Gawain sighed. "I merely spoke to him about his unacceptable behavior. He took it rather well, I'm pleased to report. How has he behaved so far this morning? Do you find him to be more sober? Behaving a little more responsibly?"

Cherish's eyes lit up with mirth. "Do you mean before or after he danced around the parlor with an egret feather on his head?"

He stared at her in dismay.

She laughed heartily. "Oh, your expression is priceless. I am jesting, Your Grace. His behavior has been beyond reproach."

"Blast it, Cherish. You had me going there." He cast her an affectionate smile, liking she felt comfortable enough to tease him.

"Sorry, but I could not resist. Ah, you must excuse me. Fiona is calling us to our baskets. What do you think? Will it be you for me so that we may finish yesterday's conversation? Or is she going straight for pairing me with Reggie?"

To Gawain's relief, Cherish called out his name. Fiona called out Reggie's name.

Poor lad.

Gawain almost felt sorry for Reggie, who obviously wished to be matched to one of the silly, giggling girls. But Gawain and Fiona were not going to let any young lady other than Cherish claim him.

He grabbed hold of their picnic basket and held out his arm to Cherish. "Let's find a shady spot before the others grab them all."

She nodded. "I'm sure there is no shortage of trees. But I would like to be far enough away from the others that we are not overheard."

"Then you've given your situation thought and come to a conclusion?"

She nodded again. "I expect it will be to your liking."

His stomach churned.

Why was he irritated about her bending to his will? She was a good choice for Reggie, and he would be a kind husband to her. "Right, let's go."

They wound up settling on the beach again, since Fiona had her staff set up several open-air tents at lengthy intervals along the stretch of sand. The day was hot and the wind off the water provided a refreshing escape from the heat.

Gawain removed his jacket so that Cherish could sit upon it while he stretched out upon the warm sand and watched her dig into the basket. "There's a tablecloth in here, Your Grace. We can spread it out so that you need not get all those little grains dug into your clothing."

He shook his head. "No, I'm quite comfortable. Besides, the tablecloth is not all that big. It'll be just enough for us to set the food atop it. What's in our basket?"

"Oh, it looks lovely. Chicken...fruit...a loaf of freshly baked bread. Oh, the aroma is heavenly. Cider for me. Looks like ale for you. Silverware and table linens. Are you hungry? I'll set it all out now."

"I am always hungry. Look at the size of me. Do I not look as though I have a hearty appetite?"

"You look quite fit for an old man," she said, purposely tweaking him.

He grimaced. "Ouch."

"You know I am merely teasing you. You are all muscle, as far as I can tell. I suppose that is due to your years of military service. You and your friends were out riding early this morning, so I expect you keep to a fit routine."

He nodded. "I am not used to idling about."

"And now you are determined to work hardiness into your soft nephew?" She drew out the chicken and a knife and began to expertly carve the bird while he poured each of them a drink. "Do you have a favorite part?"

"Breasts, of course," he said.

She blushed as he set a glass of cider beside her.

He took a swig of his ale and then sighed. "You asked; I merely responded. Every man enjoys a good breast…on a chicken. Do not read more into it than there is."

"I wasn't."

Well, he should not have added the "of course" to it. "What's your favorite part, Cherish?"

"Leg and wing."

"Excellent, then we will not be fighting over the pieces."

She laughed. "There is no need to fight when there are two of everything on the bird for us to share. But men do not think this way. They see what they want and will fight to claim all the spoils for themselves. Did it not cross your mind that we could each have had one of everything? But no matter, you are welcome to my breasts." She blushed again. "Oh, that is…"

"I know you meant the bird." He cast her a wicked grin. "See, sounds lewd even when you say it."

She cleared her throat. "We ought to discuss your nephew."

He nodded. "What have you decided?"

"I will give it a try. It would be supremely foolish of me to ignore the chance to break away from a life that can only be filled with drudgery otherwise. Nor do I trust my uncle to give me what I am owed when I reach my thirtieth birthday. According to my father's solicitor, that is when I come into the first half of my inheritance. The second part comes to me when I am thirty-five. Of course, it is all to be turned over to me immediately if I marry."

"I assume this is why your uncle left you behind at Northam Hall while he and his wife went off to visit her family. He dares not have you in the company of men while he dips into your trust funds."

"I do not know for a fact that he is using my funds for his own comforts. To my great frustration, I also do not know exactly what was left to me in trust. No one will tell me, not even my father's solicitor, who refuses to respond to me now that my uncle has gotten to him and probably warned him to keep silent. However, I know that my father was no wastrel. I maintained his ledgers to the end, so I am fully aware of what he was able to pass on outside of his entailment."

"They showed you the terms of the trust but provided no accounting of the corpus itself? Or the income it earns?"

"That's right, not a single account of anything. I thought nothing of it at first, but over a year has elapsed and I am still being put off. My fear is that my uncle's greed will get the better of him and there will nothing left for me." She emitted a ragged sigh and looked at him with her big doe eyes. "I suppose revealing my concerns puts you in a better bargaining position over me."

"No, Cherish. I would never take advantage of you in this fashion. You are to be a part of my family, and I will always protect you."

She regarded him in obvious surprise. "Thank you, that sounds quite nice. I wish my uncle had even a smidgeon of your honor. He is so loathsome. Hopefully, his failings will no longer matter once I marry. But I do have a concern."

He frowned. "What is it? Do you think your uncle will try to stop me? You are of age to consent. I do not need his permission to marry you...um, marry you off to my nephew."

He took a swig of his ale, irritated with himself for almost leaving off that last detail. His nephew. *Right*. She was to be Reggie's.

She nodded. "He is a sneaky fellow and I am too convenient to have around. He will lose an unpaid servant, not to mention now having someone powerful to hold him to account for whatever he has done with my funds. No, he will not like it at all."

Gawain growled softly. "I will eat him alive if he tries to interfere."

"Goodness, I think I am very much going to like having you on my side." She cast him a breathtaking smile that managed to wrap itself around his heart.

No. No.

Not this girl.

Not his heart.

"Would you think less of me if I admitted how eager I am to watch you give my uncle his comeuppance?" she asked, unaware of his wayward thoughts. "There is much to be said for having a big, growling duke on my side."

He could not get over how beautiful her face was as it lightened in that moment. She had a luminescent glow about her. But as lovely as she looked, her sparkle also brought home just how burdened she must have felt until now.

Despite his resolve to keep his hands off her, he found himself reaching out to tuck a finger under her chin. "I shall be just that whenever you are ready to defy him. I will fight for you, Cherish. But I am also glad you have finally come around to fighting for yourself."

"I know. It was foolish of me to put it off for this long." When he released her chin, she turned away to dig into the basket. She poured more ale into his mug and then handed it back to him. "But my problem is not really solved yet. I still have to appeal to

Reggie, don't I? Oh, I do not expect him to love me, but there has to be some little spark of affection between us or he will never accept me, no matter how hard you and Fiona push me at him."

"I do not see a problem on that score. You are the prettiest girl at the party."

The comment obviously surprised her. What had he just said? Well, *wasn't* she achingly beautiful? It was plain for anyone to see.

"Your Grace, I am not certain you and Fiona see me clearly."

"We do." He gulped down his ale. "Cherish, I am not just saying this to appease you. It is a fact. Fiona and I are not wrong."

She brushed back a few curls that had loosened in the breeze, something that seemed to happen regularly because her hair was delightfully lush and unruly. "Reggie does not think so. He hasn't ever looked my way. Perhaps at first, but that was only to dismiss me as a possible match. How am I to go about attracting him when I do not know how to flirt? I am not even a good dancer. I don't ride well, either. In fact, I am deathly afraid of horses."

He set aside his mug and leaned an arm on his bent knee as he concentrated his attention on her. "Did you have an experience riding that frightened you?"

She nodded. "I fell off the horse my father gave me as a present for my tenth birthday. I couldn't control him and wound up with a fractured wrist and an egg-sized lump on my brow. But I healed quickly. It could have been so much worse."

"I'm sorry."

She shrugged. "Wasn't your fault."

"Nor yours. I'll give you riding lessons if you are comfortable enough to trust me. Reggie enjoys riding. He's quite good at it. However, he doesn't keep to it with any regularity. Getting him off his rump and active is a trait that has yet to be instilled in him."

"Poor Reggie. You should not be too hard on him. I'm sure he finds you quite daunting and does not think he can ever measure up to you."

"But that's just it. I think he can. He simply doesn't try hard enough."

"Have you done anything to encourage his participation? You might compliment him once in a while so he does not feel defeated before he ever starts. I can see he loves you and admires you. Your words are very important to him. He needs to feel you are proud of him."

"Which I am not at the moment," Gawain admitted.

"And he feels *that* acutely."

"Cherish, are you rebuking me?"

She brushed back another lock of her hair that had come loose in the breeze. "No, I'm merely voicing my opinion. I know how it feels to be trod upon. Reggie may be feeling the same with you. Oh, I am not suggesting you are anything like my boor of an uncle. But have you ever trusted Reggie with an important project? Or shown him that you value his opinion?"

"He rarely ventures one."

"And why is that? Are you too quick to dismiss him if you disagree with what he has to say? Or if he does not express an opinion immediately? He is not a soldier who needs to be trained for battle. He does not need to have orders barked at him. Nor will he die if he requires a few minutes to make a decision."

Gawain did not wish to be lectured, but Cherish was making sense. "Go on."

"Everyone absorbs information differently. I think you are a bit of a bull, quick to decide and act. But Reggie might be more thoughtful and need time to digest all the facts before he reaches a conclusion. His way isn't wrong, merely different from yours. I think an encouraging word from you will work wonders on him."

"Maybe." He took the breast of chicken she now offered him and sank his teeth into it. After swallowing a bite, he continued their conversation. "What about your dancing skills? Why do you say they are not good?"

"Because they aren't. I have not danced in years. Attending a few of the local assemblies and hopping about to a lively reel or two when I was a girl of seventeen is not at all the same as dancing among elevated Society. I have never waltzed. Nor ever learned the steps."

"I'll help you with that as well."

She nodded. "Thank you. I think I can pick up most of the other dances without too much difficulty. Hopefully, the waltz won't stump me either. It seems easy enough. I don't think I would require more than an afternoon or two to learn it and refresh my memory on the other dances. I only need to master them enough to keep from making a fool of myself. But even if you had me dancing with the grace of a swan, I don't know if it would be enough to attract Reggie's attention."

"He'll ask you to dance. Let me take care of that part."

"Then it shall be up to me to keep him interested? Oh dear." She began to nibble her lip, looking adorably distressed.

Botheration, she is pretty.

He arched an eyebrow. "I see you will also need lessons on how to flirt with a man."

She laughed. "Desperately."

"I'll show you how it is done. Believe me, I've been assaulted by the best. We'll add that to your lessons." He took another bite of the breast, refusing—absolutely refusing—to think of *her* breasts. It was wrong on every level, so very wrong. "Cherish, you've told me everything you cannot do. Now tell me what you *can* do to impress my nephew. Surely you must have a few skills."

She winced. "I can manage an estate and am a wizard at sums. But I do not think this is the sort of thing you mean. It might attract a practical man like you, but no one else. As for the traditional feminine accomplishments, I can sing. And I play the pianoforte quite well. But that is about the extent of my talents."

"How good are you at those?"

"Fairly good, I think," she said with a shrug.

"Does Fiona know this?"

"Yes, I've played for her whenever she asks me. She often hosts recitals when she is in residence. Nothing fancy, just the local gentry and other neighbors coming around for an evening musicale or afternoon tea."

Knowing how modest this girl was, her shrug probably meant she had a voice of professional quality and an equal ability on the instrument. "Would you feel comfortable if I asked Fiona to feature your talents one night this week? Tonight or tomorrow night, since I would like to have you noticed as soon as possible. I'm sure Fiona can fit in a casual musicale after supper, or an afternoon recital."

"I suppose," she said, putting a hand to her cheek as she blushed. "As you may have gathered, I am not very good at being the center of attention."

He cast her a wry smile. "I've noticed."

"But I will perform if you arrange it with Fiona."

"Good. I'll speak to her about it as soon as we are through with the picnic." He set aside his chicken and drank more ale. "Cherish, you haven't asked me."

She frowned. "Asked you what?"

"What I will provide for you in return for agreeing to marry my nephew."

She appeared confused by his question. "He has to ask me first, don't you think?"

Honestly, this girl needed a little of the mercenary in her. If he were not honorable, he could so easily cheat her. He wasn't ever going to hurt her, of course. If anything, he had a surprisingly strong urge to protect her.

A ridiculously strong urge that would sabotage his best-laid plans if he weren't careful. "Should you not look out for yourself if our matchmaking fails?"

She nibbled her fleshy lower lip in thought. "I suppose, but what would you suggest is fair?"

The notion of Reggie nibbling those luscious lips had his stomach roiling again.

There was something about the shape of her mouth that fascinated Gawain. It had a graceful, bow-like curve, and was the slightest bit too broad for her face. The bottom lip had a plump fullness to it. The whole of her mouth had him wishing for a taste...

Oh, blast.

This would not do at all.

"Well," she said, continuing her thought when he did not immediately respond, "I could not demand a large sum of money from you to free me from my uncle. First of all, he would likely grab anything you gave me. I think my only safe way out is through marriage. So let us see how this week progresses."

"We are already three days into the week, since my friends and I arrived late. There is little time left. I think we must have an immediate plan of action."

"Ah, that's the bull in you talking again. Are you always so impatient to charge ahead?" She cast him another of her delicious smiles. "If it is clear Reggie will never ask me, then perhaps you will agree to help me find someone else. Would you do this for me? You are sharp and know the character of these men. I would trust your judgment. This is the best reward I could have, to be safe and married to someone kind."

He growled low in his throat. "I would kill anyone who ever dared hurt you."

Gad, where had that come from?

Her eyes widened and she laughed. "That ought to scare every man away from me. But what a marvelously apish thing to say. Hopefully, a worthy man won't need to be threatened by you, or he wouldn't be all that worthy, would he? Do you think Reggie might ever desire to protect me in this way?"

He raked a hand through his hair, startled by the pang of jealousy now gripping him. Him? Jealous of his own nephew?

What was happening to him?

41

CHAPTER FOUR

T HE PICNIC WAS followed by various afternoon entertainments, such as archery for the ladies and a ride through the countryside for the gentlemen, after which most guests retired to their chambers to rest up and prepare for the evening's entertainments, which were scheduled to include Cherish's singing a few tunes while accompanying herself on the pianoforte.

But Cherish did not bother to rest.

She took a moment to wash up before hurrying downstairs to the music room, where the Duke of Bromleigh was waiting for her. She paused at the threshold, hoping to calm the flutter in her stomach before she marched through the open door.

This Silver Duke was going to teach her to dance the waltz.

How was she ever to maintain her composure, especially when in his arms? "Here I am, Your Grace."

He smiled as she walked toward him. "Good—we haven't much time, so let's get started right away. I'll teach you the waltz first, since this is a dance you have yet to learn. The others, the quadrille, gavotte, reels, will likely come back to you with or without our taking the time to refresh your recollection of them."

"All right. What are we to do for music?"

"You said you can sing."

"This evening's recital will be quite painful for all of you if I can't," she said in jest.

His smile and resonant chuckle in response simply melted her insides. "How about you hum us a waltz as we go through the steps?"

She nodded. "All right."

He had taken off his jacket and opened up the doors leading onto the terrace in order to allow in a breeze. As he approached to take her in his arms, she made a quick assessment of his appearance.

Dear heaven. The man was sinfully handsome.

He wore dark trousers, a silverish-green waistcoat, and a dark green cravat that contrasted beautifully with the crisp white lawn of his shirt. Those hues brought out the deep green of his eyes and dashes of silver in his dark hair.

He looked marvelously broad in the shoulders and trim at the waist, his physique exquisite enough to make any young woman swoon.

"Um, Your Grace…" she said as he took her in his arms.

"Yes, Cherish?"

"I don't mind humming us a tune, but I would prefer to go over the steps first."

"Very well."

Tingles shot through her when he casually placed an arm around her waist and drew her to him. He seemed quite big and powerful when up this close. "Put this hand on my shoulder," he instructed her.

"Like this?" She was surprised by how solid he felt.

"Perfect. Now put your other hand in mine."

More tingles shot through her as his warm hand wrapped around hers.

"Now we are going to take three steps in fast succession and then a twirl. As I move my right foot forward, you'll move your left foot back."

They tried it several times before she caught on and managed it effortlessly.

"The object is to move in a greater circle around the room, but also to spin in a smaller circle within our own private orbit."

She smiled up at him. "I understand."

He smiled back with devastating effect to her composure. "You are doing beautifully."

Dear heaven.

Dear heaven.

Dear heaven.

She could get used to being in his arms.

However, she refused to dwell on the possibility because it would only lead to pain. Despite Fiona's schemes to match her to this Silver Duke, it wasn't going to happen, since he had made it eminently clear he wanted her for his nephew.

Which meant she could never free her heart to hope for *him*.

"Are you ready, Cherish? Start humming a waltz."

She laughed and nodded. "All right, here we go."

Her tune and their dance worked surprisingly well, and they had little difficulty circulating about the room in time to the music. She was surprised by how well their bodies seemed to understand each other. He had only to apply the slightest pressure of his hand to the small of her back to turn her this way or that. He knew how and when to guide their movements to create an effortless flow.

They were dancing as one, holding on to each other and lost in their private world. She supposed this was why matrons considered the waltz so dangerous. Hearts were lost with this dance, as hers was in danger of surrendering to his now.

She stopped singing, pretending she forgot the rest of the tune because she would lose herself to him completely if this kept up a moment longer.

They now stood unmoving in each other's arms.

Panic overcame her. "How was it, Your Grace? Was my dancing passable?"

He released her and raked a hand through his hair. "Excellent. You have a natural grace and ability. Let's move on to the next dance."

She nodded, relieved he had stepped away to cut that surprisingly strong bond between them. Had he felt it, too? She dared not call it a bond of attraction, for people did not fall in love over a simple dance.

"You have a lovely voice, by the way," he said, raking a hand through his hair again as he studied her.

"Thank you."

They went through the steps of a few other popular dances, none as intimate as the waltz. But for Cherish, these dances felt almost worse, because each touch was brief and teasing, and that left her hungrier for his next momentary touch.

They were about to go over the steps of the quadrille when Reggie strolled in. "Uncle Gawain, there you are. What are you two up to?"

"We are just finishing a dance lesson," Cherish said. "Mine, sadly. I haven't danced in quite a while. Your uncle was attempting to help me out."

"What fun. May I join you? I adore dancing," Reggie said, stepping to her side. "Which ones have you yet to go through? I can help teach you, since your tutor appears to be tiring. Uncle, have a seat and rest your weary bones while I take over. You don't mind, do you? It must be a relief to get off your tired feet."

Cherish stifled the urge to laugh, for the duke appeared ready to bludgeon his nephew for the smart remark.

Tiring, indeed. The man could go on for several hours more without breaking a sweat, he was in that good a shape. But Cherish did enjoy the way Reggie managed to tweak him. Was it not the point of this exercise to make herself competent enough to gain Reggie's notice?

And now she had his undivided attention, so why not take advantage of the unexpected opportunity?

"That would be lovely, Lord Burton," she said before the duke snarled at his nephew and chased him out. "I noticed you dancing the other night, and you were divine."

"Really?" Reggie preened.

"Yes, easily the best man on the dance floor." She did not

mention that most of his friends were not sober enough to stand up straight those first nights before the Silver Dukes arrived. "Your uncle was about to review the steps of the quadrille with me."

Reggie took her hand and led her into the center of the room. "Let me show you how it is done."

Cherish batted her eyelashes at him.

She was certain she heard the duke growl.

How marvelous.

But she was not going to look back at him, for she would likely give herself away. She ached to be back in his arms. This was the worst possible thing she could do for herself, since he had stated quite plainly that he would never marry.

He had also told her to start looking out for herself and urged her toward his nephew. Well, it was suddenly happening, and she was not going to kick this chance away. If she could not have love, then she would accept kindness.

She could tell by the way Reggie held her and guided her through the steps that he was a good and warm-hearted man. There was nothing rough in his motions, yet he was not soft, either. He was simply pleasant and complimentary.

Yes, she would accept kindness, because falling in love with this Silver Duke, despite Fiona's schemes otherwise, would only lead to heartbreak. If he was determined never to marry, then she would have to settle for something less than marriage if she wished to be with him.

No matter how deeply she could grow to love the Duke of Bromleigh, she would never accept becoming his mistress. It did not matter that she might crave to be held in his arms every night for the rest of her life. To be at his mercy, a mere bauble for his amusement, was a fate worse than spending her life as a drudge at Northam Hall. No, she would never be with any man who had the power to toss her away with the promise of a few coins to ease his conscience.

"You did brilliantly, Lady Cherish," Reggie said when they

finished going through the first round of steps.

"You made it easy for me, Lord Burton," she replied, genuinely pleased he approved of her attempts. "I cannot thank you enough. I was so afraid to make a fool of myself, especially at tomorrow night's formal soiree."

"You shan't, I assure you." He glanced over at his uncle, but quickly returned his attention to her. "I shall claim at least one dance from you. Perhaps two, if it is permitted."

He bowed over her hand and kissed it gallantly.

She heard the duke softly growl again.

Had Fiona told Reggie about her plot to match her and the duke?

Because it truly felt as though Reggie was having jolly good fun playing the role of attentive beau. After ignoring her for the past three days, she had to question his sudden interest in her. It was not possible for him to be infatuated with her.

Fiona must have let him in on her plans and he was joining in with hearty approval. That was all it could possibly be.

But what if his sudden notice of her was real?

No, there had not been the hint of attraction between her and Reggie until supposedly this very moment...and the way Reggie kept sliding glances at his uncle was telling. Yes, he had to know of Fiona's plan.

Cherish now felt caught in the middle. But she could not weaken toward the duke so long as he held to his conviction of never marrying. Did she not have herself to think about? And had the duke not insisted that he wanted her for his nephew?

Cherish shook her head. It was all getting a bit too complicated for her. She decided to simply go along with whatever was happening and do her best to get to know Reggie. Time would reveal how everyone's plots were to play out.

Reggie cleared his throat. "I plan on going for a morning ride tomorrow, Lady Cherish. Would you care to join me?"

Honestly, had Fiona primed him?

She smiled sweetly. "What a coincidence that you should

mention riding. Unfortunately, I am afraid of horses. Your uncle was going to help me get over my fear."

"He was? How splendid of him, but not at all necessary. Allow me to assist you. I'll attend to it, Uncle Gawain. I'm sure you have better things to do with your time. Perhaps you ought to sleep in late, recover from today's strenuous activities."

Cherish covered her mouth to prevent a strangled laugh from escaping her lips. She masked it with a quick bout of coughs.

"How in blazes is a picnic strenuous?" the duke grumbled, now striding toward them and looking not at all pleased.

She stood between the two big men, feeling the flames of defiance shoot back and forth between uncle and nephew.

But she silently cheered, for Reggie was not spineless after all. Good for him.

As for the duke, he appeared as stoic as ever. However, there was something in his eyes...could it be jealousy?

No, impossible.

Yet as silent and unmoving as he was, she could not help wishing he would be a raging ape on the inside. Bouncing off walls. Tossing chairs. Wildly jealous and beating his chest while grunting, *Mine. She is mine.*

"The riding lesson is not important," she said, dismissing her fanciful notion and addressing these two before they came to blows over her. Well, that was also ridiculous. These men were family to each other and hardly likely to come to blows over *her.*

However, they were challenging each other, and she did not like to be the one creating a split, no matter how harmless, between these two. "I am always going to be afraid of horses, and that will not change. Why don't you two go off together for a morning ride? I'm sure tomorrow will be a lovely day for it."

The duke cast her a soft look. "No, let my nephew help you out. He has an excellent way with horses. In truth, he's much better around them than I am. You'll be in good hands with him."

Reggie glanced at his uncle in surprise. "Thank you. I never realized you thought so."

"I should have told you more often," the duke admitted, and Cherish realized he had taken her earlier words about being kinder to Reggie to heart. "How about we all share a lemonade on the terrace before retiring upstairs to ready ourselves for tonight? What does Fiona have planned for us after the musicale?"

Reggie laughed. "What? You haven't checked Cousin Fiona's schedule? Musicale first, in which we shall all delight in hearing Lady Cherish's dulcet tones."

She blushed. "Well, I shall sing. Hopefully, you will find it pleasant."

"I am sure we shall all be transported," Reggie said, taking her hand and giving it a light kiss as he bowed over it again. "Then we all go into supper. Afterward, it is to be parlor games. She is setting us up in teams of four to compete against the other teams of four. Fiona has already put her list together but won't show it to anyone yet."

The duke winced. "Oh, hell."

Cherish stifled the impulse to laugh again, for she was having far too much fun watching him squirm. This big, powerful man was such a marvel of contradictions. He had survived years of battle, harsh conditions, painful wounds, and other difficulties beyond her comprehension, yet he grimaced at the thought of having a silly young lady or two placed on his team? "Your Grace, I am sure it is all meant to be in fun. You will survive these games no matter what diabolical designs Fiona has in store for you."

"She'll stick me with all the peahens, I'm sure," he muttered.

"Well, Lady Cherish certainly is no peahen." Reggie held out his arm to her. "I hope you are on my team."

"Oh, thank you. I would love to be on yours." She placed her hand in the crook of his offered arm.

The duke stepped back to retrieve his jacket, and then followed them out. But he was stopped before catching up to them by Lady Margaret, who had been carrying several books and now dropped them at his feet. "Oh, dear. Do forgive me, Your Grace."

"Not at all," he said with resignation at the obvious ploy for his attention, and knelt to pick them up for her.

"I thought I could manage them on my own," Lady Margaret said with a nervous titter. "I do enjoy a good read. Don't you, Your Grace?"

Cherish was surprised when Reggie did not rush forward to assist her, leaving the chore entirely to his uncle. Was Margaret not one of his favorites? She was very pretty and knew how to flutter about in that helpless way all men seemed to adore.

But Reggie merely looked on and grinned. He also held Cherish back when she started forward to help pick up one of the books. "Come with me," he whispered, and led her off to the terrace.

He held out a chair for her and then settled in the one beside her. Only then did he dare to emit the burst of laughter he must have been struggling all the while to hold in. "Lady Margaret wasn't planned. But wasn't her timing perfect? If that girl can read, then I'll eat my shoe. Did you see the books she dropped? One of them was in German and the other two were written in Latin. Did you see my uncle's face? Gad, how I love to see him caught off his guard. He's always so perfect, it is maddening."

Cherish joined him in a mirthful chuckle. "I knew it. I gather Fiona has told you of her plan."

"To match you with my uncle? Yes, and I think it is brilliant. He wants to match us, and I am determined to see that plan blow up in his face." He suddenly realized he might have insulted her and hastened to apologize. "I did not mean... You are clearly a lovely young woman. Do forgive me. I certainly meant no insult."

"None taken."

"Thank you, Lady Cherish. I can see why Fiona adores you, and I am convinced my uncle is not indifferent to you either. As for me, I am not of a mind to marry yet. Besides, my uncle is right about my needing to grow up a bit before I make a suitable duke or proper husband."

She shook her head. "It is quite all right. I am not at all offended. I think you are a good soul, although..."

"What, Lady Cherish?"

"That woodpecker laugh of yours. Is it real or merely put on?"

He grimaced. "It is real, but only when I am drunk. You must think me an idiot."

"Not at all. But I do prefer you when you are sober."

"Well, I am almost grown out of these drunken revels. I'm sure within another year or two I shall be a model citizen." He called over one of the footmen and ordered lemonade for them. "And three glasses. Oh, and move this chair away from Lady Cherish. Put it to the right of mine."

They had taken seats at a wrought-iron table with three matching chairs surrounding it. The empty chair had been beside her. But the footman now placed it beside Reggie. Cherish was disappointed that the duke would be forced to sit next to Reggie and not her, but it was in furtherance of Fiona's plan to make the duke realize he, not his nephew, was the right match for her.

Even if everything they did failed, as Cherish truly thought it would, it was still worth the attempt. She was so strongly attracted to this man, and not because he was a duke. In truth, his title was an irritating impediment. It sat atop his big, strong shoulders like a giant chip. He had grown so wary of everyone's motives that he refused to ever let down his guard and allow anyone in.

The duke joined them a few moments later, striding onto the terrace in all his magnificence.

He frowned upon taking in the seating arrangement, but said nothing and settled his large frame on the chair beside his nephew. "Stupid trick," he muttered, spreading his longs legs before him. "I'll wager my entire estate that girl has never read a book in her life."

Cherish thought he was likely right, but Lady Margaret was young and it was not her fault that her family chose to have her trained in the art of flirting rather than academics. Yes, she was never going to expound on important scientific theories. But she was very likeable and did not appear to have a malicious bone in her body.

In truth, Cherish liked Lady Margaret and felt sorry that her family was pushing her toward this Silver Duke when it was obvious she liked Reggie. "Do not be too hard on her, Your Grace. You ought to be flattered the ladies are interested in you."

"That's just it, they are not." The duke glanced at his nephew. "Lesson number one, Reggie. When you are duke, everyone will desire you for your wealth and title. They will not give a fig about who *you* really are."

Reggie leaned forward, his expression dispirited. "Not everyone, surely."

"There are a few good people, but spotting them is a talent you must develop for your own protection. Some liars are easily detected because they are so obvious, one can spot their falsehood before they ever open their mouth. But the best ones often are not so easily spotted. They will work slowly and quietly, sowing seeds of doubt so that you no longer trust your good friends. Their motives are insidious. Their goal is to separate you from your family and anyone else who may have earned your trust."

Cherish was surprised by his comment. He was stern and a bit bullheaded, but she had not expected to find him holding such a level of distrust in others. "I think you are too cynical, Your Grace. We are not living in Shakespeare's *Othello*. There are many good people around who are not as villainous as Iago."

Was this the reason for his determination never to marry? Had someone hurt him terribly in his younger days? Someone to whom he had given his heart?

His eyes now held the glint of steel. "I do not mean to suggest everyone is venal, Lady Cherish. But it is important for my nephew never to let down his guard. Even now, he is a target for the unscrupulous. As am I. But many steer wide of me because they fear to face my wrath."

Reggie frowned. "And you are worried that I will be a dupe to everyone's schemes? I hope I am not that foolish."

"I know you are not, Reggie. But you are not yet fierce. To protect yourself, you have to develop a bit of the ruthless in you or the bad actors will swarm all over you like bees to honey. Ladies are the most dangerous, for they can get very close and sting you hardest and deepest."

Cherish quietly held her breath.

So, there was a woman in his life.

Who was she? And what did she do to hurt him so badly?

CHAPTER FIVE

G AWAIN ENJOYED CHERISH'S recital, for her voice was soft as a gentle rain and her fingers were nimble and light upon the piano keys. She played two popular songs and encouraged others to join in singing along with her.

The ladies particularly enjoyed this, but Gawain just wanted to hear her sing. Was there anything he did not like about this girl? She surely was something special.

After supper, Fiona announced the start of a night of parlor games. Gawain, to his dismay, was teamed with two peahens, Lady Yvonne and Lady Eugenia, and one of Reggie's friends, a young man he had yet to see sober, Lord Pershing. If Fiona was trying to torture him, she had managed to do a wonderful job of it.

It wasn't that Gawain was completely against parlor games, and he had to admit the ladies assigned to his team were quite beautiful. Unfortunately, there was not a hint of brain matter between their ears.

He had participated on occasion in some fairly naughty games contrived by some infamous hostesses who lived on the fringes of elegant Society. Almost nothing was out of bounds, and clothes often came off at those soirees popular with the *demi-monde*.

But Fiona's guests were proper Society, and nothing shocking or remotely interesting was going to happen tonight. He would endure and play along with the silliness because he was supposed to set a proper example for Reggie, but what he really wanted to do was spend more time alone with Cherish.

As his teammates joined him, he smiled and resolved to behave himself.

Cherish was teamed with Reggie, Lady Margaret, and another friend of Reggie's by the name of Lord Durham. Durham and Reggie had been friends since childhood, and Gawain quite liked the boy. Well, he was a few years older than Reggie and had always had a good head on his shoulders, so this "boy" had to be close to thirty years of age by now.

The first game was to be charades. Fiona quickly went over the rules. "One teammate is to convey the clues only by gestures. The others are to guess what is written on a square of paper drawn out of this hat."

Gawain had already resigned himself to losing. One drunken sot and two young ladies with nothing but air between their ears was a handicap impossible to surmount.

Fiona selected him as captain of his team and handed him the hat from which he was to withdraw the square of paper. "Good luck, Gawain," she said, unable to contain her laughter.

"I'll get you for this, Fiona," he replied with a pained chuckle.

He unfurled the paper and saw the answer written was Westminster Abbey. Not very difficult, but he already knew his team would never figure it out.

He hated losing.

Fiona, Reggie, and even Cherish were grinning at him. Had any of them been on his team, they would have guessed the answer within a minute. But *these* teammates?

He turned to Yvonne, Eugenia, and Pershing with a groan. "All right. Pershing, open your eyes."

The ladies giggled. Pershing weaved.

Gawain sighed and pointed west. He may have been pointing to the moon for all the good it did.

"Pointing!" Lady Yvonne shouted out with glee.

"Outdoors." Lady Eugenia began to hop up and down. "Swimming! Trees! Kittens!"

Huh?

He tried to convey a setting sun. Apparently, none of his teammates realized the sun set in the west. He gave up and moved on to the third syllable and pretended to hold a bowl, the contents of which he was stirring. Surely they had to get *stir* out of Westmin*ster*. But they hadn't gotten the *West* or the *min*, so he was not all that surprised when their guesses were still inane.

"Spinning!" Yvonne shouted.

"Whirling! Dancing! Twirling!" Eugenia squealed.

Pershing merely snored.

"Time's up," Fiona said. "I'm sorry, but your team has lost your point."

Gawain truly, oh so truly, hated to lose, but he tried not to show it. After all, no one could possibly blame him when they came in dead last. But for pity's sake, what was so hard about guessing *stir*?

As the next team got up to take their turn, he sank into the vacated chair beside Cherish and moaned. "This is utter agony."

She smiled sympathetically as she leaned toward him and whispered, "They don't cook. They've probably never set foot in their kitchen or seen a mixing bowl, so they do not understand the concept of stirring. Well, Pershing might have understood stirring one's drink. But he was off snoring and not watching your brilliant enactment. Nor have any of them been taught anything remotely scientific. They do not realize the sun sinks in the west."

"I shall address this oversight the next time Parliament is in session," he grumbled. "Women must be given a rudimentary education on the sciences, mathematics, and politics."

Cherish gave a doubtful snort. "They will shoot you down so fast, you won't know what hit you. Few men care to give ladies the power of education."

"You are educated, are you not?"

She nodded. "Mostly self-taught, but my parents encouraged

it."

He leaned closer to continue their conversation as the noise level in the room escalated. Talking proved impossible, but he did not mind drawing closer to Cherish because he liked the scent of her, something wild and fruity that mingled perfectly with the soft warmth of her skin.

If he wasn't careful, the desire to taste her might very well overwhelm him. That would not do at all. He was not supposed to be having these feelings for her.

Fortunately, her team was up next, so his torture at their closeness was short-lived as she left his side to join the others.

Durham, Reggie, and Cherish were smart, and Durham was chosen to give the clues. He stared at the paper a moment and then began to gesture falling asleep. Lady Margaret, the weak link in their strong chain, was hopping about like a clueless pup, shouting out inane responses to the clues Durham was giving.

Gawain immediately realized it was a quote from a Shakespeare play, Hamlet's famous soliloquy. Every schoolboy knew the start of the passage... *To be, or not to be.*

Cherish and Reggie guessed it at the same time, together reciting lines from that famous passage. *"To die, to sleep. To sleep, perchance to dream,"* Reggie said.

Durham nodded and motioned for them to continue.

Cherish finished the verse. *"Aye, there's the rub, for in this sleep of death what dreams may come."*

"Yes!" Durham shouted. "That's the answer. What dreams may come."

Margaret looked on and clapped, probably having no idea what her teammates were talking about.

Cherish, Reggie, and Durham, with Lady Margaret as their little albatross, were handily in the lead as the night progressed. Gawain's team was dead last.

He tried to tamp down his own apish instincts to win, knowing it was an impossibility. What choice did he have but to take his loss with good sportsmanship?

Lord, Lord... Oh, how he hated to lose.

Fiona and Reggie were taking too much pleasure from his suffering. Gad, were all relatives this irritating?

But he knew he was the one behaving like an uncivilized ape because he could not even let this simple game pass without turning it into a battle. Yes, he'd been raised in the military, and the training to win was ingrained in him. He wasn't angry so much as frustrated.

The last game was to be bobbing for apples.

"Simple enough," Gawain muttered as they were all herded into the garden, where four barrels filled with water were set out on mats. Fiona dropped one apple into each barrel. Footmen stood close by with towels in hand because everyone who played was going to get soaked.

They were four teams of four who were to participate, so sixteen players in all.

How he got roped into this, Gawain did not know. But he owed it to Fiona to endure this night of torture, since she was helping him out with Reggie.

"It shall be the men against the ladies in this one," Fiona announced. "If I were to pit you men against one another, you would try to drown each other. So I shall assign one man on each team to a lady on the opposing team. First one to come up with the apple in their mouth wins."

They played in turns, and the first teams selected were not his or Cherish's team.

He stood watching beside Cherish as she cheered and seemed to take genuine delight in watching the mayhem of the game. Everyone on a team took a turn, but each game was limited to two minutes, so no points were awarded if neither player came up with the apple in time. Few players came up with the apple, so only two out of the first set of challengers were awarded a point.

No one seemed to care if they won or lost. There was an awful lot of accidental kissing as both sets of lips were vying for the same apple. A time or two, the apple was forgotten and the contestants went straight to the kissing part.

Then his team was called up, Gawain was not surprised to be pitted against Cherish, because Fiona was diabolical when she wanted to be and had to know this would irk him. By this time, all of the men had removed their jackets, cravats, and waistcoats so as not to ruin the expensive fabrics as they were sloshed with water.

The ladies were given towels to wear as bibs to protect their gowns and they each were provided mats to prevent grass and mud stains on their clothing as they bent on their knees and dipped their head in the barrel.

A fresh apple was dropped into the barrel for each round.

Cherish smiled at him. "Are you ready, Your Grace?"

"Something tells me you are an expert at this game."

She laughed. "Not at all. If anything, you have the advantage, since you have the bigger mouth to grasp that apple. But I've forgotten what silly fun these games can be. It feels good to take a simple pleasure and not worry about what others think."

He saw the enchantment in her features again, the shimmering joy in her beautiful eyes.

"Ready! Set! Go!" Fiona called out, and everyone's face hit water as they began to chase the bobbing apple.

Too often, Gawain missed the apple and wound up with his lips on Cherish's cheek or nose. His entire body exploded in heat when the apple slipped away and his lips wound up on hers. Yes, that was hardest to draw away. She had the sweetest lips.

Suddenly, all he wanted to do was kiss her.

Kiss her wet. Kiss her hard. Just kiss her.

He was spared his continuing agony when Fiona called time and no one on the four teams had caught their apples. But the end of his round did not mean the end of his spurt of heat over Cherish.

As for Cherish, she appeared completely unaffected by the innocent touch of their lips. She left his side and now took over as timekeeper when Fiona's turn came up. Fiona groaned when she realized she had to face Pershing, who had finally awakened from his drunken stupor. "I'm sure there must be some mistake," she muttered.

Gawain could not stifle his grin. "You're the one who set up the game. Serves you right, Fiona. I had that idiot on my team the entire night. Now he is all yours."

To no one's surprise, the stupid sot of a lord almost drowned when he passed out in the water, and Gawain had to lift his head out of the barrel when it did not bob up after the apple.

He turned with a scowl toward Reggie. "If you ever behave like this idiot, I will drown you myself."

"Botheration, what did I do?" Reggie griped back at him.

Gawain sighed. "Nothing, just don't ever be like him."

"Fine, I'll be just like you and hold myself out to be such a paragon that no woman will ever be good enough for me. I cannot wait to die alone in a cold bed."

Cherish had been standing beside them all the while and now turned to them with a gasp. But she quickly turned away again and continued to keep time on the other players.

Gawain felt his nephew's words acutely because the boy was right and the barb had struck straight in his heart. He strode off toward the beach, knowing the games were now at an end and everyone would soon return inside to chat, play cards or billiards, or simply retire to bed.

He would not join them, for he was not fit company. Losing always put him in a bad temperament.

It was foolish of him to behave like a spoiled child and resent someone else's win over something utterly inconsequential.

Yes, he failed miserably at being a good sport. Perhaps winning mattered to him because Cherish was watching and he wanted to look like a conquering hero in her eyes.

Bah, it was the opposite of what he ought to want.

Bloody blazes, he was still reeling from that brief touch of her lips.

He stopped at the top of the stairs and simply looked out

across the water as the sun began to set. The colors of the sky were a brilliant mix of orange and lavender, and the sea glistened. There was a lightly salty tang to the air as a soft breeze wafted across the white-foamed waves toward him.

The magnificent view and pleasant breeze ought to have calmed him, but he remained too riled to fully appreciate the beauty of his surroundings or this sunset.

He had been so determined to find the right girl for Reggie that it never crossed his mind that Cherish would feel so right for *him*. But he would have to get over this unexpected longing for the girl. For pity's sake, he had only known her a few days. Not even a week. Not even *half* a week. That Fiona had been writing to him about her for several months did not count other than to explain why he felt so comfortable around her.

His heart hitched when he sensed Cherish approaching. *Oh, great.* Now he could *feel* her presence before he ever set eyes on her.

This was very bad.

He heard her soft laughter a moment later, so he turned to her with a frown. "Don't you dare berate me."

She came to his side and smiled up at him. "Fiona sent me to calm you down and return you to the party. She said to tell you that she apologizes profusely for saddling you with the three silliest guests at her party and..." Cherish burst out laughing. "Oh, please forgive me. I hope you know I am laughing at the situation and not at you. I would never laugh at you."

He groaned.

"Truly, I had no idea Fiona was so diabolical. It was such a wicked, wicked thing for her to do to you, especially knowing your nature. I could almost see smoke pouring from your ears each time your team botched an answer. The frustration you must—"

"I thought you said Fiona had sent you to calm me down."

She nodded. "Oh, yes. Sorry, but do allow me to tease you just a little. You are so perfect in everything you do, it is quite daunting to us all. So, to see you brought low in this harmless way... And it was harmless, you must admit. But how you must have gritted your teeth and tried to slog through the evening. You looked so..."

"Foolish?"

"No, *dismayed* is the better word." She laughed again, unable to stifle her melodic trills. "Oh, do ignore me. I am so relieved to find you are actually human and not this unreachable paragon. She pushed you too far and asked me to convey to you that she is truly sorry."

Gawain shook his head. "No, I should not have stalked off as I did. These were simple parlor games. Harmless, as you said. I was a poor sport and took it out on Reggie when I lost. He's a good nephew, and I've been coming down on him like a hammer over the head. He is nothing like that dolt Pershing and will never be, even on his worst days."

The wind blew softly through Cherish's curls as she nodded. "He is handling it well. In truth, your coming down on him harder than warranted is bringing out the strength in him, don't you think? Perhaps we all need to face a little hardship to bring out the better part of us."

He met her gaze, loving the warmth of her eyes. "And what about you, Cherish? Do you really believe living under Northam's roof has made a better woman of you?"

"It has forced me out of my complacency and made me think of my own needs." She shook her head and sighed. "To be honest, I am not happy about having to toughen myself up. Oh, I am eager to be away from my ogre of an uncle, but it still feels cruel to manipulate some innocent soul into marrying me simply to enable me to escape an intolerable situation. I cannot find it in my heart to use someone that way."

"And if that someone loved you?"

Her expression turned soft as a dream. "That would be an altogether different matter, especially if I loved him back. That would be bliss."

She appeared ready to say something more, then shook her head again. "It is a lovely sunset, isn't it? The same can be seen from my home... Well, what used to be my home. I was sure my father would leave it to me, since it is not part of the entailment. But my uncle and my father's solicitor claim he did not."

"And you trust their word?"

"I would never trust my uncle, but why would my father's solicitor lie to me? Well, I did not question him at first, but now I am not so certain. Yet it seems so far-fetched that he would collude with my uncle regarding this estate. He insists it is Northam's now, and I must accept it."

"But you haven't?"

"No, it sticks in my craw. It feels wrong, but how am I to challenge it when the solicitor has all the documentation and I have none? So, it is time I accepted the harsh fact that Northam Hall is not mine and will never be mine. Otherwise, I will never have the courage to distance myself from all the memories I hold so dear and move on."

She placed her hand on his arm when he said nothing in response. "We ought to return to the others."

"You go on ahead, Cherish. I am not fit company yet."

As ever, the breeze softly whipped through her curls while she remained standing beside him and feeling too right for him to dare believe possible. "I'll stay with you, Your Grace. Would you mind terribly?"

He shrugged. "Do as you wish."

"What I wish is to talk to you. But you just want me to leave you alone and go away. Are you thinking of the woman you once loved?"

The question startled him. "What business is it of yours?"

"None at all. I have never been in love. Goodness, I have never even been kissed. The closest I've ever come to any man's lips on mine was tonight when our lips accidentally touched while bobbing for apples. Oh, I know that does not count as a kiss."

That all-too-brief encounter still had his body in turmoil. His heart, too.

"What does it feel like?" she asked. "I mean, to really kiss someone. To be in love and kiss that person with all the strength of your being. Obviously, falling in love left you in tremendous pain. Is it not ironic that something capable of bringing you so much joy can also leave you with unbearable pain?"

"Cherish, I do not wish to talk about it."

"You needn't. I am doing all the talking. Ignore me if you would rather not comment while I sort it out for myself. My problem is not love but indifference. I think indifference is worse than anything else. This is what I am facing, the prospect of living my life as a shadow, ignored by the family who ought to love me and yet left me without resources to do something about it. I thought I could endure my lot and not care."

"But you are discovering that you cannot?"

"It is awful. I've tried to harden myself because Fiona insists I am too soft and think too much with my feelings instead of my brain. But never feeling anything makes the entire point of living meaningless, don't you think?"

"Cherish, if you are trying to get me to open up my heart and confide in you, forget it. I am not going to talk about myself."

She nodded. "I was talking about me. You have made your decision to close yourself off to the world. That is your choice to make. I thought I had made the same choice, but I cannot do it. At least you are a duke and will have an impact on the lives of others no matter what you do. But I am no more than a leaf on an autumn breeze that will soon wither and die."

"You are nowhere close to withering." She was a summer rose, delightful to the scent and the eye. He just wanted her to go away before he gave in to desire and kissed her in the full and glorious way he ached to do.

"How does one know when love is real?"

He gave a groaning laugh. "Why don't you ask me something simple, like explaining the theory of gravity? Or the origins of the moon and stars? Obviously, I am the wrong person to ask about love."

"Because you were burned once and now hide from it forever?"

He placed his hands on her slight shoulders and made certain she was looking straight at him while he frowned at her. "What I do is none of your business," he repeated, irritated by how easily she got under his skin. "I think you need to go back inside with the others now."

"Why?"

"Cherish, you do not want to learn about love from me. I would only hurt you."

"Thank you for the warning. I shall take it to heart. But answer me this about the woman who turned you into this closed-off person you've become. If she were to come back into your life, what would you do?"

"Run as fast as my legs would carry me in the opposite direction. Satisfied? Will you go now?"

"All right. But I hate to miss this lovely sunset. I'll just stand apart from you and watch it. Am I not allowed to think of my future, too?"

"Must you do it right here?"

"Is there a better spot?"

He sighed. "Come here." He tucked her hand in the crook of his arm as they stood together watching the last golden rays of sunlight disappear over the horizon.

What was he to do with Cherish? Besides ache to kiss her into forever?

CHAPTER SIX

T HE NEXT FEW days passed quietly and everyone was forced indoors due to a succession of rainy days. Gawain hid out in the library most of the time, leaving Fiona, with the assistance of Reggie and Cherish, to fill in the hours for her guests.

As it turned out, Cherish was indeed quite accomplished on the pianoforte and had a large repertoire of songs. Yesterday afternoon and again that evening after supper, she entertained everyone with her lively tunes while the others danced. Gawain had retreated to the library because he did not wish to be accosted by the peahens who would expect him to participate.

If Cherish was not dancing, then neither did he care to dance.

This afternoon, the young ladies were again enlisted to entertain the gathering with songs. Cherish, not wishing to be featured once again, volunteered to accompany them on the pianoforte. He almost felt guilty for not helping out, but Reggie had stepped up and was doing an excellent job of organizing entertainments for Fiona's male guests. On top of it all, he had done it while sober.

But Gawain knew it was time for him to step in when he heard Reggie's woodpecker laugh resounding through the hall.

This meant his nephew had been drinking again.

Not that he blamed Reggie, for all the young men had spent the past few days foggy with drink to relieve their boredom. Many of the ladies had tippled, too.

He set his book aside and was about to rise from his comfortable reading chair when he heard a light rap at the door. "Come," he intoned.

A moment later, Cherish stepped into the library. "Um, Your Grace..."

He had avoided the girl fairly easily these past rainy days, but the sight of her now simply took his breath away. She was a ray of sunshine and her radiant smile had his heart beating ridiculously fast. How did she manage this?

Her gowns were nothing fancy, including this one she had on, which was a dark green muslin barely trimmed with silk. It had little white flowers embroidered around the bodice and hem that added just the slightest frivolity to her otherwise serious nature. Her throat was bare, as usual. All she had on were those small gold earrings dangling from the lobes of her little ears.

Gad, she drove him wild. He wanted to spend the night nibbling her ears, her throat—

Which was why he had made it a point to avoid her in the first place. "What is it, Cherish?"

"Fiona needs your assistance."

He cast her a wry smile. "I was just about to seek her out. I heard Reggie's woodpecker laugh."

Cherish arched a delicate eyebrow and tossed him another smile. "It is hard to miss, but don't judge him too harshly. The young men are bored and have little to do other than dance and drink."

"I know. I was young once, too." He held her back a moment before they walked out. "How are you and Reggie getting along?"

"He is very nice, but..."

"Are you irritated that he is drinking?"

"No, they all are. He is actually more sober than the rest... Well, Lord Durham also has his wits about him. He's another one like you who always prefers to remain in control of his senses."

"Then what is your hesitation?"

She cast him a look of dismay. "I am not hesitating. In truth, I have been mingling with the others and quite enjoying myself. But...besides your nephew, I think there may be another young lord interested in me."

"There is?" That she should have a genuine suitor hit Gawain hard. To his dismay, he felt a sudden heaviness course through his body, as though he were about to be buried beneath a crushing pile of stones.

She nodded. "But I doubt it will lead to anything. Who would seriously offer for me without knowing the details of my dowry? It is absurd that I am left completely in the dark about my trust fund or any other arrangements my father made for me before his passing."

"Who is this other man?"

"Oh, he isn't important. It will never come to anything anyway. I think he truly likes me, but he needs to marry an heiress."

Gawain's insides began to churn.

Obviously, the man's taste in women was excellent and could not be faulted. What if he decided Cherish was worth more than any advantage an heiress could give him, and offered for her?

It was all he could do to tamp down the apish part of him.

He did not press her for the name of this new suitor because right now he wanted to rip the man's head off.

Bollocks.

What was happening to him? He had never felt this way about any woman, not even the one who had betrayed him all those years ago.

"Reggie will have you no matter what you bring to the marriage. I will provide for you if your father has failed to do so. As I said, it is your intelligence and charm that is important. This is what Reggie needs above all else."

She did not look happy about his comment.

As for him, he was amazed that he managed to sound so unaffected. "Are we clear on this?"

"Yes, we are clear. But do not expect me to cheer over this, Your Grace. I am not comfortable about your plans, and it still feels quite mercenary."

"Mercenary? Cherish, you have not asked me for a blessed thing." He stared at her. "There is a business aspect to every marriage. You cannot deny it. Will it ease your mind if we set terms down in writing?"

She laughed. "No, although any young lady with half a brain would insist on it. But this appears to be the missing part of my brain. I don't want to be *paid off*, and I am not interested in your wealth. My concern is about matters of the heart."

"Mine? I can assure you, I will not think less of you if you negotiate hard to protect your future."

"No, I am speaking of your nephew's future. Does he not deserve someone better than me? Someone who adores him and cannot breathe whenever he stands close? I've noticed this is how Lady Margaret behaves whenever she is around him. She genuinely cares for him."

"Her?"

"Yes, and I like her."

"If she is enamored of Reggie, then why is she constantly tossing herself in my path?"

Cherish pursed her lips. "That is her family's doing, not hers. She is happiest and most relaxed when she is beside him. In truth, I think she and Reggie suit quite nicely. He is very kind and protective around her."

"And your point?"

"It feels cruel to save myself by marrying Reggie when I cannot make him as happy as he deserves to be."

"And you think a little peahen like Lady Margaret can make him a better wife? He needs a woman with brains. You will be a good wife for him because you also have a caring nature and will do all in your power never to hurt him."

She did not appear convinced. "Well, I wanted to be honest with you about my feelings. But if you and Reggie are all right with it, then I shall try to be as well. I may not succeed. It feels very wrong, and this is difficult for me to overcome. Your nephew and Margaret seem so right together."

"Few *ton* marriages are based on love, Cherish."

"I know, and I think it is a very sad thing. Oh, I understand the business need for many in the Upper Crust to secure their assets or enhance their fortunes. I shall speak no more about love or the hope of it. But do not be angry with me if I quietly keep wishing for it."

They strode down the hall and walked together into the parlor, where Fiona obviously had her hands full trying to keep her guests entertained.

Everyone sprang to attention when Gawain strode in. Reggie staggered to his feet and swallowed hard. "You aren't going to berate me, are you?"

"No," Gawain said. "Just lay off the brandy for a while."

Cherish darted away when the peahens began to cluster around him. He took his punishment with manly grace, smiling all the while they chattered at him and split his head open with their inane comments.

He held his smile as they shamelessly flirted with him and did not bother to ask him a single question about his likes or dislikes, his feelings, his thoughts on anything.

Well, why should they? Their parents must have pounded all the relevant facts about him into their head. His noble lineage. How he acquired his peerage. The extent of the Bromleigh holdings. The ladies he had escorted in the past.

How best to lure him into a compromising position.

Cherish was the only one who stood to the side and did not bother to vie for his attention. Well, he had firmly chased her away by now. He'd shoved her at Reggie.

Why did it feel like the biggest mistake of his life?

When the rain finally stopped and the sun burst through the thick layers of clouds, he took it upon himself to organize a shopping excursion into Brighton. The ladies were thrilled. Even the gentlemen were eager to get out of the house. Some chose to join the ladies and others chose to remain behind and go for a ride. Reggie and his friend Durham agreed to attend to the men who wished to ride.

Gawain was not sure riding across the countryside was a wise idea, since the ground had to be wet and quite slippery because of the falling leaves.

In addition, they had all been drinking. Well, they were grown men. Durham and Reggie were only mildly soused and could be counted on to keep their wits about them.

"You are frowning, Uncle Gawain. Don't worry about us."

But he did worry about Reggie. After all, the lad was his only nephew, and Gawain did not want him doing anything reckless.

Durham patted him on the back, a familiarity he allowed because Durham was one of those rare young men of quality. "We'll keep it short and likely return to the house before you and the ladies do. A round of billiards or card games will do for us while you are still off in town. Reggie and I have it all under control."

Fiona called for several carriages to be brought around. Gawain had his own mount saddled, an enormous gray by the name of Odin who had been bred for battle. The big beast scared the wits out of Cherish, and she would not go near him. His heart went out to her, for her fear was real and a palpable torment to her. She had probably made things worse for herself by pretending to be strong and keeping her dread bottled up inside. It had now built up to a point that she might never get over it.

Gawain made certain to keep Odin a safe distance away from her.

"Will you not ride with us, Gawain?" Fiona asked as the ladies went to the waiting carriages to climb in.

"No, I'll be fine serving as escort." He had no desire to remain trapped inside one of those carriages with no escape from the ladies or their endless giggling and prattling. Not that what *he* spoke of was always highly intelligent or of particular note, but it was not conversations about lace gloves or how many curls to style in one's hair.

"Are you sure?"

"Yes, there'll be more room for you ladies if I ride," he responded when Fiona regarded him quizzically.

Cherish had already climbed in and was gazing at him and Fiona as they spoke.

Lord, her eyes. They truly were a mirror into her soul.

He could hear her thoughts as though she spoke them aloud, her desire to prove herself brave and her distress in knowing she had not yet conquered her fears. Mixed in was the desire to prove herself to *him*.

Of course, there was no need. If only she knew how much he…

No, he dared not consider his feelings for her.

As the carriages rolled away, a few of the gentlemen chose to join Gawain. They rode beside him as they escorted the ladies into town.

It was still early afternoon when they arrived in Brighton. The sun had burned the clouds away by the time the conveyances drew up along the high street, where all the finer shops were located.

Fiona, being a bit of a mother hen, guided the ladies into the nearby shops. The merchants were delighted to be descended upon, and even more delighted when Gawain told all the ladies to buy a little gift for themselves and it was his treat. While the other gentlemen followed them from shop to shop, Gawain made his payment arrangements with the merchants and then stood beside the carriages to await everyone's return.

To his surprise, Cherish did not go into the shops but merely browsed from outside, doing nothing more than peering into the windows and staring at the colorful displays.

Gawain strolled over to her. "I've told the merchants to charge everyone's purchases to my account."

She smiled up at him. "Is that your way of atoning to Fiona for hiding out in her library these past two days?"

He chuckled. "Yes. Go in and choose something pretty for

yourself."

"It isn't necessary."

"Why are you so reluctant? What is it, Cherish?"

She blushed. "I don't want anything from you."

The comment surprised him. "It is a harmless gift that I've offered to all the ladies. No one will make anything of it. Why not choose a ribbon or a bit of lace? Or even a pair of earrings." He tugged lightly on her ear. "It is the only jewelry I ever see you wear."

She fidgeted a moment, and then released a soft breath. "My uncle will take away anything he thinks is of value. After my father died, I expected him to claim my mother's pieces, for many of them were part of the Northam family jewels. But he also took my rings and necklaces, claiming they were Northam property even though they had nothing to do with the family's heirloom collection. He's just a toad that way. There was nothing expensive among them, so I really should not have cared."

"Of course you should have. Especially since they held sentimental value for you." Gawain knew he was going to haul off and punch Northam if the man ever dared approach him. "And you are all about sentiment, aren't you?"

She nodded. "Yes, silly me."

"Not silly at all. Come with me." He did not give her the chance to argue, but took her by the elbow and nudged her into a nearby jeweler's shop. "Choose something."

She coughed. "Good afternoon, Mr. Sloane. How are you today?"

The proprietor's gaze shot back and forth between the two of them. "A lovely day now that the rain has ended, Lady Cherish. What can I do for you?"

"Nothing at—" she started, but Gawain cut her off.

"I am buying a gift for each of Lady Shoreham's guests, but this young lady is being quite stubborn and will not choose anything for herself. I will not have her return to Lady Shoreham's manor empty handed. Let me see your selection of lockets.

Heart lockets, if you please." He regarded several display cases. "Let me have a closer look at these, too," he said, pointing to a row of cameo brooches. "These might do. Something simple but elegant."

"At once, Your Grace. Let me show you my finest." Mr. Sloane hurried into his back room to fetch his samples.

"Why are you doing this? Northam will only take away whatever I choose," Cherish whispered, obviously irritated with him and also feeling humiliated over her circumstances.

"Fiona will let me know if he does, and I will come down on him like a Viking horde. I assure you, Lord Northam will not touch this gift if he values his life."

She rolled her eyes at him, but he caught the glimpse of a smile that she was trying hard to hide. "You are being apish again, you know."

He grinned. "I know."

"I think you rather like flexing your muscles from time to time."

His grin broadened. "I do. So let me have my pleasure, will you? I cannot abide grasping people. It sets my blood boiling, especially when they grasp what they can from someone who is not in a position to fight back."

"I should fight back," she said with a nod. "I am ashamed I haven't done so yet."

"Cherish, no. I did not mean to admonish you in any way. None of this is your fault. You could not possibly defend yourself without my assistance, since our English laws are stacked against you. Now, come look at what Mr. Sloane has brought out and choose something lovely for yourself."

Since he gave her little choice, she chose a cameo brooch—a carving of a lady with a book—and pinned it to the lace fichu at her bosom so that it sat snugly just atop the cleavage of her breasts. "What do you think, Your Grace?"

That he was in serious trouble over this girl. His heart was in an uproar.

"Perfect."

He led her back outside. The ladies all showed him their purchases. He smiled and nodded and pretended to care. Well, he was pleased they had all enjoyed their shopping outing and the gift each chose for herself.

However, every last one of them noticed Cherish's cameo brooch. Dear heaven, did all women have such sharp eyes? They ought to be tossed into military service and trained as sharp-shooters.

Fiona came to his rescue before gossip got out of hand. "Oh, thank you, my dear Bromleigh. Lady Cherish has been so helpful to me," she explained to the others. "I begged for his help in selecting something special for her. I knew she would adore this cameo brooch as soon as I spotted it in Mr. Sloane's shop. Did he have it set aside for us as I requested?"

Gawain cast her a wry smile. "All attended to."

"Good." She leaned forward, kissed his cheek, and then whispered, "You dolt. Whatever possessed you to buy her something sure to raise eyebrows? Is she not in a bad enough situation? Did you have to put her at risk of being labeled your paramour?"

"She is not in any danger of it."

"Only because I jumped in and rescued her in time."

He drew away.

After assisting all the ladies back into their carriages, he strode to his mount and prepared to ride home along with the other men. But his mind was caught up in thoughts of Cherish. So what if he had bought her that trinket? It wasn't a diamond necklace or anything remotely sparkling. Nor had it made a dent in his pocket change. One would think he had given her a Crown jewel for all the fuss.

The look of pleasure in Cherish's eyes once she had resigned herself to accepting it was worth everything.

He had just climbed onto his saddle when someone called to him from a passing carriage. His blood turned to ice.

Katie.

The young woman who had broken his heart all those years ago. Only now, she was Countess Albin.

The widowed Countess Albin.

What was she doing here? And what else was she going to do to ruin his life?

CHAPTER SEVEN

FIONA RUSHED INTO Cherish's bedchamber as soon as they returned from their shopping excursion. "Trouble," she said, her face looking quite pale as she shut the door behind her and then leaned against it with a groan.

Cherish had been about to stretch out on her bed and read a book, but she immediately set aside her reading material and rose to rush toward her friend. "What's wrong? Are you feeling unwell?"

"I am in the pink. It is *that* woman."

Cherish shook her head. "What woman?"

"Did you not notice a fine carriage draw up beside ours just as we were leaving town?"

"Yes."

"Then you must have seen the brazen hussy who popped her head out of the window and called to Gawain. Shameless, evil woman."

Cherish arched an eyebrow. "Friend of yours?"

"Do not even jest about this."

"Very well. Yes, I saw her. She is quite beautiful. Who is she?"

"She is the widowed Countess Albin now, but she was Gawain's childhood sweetheart, Katherine de Montville."

Cherish's heart sank into her toes.

No, not merely sank, but *plunged* to her toes.

She sat down heavily on the bed. "Oh."

"Oh, indeed. She is going to ruin all our plans."

Cherish felt numb.

How was she ever to compete with this woman who was classically beautiful and obviously wealthy, if her elegant carriage and the gleaming jewels dangling from her wrist and throat were any indication? This meant she had been provided for by a husband who understood his duty in protecting the financial security of his loved ones.

Why couldn't her father have been such a man?

But her toad of an uncle had fooled them all, pretending to idolize and adore his elder brother even though they were only brothers of the half-blood. He had hidden his jealousy well.

But she and her parents were also to blame for allowing this situation to befall her. They had been naïve and simply accepted the vile toad despite telltale signs they would have spotted had they been the least bit cynical.

Well, too late now. What was done was done.

She turned her thoughts to Lady Albin. Cherish had caught a mere glimpse of her, but it was enough to notice how sophisticated and exquisitely striking she was with her catlike green eyes, a perfectly formed nose, creamy complexion, and stunning, dark curls. And now to be told she and the duke had known and adored each other all of their lives?

How could she compete with this?

Fiona began to pace across the exquisite Aubusson carpet that covered the hardwood floor of her bedchamber. "Blast the conniving woman. She cornered me and I had to invite her to supper this evening. I'm so sorry, Cherish. This is an awful turn of events."

Cherish felt too numb to respond.

Fiona paused in her pacing and stared at her. "I hate that woman for how badly she hurt Gawain."

"What happened between them?" Cherish asked, barely managing a breath.

"Plenty, I'm sure. I mean, she could not have been a virgin

when she entered into her marriage."

"Fiona!"

"Well, it is true. Who can resist Gawain? But he was no cad. He was born noble and would never hurt a genteel young lady in that way. He wanted to marry her. He thought she wished for the same or he never would have claimed her in *that* way."

Cherish tried not to ache over what her friend was revealing. "Obviously, something went wrong between them."

"It wasn't his doing, that I can assure you. He loved her and would have moved heaven and earth to marry her. But she went to London for her debut Season and not three months later came home married to the Earl of Albin. Gawain was devastated. She had been proclaiming her love for him all the while, but he now realized she had been lying to him all along."

"Perhaps her family situation required her to—"

"Make the sacrifice and marry Albin? No, she was quite secure. But now she has doubled or tripled her wealth and gained a title, too. She never once told Gawain she was sorry. In fact, she was surprisingly mercenary about it all. She assured Gawain that she did not love Albin, and then told him they could be together whenever Albin wasn't around."

"Good heavens," Cherish said, placing a hand to her stomach as it roiled, "even I know he would never do such a deceitful thing, and I've known him less than a week."

Fiona nodded. "I am completely overset by her sudden reappearance. We were doing so well in our plan and now it has been completely undone."

"*Your* plan, Fiona. It was never mine." But Cherish ached so badly inside, for she had held on to a slim hope of gaining his love.

Well, it would never happen now.

Fiona resumed her pacing and then paused again to stare at her. "Perhaps we ought to go along with Gawain's plan and match you to Reggie."

"No." Cherish shot off the bed. "First of all, it isn't fair to

Reggie. Second of all"—she emitted a long, ragged breath—"I have fallen in love with him, Fiona. Oh, how could I be so stupid as to lose my heart to that Silver Duke? I knew your scheme was dangerous, but I could not stop myself. There were moments I thought he might like me in return, but it was all fanciful wishing on my part. I see this now."

"No, you were not imagining it," Fiona said, coming to her side and taking her hands in her own. "He does like you. Very much, I'm sure. I've noticed how he responds whenever you walk into a room. His eyes light up. And he turns into a jealous ape whenever some other man dares approach you."

"I've never seen it."

"Because he tries to hide his feelings from you. So typical of him," she muttered, shaking her head. "But I know my cousin and see right through him. There is something between the two of you, I am certain of it. If only she hadn't walked back into his life to interfere."

Unfortunately, the woman *had* shown up, and Cherish did not know what to do about it. "How can I compete with someone he once loved that fiercely?"

Fiona pursed her lips and frowned. "By being you. Gawain is older and wiser now, and more cynical. He has to know better than to ever trust her again. But he trusts you, as well he should. You are loyal and honest. Frankly, you are good to a fault. You have to fight for him, Cherish. We cannot let that horrid woman win."

Cherish hated when her friend got that determined look in her eyes, but said nothing when Fiona released her hands and resumed pacing while she thought aloud. "We have several things working in our favor. First, Gawain will never forget what she did to him. She is the one who betrayed him and turned him into the cold Silver Duke he has become. Second, and more important, I doubt she has changed her character. We must use this to our advantage. He has to see her for the mercenary and unfeeling woman she has always been."

"But what if he cannot or will not see through her feminine wiles? He is a duke now, and she will certainly accept his offer of marriage."

"Assuming he proposes to her." Fiona gripped her by the shoulders. "He never will if he is in love with you. This is a war, and you need to fight it. Only you are capable of defeating her."

"Fiona, how am I ever to do it? I am not an accomplished flirt. I have no dazzling gowns. And I am no competition for her in looks."

"You are completely wrong about all of it, especially in the matter of looks. You are far prettier."

"Says my best friend who is wonderful and supportive, and blinded by the fact that she adores me," Cherish said with a chuckle. "Honestly, Fiona. You have to look upon the situation objectively. It is a lost cause."

"Never say such a thing. You cannot give up before you have even tried. Gawain would not want you to."

"Gawain, is it? One look at her and he has forgotten I exist."

Fiona sighed. "Let's just see how this evening progresses. Perhaps we are in a panic over nothing."

Cherish knew the danger was quite real.

She wanted to fight for him, but she was so inexperienced around men. Nor was she the sort to shimmer and glitter around them like a sparkling butterfly. She was a miserable failure at the art of flirtation. How was she ever to win his heart?

Well, she could not be anything other than herself.

He had already been hurt deeply by one woman lying about her feelings, so Cherish was not going to make that same mistake and put on a false face to tempt him, no matter how well intentioned her motives.

Fiona was already digging into her armoire and sorting through her gowns. "Oh, yes. This one will do quite nicely."

She withdrew a silk gown in a copper hue that Cherish rarely wore because the neckline plunged too low for her taste, although it was considered quite fashionable and appropriate for tonight's supper. Whenever she did wear it, she attached a bit of lace at her bosom for modesty.

Fiona seemed to read her mind. "Do not take out your lace. I shall burn it if you dare pin it to the gown. You have the perfect cleavage, and Gawain's eyes will pop wide at the first sight of you."

Cherish laughed. "Fine, your not-so-subtle hint is understood. I happen to agree with your choice of gown. I can wear the cameo brooch with it, and I think that is important. He was so pleased when he helped me choose it, and I want him to be reminded of that."

"Now you are catching on," Fiona said with a smirk. "Let me find you a bit of silk ribbon to match, and we'll make a choker out of it to hold the cameo at your throat. I'll have my lady's maid attend to your hair. She is a wonder. I'll direct her exactly how to style it, and you are not to touch a wisp or curl of it. Trust me, Cherish. This is all-out war—and we are going to win it."

Dear heaven.

But Cherish was pleased. The Duke of Bromleigh and his cousin were both competitive and hated to lose. She could see the similarities in their natures. Despite their compulsion to always win, they were also exceedingly honorable, loyal, and clever. Cherish would also add compassionate to their fine qualities. The duke gave the appearance of being icy, but she had no doubt he would be the first to run to the aid of someone in distress.

By the time Fiona's maid finished dressing her, Cherish did not recognize herself. She had never in her life considered herself sultry, but she was exactly that now. Every curl, every nip and tuck of silk, every detail, was designed to draw the duke's eye toward some part of her body that was considered sensual.

She clapped her hands, not nearly as appalled by her alluring transformation as she ought to have been. "Take that, Your Grace," she muttered to herself. "What do you think of me now?"

Reggie and Fiona stopped by her door so the three of them could walk downstairs together. Reggie's eyes bugged wide the moment he caught sight of her. He burst out laughing. "Spectacular! What did you do? My uncle is going to bounce off the walls like a great ape."

Cherish could not contain her own mirth. "The credit goes to Fiona and her maid. I had nothing to do with it."

He shook his head. "Oh, you did. This is all you, Cherish. Well done. You are absolutely sparkling. I am in raptures over you myself."

She blushed.

"Oh, gad! Blush like that when my uncle compliments you, and you will have him eating out of the palm of your hand. He will be completely undone."

She doubted it, but was pleased they considered her much improved.

Her heart was pounding by the time she entered the parlor to join the others already assembled. To her disappointment, the duke was not there.

However, several men suddenly cast her admiring looks. One in particular, a handsome gentleman by the name of Lord Fellstone, had been circling around her for several days now and showing her particular attention. He noticed her and approached, requesting the privilege of escorting her into supper. Fiona had prepared her for the possibility of attracting suitors and advised her how to respond. "Why, yes. I should be delighted."

Fiona had also instructed her to pay attention to everyone but the duke tonight.

Reggie had seconded it. "You have to pretend he doesn't exist, Cherish. He has to be made to feel as though he is losing you."

This would be hardest for her. She was so drawn to him, but also understood the necessity. He would never own up to his feelings unless desperate measures were taken. The ploy would either work spectacularly or completely blow up in her face. She feared the latter outcome, but was determined to see this scheme through to the end.

Fiona and Reggie would watch him and report their findings. They could then adjust their tactics as required.

Their battle plan suffered a tremendous blow when the duke walked in with Lady Albin on his arm. She wasn't so much on his arm as clinging to it possessively, her cat eyes scanning the room for any rivals, and her claws firmly dug into him.

Cherish tried to appear indifferent, but she was so bad at these games.

To her surprise, his gaze shot to her almost immediately. He noticed the cameo brooch at her throat and cast her an affectionate smile. She placed a hand lightly to her throat and smiled back.

The exchange could not have lasted more than a heartbeat, but his wicked countess immediately caught on.

Oh, her claws were definitely out.

Cherish wished she had some claws of her own, but then she would not be herself. In all her life, it had never crossed her mind to be cruel to anyone. Well, there was nothing to be done but see how this night played out.

When the supper bell rang, Lord Fellstone led her into the dining room. "Fate is smiling upon us," he said, noting Fiona's seating arrangement. "Look, we are placed beside each other."

Reggie sat to the other side of her.

Fiona, being hostess, was seated at the head of the table. Since the Duke of Bromleigh was her cousin and the highest-ranking gentleman present, he was placed at the opposite end and anchored that part of the table. Cherish was not sure why Fiona had chosen to seat the wicked countess beside him, but being a dullard about such strategies, she had to trust Fiona to know what she was doing.

Ignoring the Duke of Bromleigh was so hard for Cherish, but she tried her best. Lord Fellstone was quite charming and determined to occupy her attention. He appeared to sincerely enjoy their supper conversation, although Cherish was not certain why he had remained attentive even after learning of her reduced circumstances. Had Reggie and Fiona bribed him to appear besotted with her?

It was just an evening's conversation, so she would not make too much of it.

Lord Fellstone was not the only gentleman she spoke to as they dined. In fact, she engaged in conversation with everyone at her end of the table and was now certain Fiona had planned this seating arrangement on purpose.

Lord Durham and Lady Margaret were seated immediately across from her. Cherish's heart went out to Lady Margaret, because the conversation was a bit too intellectual at their end of the table and the girl appeared to be struggling to keep up. When the conversation reached a lull, Cherish commented on Lady Margaret's necklace. "It is beautiful. Is it an opal?"

The girl cast her an appreciative smile. "Yes, a gift from my uncle. He is an admiral in the Royal Navy and was assigned to the South China Seas most recently. He brought this necklace back for me. I think it is quite beautiful, too. Prettier than diamonds or emeralds. And your cameo is lovely, Lady Cherish. I love those, too."

The conversation then turned to her uncle's travels and those of the gentlemen at the table. Lord Durham was surprisingly well traveled. "I spent quite some time in Italy and Greece, in addition to seeing much of the world. There is no denying their ancient sites, their food and culture, are all fascinating. But there is no place as beautiful as England. I am happy to be back home and in the company of my closest friends."

Cherish had to admit she was enjoying herself despite her heartache. She tried very hard not to glance down the table to where the duke was seated, but curiosity finally got the better of her, and she looked.

To her surprise, he happened to be looking back at her.

She smiled at him.

Oh, she probably should have sniffed and tossed her chin into the air. Or ignored him and turned away. But her instincts were to be honest, even if she were ultimately humiliated by her feelings. He had gone on about how no one knew who he really was or cared to know anything about him beyond his title and wealth. He detested insincerity and dishonesty.

If she were to win him, she sensed it would only be done by remaining true to her natural self with all her faults, flaws, and foibles laid out in the open for him to view. But she had many good qualities for him to notice, as well.

A few minutes later, they exchanged glances again. Once again, she smiled at him because she sincerely liked him and it felt like the right thing to do.

He took a sip of his wine and then smiled back. Her heart lurched when he took another sip and then winked at her. She also blushed, the heat immediately coursing up her neck and into her cheeks.

Well, so much for coming across as sultry.

She looked down at the food on her plate, a crisped duck atop a bed of cauliflower and potatoes, and took a hasty bite. Delicious.

She tried not to look his way again.

"I understand we are to have dancing again tonight," Lord Fellstone said.

Fiona nodded. "A full orchestra this evening so that Lady Cherish is not chained to the pianoforte while we are all having fun. You must claim two dances from her, Lord Fellstone, in order to make up for those nights she lost while helping us out."

"It will be my pleasure," he replied with a nod, then asked Cherish if she would allow him to claim a second.

She nodded. "I would like that very much."

Fellstone was about Reggie's age and quite nice looking. Fiona had already filled her in on most of his details. She knew he was the eldest son of a profligate earl. She also knew the old earl, having lived a life of excessive drinking and gambling, was no longer in the best of health and not expected to survive the year. This meant Fellstone would inherit an earldom that consisted of a rather run-down estate.

It was a shame, for Fellstone appeared to be a clever and kind fellow, not at all inclined to follow in his father's wastrel footsteps. Given the choice, he was the sort who would have chosen a love match for himself. But he was soon to be saddled with a ruined earldom, and this would require him to find an heiress unless he wished to spend his life struggling to bring the estate back to profitability during his lifetime.

For this reason, Cherish doubted he was free to pursue her in earnest.

This also assumed he was genuinely interested in her and had not been bribed by Fiona or Reggie. Well, it did not matter. She resolved to have a good time and not dwell on anything serious tonight.

However, maintaining a light and jovial façade was not as easy as she'd hoped. Her heart was lost to the Duke of Bromleigh, and seeing him with his first love was quite hard to endure. Settling her feelings elsewhere was impossible while she still loved him.

Still *loved* him?

What was wrong with her? She had known him only a few days. How could she love him at all upon so short an acquaintance?

And yet she *was* in love with him. It was ridiculous, but how could she deny her feelings? He had claimed her heart, and she could not move on until all hope of his reciprocating that love was lost.

She stared into her lemon syllabub, taking small bites of the creamy dessert with her spoon, grateful Fiona's cook had put very little white wine in it. That would have turned the dessert to liquid and made it more of a drink than a sweet treat to end their repast.

Wine had been poured liberally throughout their meal, and Cherish found herself a little giddy by the time the ladies rose to take their tea and sherry in the parlor while the men remained behind for their ports, brandies, and smokes.

She tried not to glance at the duke as she passed by his chair on her way out, but he was awfully hard to ignore as he stood along with the other men, looking magnificently sleek and powerful.

The wicked countess had remained beside him, no doubt curious to see what he would do as she passed. Goodness, this woman was crafty and manipulative.

In the next moment, the evil woman stuck her foot out and tripped Cherish. She cried out, finding herself about to fall.

"Cherish!" The duke caught her before she tumbled. "Are you all right?"

She nodded, having safely landed in his arms. "Yes, how clumsy of me," she said, her heart racing at the near disaster. "I...I must have tripped on something."

How could she tell him that his first love had purposely stuck out her foot to send her toppling? Would he believe her?

His arms remained circled around her. "You look a bit unsteady on your feet. Fiona's cook put a little extra spirits in everything tonight. Take a moment to catch your breath. I have you."

She nodded again, just wanting to stay in his embrace all night.

"You look exceptionally pretty, by the way. What have you done differently?"

"Fiona had her maid help me with my hair, and she chose my gown. Otherwise, I would have looked like my usual country mouse self."

He frowned. "You have never looked like a mouse. But tonight"—his frown melted away and he grinned—"you are a breathtaking angel."

Truly? Did he think so?

She laughed. "Fiona will be pleased her efforts were a success."

"Top marks for her," he said in a husky whisper, and then released her.

She walked off to the parlor, knowing she had made an ene-my of the countess, who now followed closely behind. Cherish felt the icy feline gaze at her back. The woman's scheme to trip her had worked to throw her into the duke's arms instead. Not at all what that evil woman had intended.

Lady Margaret approached Cherish as she entered the parlor. The girl was frowning and appeared worried. "Lady Cherish, may I have a word with you?"

Cherish nodded. "Of course. What is wrong?"

Margaret led her aside so they could speak in private. "My parents are pushing me toward the Duke of Bromleigh, but he is too old for me and I do not want him."

Cherish smothered a chortle. "Well, he is not all that old."

"He is almost my father's age, and... Well, he is always scowl-ing, and he frightens me. I rather like his nephew, Lord Burton. He is fun and cheerful, but he enjoys your company far more than he does mine because you are so clever and I am not. He likes intelligent women, and I shall never be that. In truth, I have never felt more stupid than at supper tonight."

Cherish put her hand lightly over Lady Margaret's. "No, you were pleasant and charming. Everyone thought you were delightful."

"I was a dolt and everyone knew it. I could hardly follow any of the conversations until you turned the topic to my opal and my uncle's travels. Thank you for that. It was a much easier topic for me to follow, and I could actually speak on the subject without sounding like the peahen they all think I am." Margaret emitted a ragged sigh and continued. "You are so very smart, and I much admire you. Can you teach me to be clever?"

"So that you can impress Lord Burton?"

She blushed. "Yes, but do you mind? I know he likes you. Even if he did not, I would not interfere if you liked him. He deserves someone as wonderful as you."

"Oh, Margaret, I do not think I am all that wonderful. But I do hope you and I shall become friends."

The girl nodded enthusiastically. "I would love that."

"As for Lord Burton, he and I are friends and that is all. If you care for him, then by all means, go after him."

Margaret's eyes rounded in obvious surprise. "Then I have your permission?"

Cherish had noticed Reggie's growing attraction to Margaret as well. But the girl was right in believing he did not take her seriously enough yet. He thought she was fun and quite pretty, but he was used to smart women like Fiona, so it was very possible he would dismiss Margaret as a frivolous bauble unless Cherish and Fiona helped her out.

On top of that, Reggie was distracted with their scheme to lure the duke into marrying *her*. The ups and downs of that subterfuge confused even her, and she knew what was going on. How was Margaret ever to compete with that?

Not that Cherish approved of Fiona's schemes or Reggie's eagerness to participate in them. She was participating as well, she supposed. But only because she truly believed she had fallen in love with the duke.

Did it count as scheming if one was truly in love? She hoped not, because she did not like to consider herself as nefarious as Lady Albin.

Margaret hugged her and then left her side after Cherish assured her that she would give her lessons on the topics men found interesting. But the moment Margaret happily flitted away, the wicked countess approached.

Cherish's heart beat faster and her palms became moist and clammy. However, she tried her best to hide her turmoil and appear composed. "Good evening, Lady Albin."

The woman eyed her. "You are not his sort, at all."

What sort was that? Heartless and selfish?

Cherish kept her chin raised so that she squarely met the woman's gaze. "To whom are you referring? I have so many gentlemen after me, it is sometimes hard to tell."

Oh, dear heaven. What possessed her to spew such drivel?

"Bromleigh, of course. There is no one else here worthy of notice."

Cherish nodded. "Yes, he is quite noteworthy."

"But he is mine, so keep away from him if you know what is good for you."

Cherish had never been threatened over a man before. It was laughable, but also worrisome because the threat came from the countess. Well, she would consult Fiona and Reggie about it later. The woman could do her little harm while she was surrounded by others. Tripping Cherish, as the countess had done earlier, was relatively harmless.

But Cherish hated the thought of that evil woman spilling something on her lovely gown to ruin it. Well, she would make certain to avoid her if she had any food or drink in her hands. A simple enough solution.

The men joined them soon afterward, and Lord Fellstone immediately strode to her side to escort her into the music room, where the orchestra was now setting up. "I thought I had better claim the first dance," he said, tossing her an appreciative smile. "You look lovely tonight, and all the gentlemen have noticed."

"That is curious." She dismissed his comment as flattery, and was surprised when others indeed approached to claim a dance.

Her jaw dropped when the Duke of Bromleigh approached her as well. "The first waltz is mine."

She nodded. "Yes, I did promise it to you and haven't forgotten." After all, he had been the one to teach her the steps, and she did not trust herself yet in the arms of anyone else. He understood it would not only be the first waltz of the evening, but her very first ever attempt at a waltz.

She counted the minutes. She danced the opening quadrille with Lord Fellstone and then two country reels with other gentlemen.

Then suddenly, her Silver Duke was by her side in all his radiance. It was curious she thought of him as some sort of a sun god, because he always wore dark clothes and had not a hint of popinjay colors on him. Even his cravats and waistcoats were rarely anything other than gray or a deep emerald green.

Cherish forgot to breathe.

A smile teased the corners of his lips, and his hand felt warm and comforting as he wrapped it around hers to lead her onto the dance floor.

Lady Albin was prowling along the edges like a predatory cat, her movements graceful and feline, but obviously agitated. This woman did not like to lose.

Neither did the duke.

Cherish hoped she was not about to be embroiled in another game. Had he insisted on dancing with her only to make Lady Albin jealous? It did not seem to be his style. He was not the sort to use people, especially not her. He had wanted her for Reggie and been honest about it from the start, sparing not five minutes before telling her the truth about his purpose. Cherish knew she could trust him.

"Your Grace," she said, taking in the wonderful scent of bay spice on his skin as he put one glorious arm around her waist and drew her close. "Why are you scowling? We needn't dance if—"

"I want to dance with you, Cherish. Forgive me if you thought I was scowling at you."

"What is troubling you, then?"

He regarded her quite seriously, focused on her and paying no heed to the chatter going on around them. "Lady Albin was the one who tripped you, wasn't she?"

Cherish nodded. "Yes, but I am sure it was an accident."

"Why are you protecting her?"

"I did not think I was. I merely meant to give her the benefit of the doubt."

He snorted. "Do you seriously have a doubt as to her intention?"

"No," she admitted. "Are you going to pass a remark to her? She will deny doing it on purpose."

He did not reply.

Instead, he twirled her in time to the music, holding her in his arms as though she were someone precious to him. It was simply his way, and she refused to read more into it. He was experienced with women and must have learned early on how to make them feel special when in his arms.

As for her, she was completely overwhelmed. She closed her eyes and pretended no one existed but the two of them.

When she opened them, she found him looking at her with a smoldering gaze that shot flames through her.

Dear heaven.

It was ridiculous, of course. He meant nothing by it. They were twirling on a crowded dance floor and his former love was pacing on the sidelines, following their every movement.

Cherish looked up at him. "Your Grace, I am not familiar with the games played in your elite *ton* circles."

He frowned lightly. "Do you think I am playing a game with you?"

"No, that is… I'm not certain what is happening just now. Would you kindly explain to me what is going on?"

CHAPTER EIGHT

"**N**OTHING IS GOING on," Gawain responded with a soft growl, twirling Cherish in his arms to the strains of a waltz, marveling how perfectly she fit against him and moved with him.

She regarded him dubiously—for good reason, he supposed.

His denial was partially a lie.

There *was* something going on between him and Katie, the now widowed Countess of Albin, but he wasn't sure what it was yet. He certainly did not want to entangle himself with her again, but she was determined to insert herself back in his life, and this had thrown him off his stride.

He wanted her to leave, and would demand it if she did not soon reveal her motives in approaching him after all these years. He did not trust her and did not want her back in his life again.

But he and Katie had so much history between them. How could he dismiss her without a thought? Yet she was nothing as he remembered her. Gone was her youthful embrace of life and the allure of her smile. Seeing her around Cherish with her claws out and filled with malice had surprised him.

Shocked him, actually. Had she always been this way and he had been too young and foolish back then to notice?

"You seem to be doing quite well for yourself tonight, Cherish," he remarked, guiding her through another spin. "You've captured the attention of several young men."

She shook her head and laughed. "Remarkable, isn't it? But I cannot take credit for it. I think it is the gown and the fact that I am showing off more of my attributes than usual," she said, glancing down at her bosom. "Obviously, I did not dress myself."

"It is evident Fiona had a hand in making you over. She wasn't going to let you hide away, and I'm glad of it. You look lovely. Dare I say it? You sparkle?"

She stared up at him again, her eyes wide and shimmering. Her expression was sweet and soft, far more alluring than any of Katie's practiced looks. "Thank you, Your Grace. I'm glad you think so."

They danced in silence for another turn about the room, but he could see Cherish's thoughts were elsewhere. "What is on your mind?" he asked.

"Are you still in love with her?"

He tensed. "I am not discussing Lady Albin with you."

He was still trying to make sense of his old flame's behavior. Strength and determination were good qualities, or at least he had always thought so. But when driven by jealousy and malice? It sickened him to think he had once been so taken with her.

"I see." Cherish pursed her lips, and now her lithe, little body was as tense as his.

Botheration.

He was in turmoil because Cherish felt so right, but Katie had also felt right all those years ago. He did not know why he was holding on to that thought when it was abundantly clear he had never truly known his childhood love.

"Cherish, stop thinking about her." He could tell by the nibbling on her lip and the expression on her face that she was troubled. Why could she not let Katie's reappearance in his life pass without additional comment?

She grimaced as he led her into another sweeping turn. "Please don't be angry with me, but I must get this out."

"Don't. You have no idea what I am thinking."

"But isn't this entirely the point? You are very good at hiding your thoughts, and I am worried they might lead you in the wrong direction. Are you hoping to resume your acquaintance with her? Do you think you can resist her wiles now that you are older and wiser? It is not so. You will be burned by her, just as you were the first time."

He ought to have been irritated by her meddling, but she appeared to be sincerely worried about him, and he could not find it in himself to growl at her. "Do you think I do not know this?"

"What I think is that you might be too confident because women so easily fall at your feet."

"Stop, Cherish. Most of them ignored me until I became a duke."

"I cannot imagine anyone ever ignoring you."

"Well, perhaps they were attracted to me, but they were never going to marry the third son of a duke. Encourage a dalliance, yes. But there was never a doubt any of them would choose what they thought was the more secure path for marriage."

"Which is what Lady Albin did. Are you bitter about it?"

"I do not forgive easily, if this is what you mean."

"You did not strike me as the sort who would. Honesty is very important to you. How hurtful it must have been to lose the one you loved with all your heart."

"I did not love her with all my heart." He shrugged. "Perhaps at the time it felt that way, but I got over her long ago."

"But you kept yourself off the Marriage Mart."

"Only because I was never interested in marrying for purposes of a business arrangement, and that is the primary purpose of that elegant meat market. However, I did not shun all events. I went to the elegant balls and fashionable soirees. Dinner parties, musicales. The theater. Occasional house parties such as this one," he added with a wry grin.

"Still, you were not open to courting another. Are you sure it was not because you remained in love with Lady Albin? I understand completely how difficult it is to get over someone you care about. Aren't I the same? Stupidly trying to hold on to my childhood memories of Northam Hall and hardly protesting as I was slowly turned into little more than a servant? I was stuck being true to my heart when I ought to have been more mercenary and looked out for myself. Is it not terrible? I was stuck on a *thing*, not even a person."

He could not help casting her an affectionate smile. "This is what I like best about you, that soft and sentimental heart of yours."

"It is awful," she said with a shake of her head. "I shall condemn myself to a life of misery under Lord Northam's tight fist if I do not change my ways. I don't think it was easy for you to move on, either. It isn't easy for me, and I came to this party not in love with anyone."

"And now?"

"I have not even been kissed yet. How am I to know what I should or should not be feeling? But I think when I fall in love it shall be once and always. How does one move on from this?"

"Do not look to me for an answer. Apparently, you believe I have done a terrible job of it. But I have moved on, and so shall you."

She regarded him with a tender expression that wrapped around his heart. "Your Grace, I know you believe you are in full control of your feelings. You certainly hide them far better than I have ever done. But I do not think you have quite moved on from Lady Albin."

"Is that so? If you are able to see through me so well, then tell me what else I am thinking."

"I am not very good at reading people when it comes to matters of love because I have no experience with it. But your outward calm does not fool me. I know you are in turmoil. Please do not make any rash decisions. You must think things through before renewing your acquaintance with Lady Albin. You have come a long way since your days as a third son and are now one of the elite, sought-after Silver Dukes. But this does not mean your heart is impenetrable."

They took another spin in time to the music. "Oh, I've done a fairly good job of building up those thick walls."

"You may think she is safe because you do not have to marry her. Is this not the appeal of widows such as Lady Albin? But you cannot carry on a liaison with someone like her."

He liked Cherish and always enjoyed listening to hear her thoughts, but not about this. "I am not a little boy who needs to be warned to protect his manhood."

She emitted a shaky breath. "She will eat your soul."

He laughed.

"I am serious. Everyone thinks you have ice in place of a heart, but you don't. You have a wonderfully caring heart that will not behave according to your will. Hearts never do what you want them to do. I just don't want yours to betray you."

"And yours, Cherish?"

She groaned. "My heart is completely misbehaving, and I am in agony over it."

He twirled her off to the side near the glass doors leading onto the terrace. With one more spin they were on the terrace, and he stopped dancing upon reaching a torch-lit corner. He drew her behind one of the pillars but continued to hold her close, slowing their dance so that they were hardly moving in time to the music. "Why are you in agony?"

"To toss your words back at you, it is none of your business."

"Has someone hurt you? One of those new suitors?"

Pain shot into her eyes. "No."

"Blast it, Cherish. You are a terrible liar."

"I know."

"Has someone insulted you? Tell me who and I shall have a word with him." He continued to hold her, their shadows barely visible in the dim light. The night sky was clouded over so that one could not make out the stars or moon.

Cherish looked quite pretty by the light of the lone torch.

"I am not so inept as to require your assistance," she insisted. "No one has said or done anything unkind to me, other than your paramour."

"Don't call her that."

"Then what is she to you?"

He released Cherish, no longer maintaining the pretense of dancing with her, and walked over to the balustrade. "I don't know what she is. I don't know who she really is or whether I ever want to see her again. There, are you satisfied?"

"No, but I am truly sorry you are so turned upside down by her."

"I'm not turned upside down."

She shook her head and regarded him with irritating patience. "Now who is lying?"

Perhaps Cherish was right and he was merely deluding himself. As much as he did not trust Katie, he suspected they could easily fall back into an intimate relationship. Since she was a widowed countess with means of her own, she would suffer little if the gossips found out about their renewed acquaintance. He could bed her without the need to marry her.

Was this not what Katie was offering? An open invitation into her bed with no strings attached?

Even Cherish, as untried and innocent as she was, could see where it was certain to lead.

On the one hand, renewing a casual acquaintance with Katie would allow him to remain free to do as he wished with his life. He could continue to be the Silver Duke everyone desired but no woman could ever catch.

Pursuing Cherish, on the other hand, meant surrendering completely. She would require a vow of commitment. Marriage. Faithfulness. Till death do us part.

Even kissing Cherish was dangerous.

He knew how to kiss a woman, and expected he could steal Cherish's heart with just one kiss because she believed so wholly and completely in the enchantment of romance. She also believed in abiding love. Unbreakable, enduring love.

He could sweep her away with such feelings.

And yet she might do the same to him, because her innocence and this sincere belief in love's existence was incredibly appealing to him. She spoke from her heart, and therein lay pure truth.

More than that, she had magic in her heart. Perhaps this was what he had always been waiting to find, that one person who could make him feel the magic.

And here she was before him.

Cherish.

The orchestra now played the last strains of their waltz. Gawain knew she would now be claimed for the next dance. He was about to offer his arm to escort her back inside when Reggie spotted them. "Ah, there you are," he said to Cherish, sounding annoyingly gleeful. "Our turn to dance."

She smiled in obvious relief and walked off with him.

Gawain was left standing alone on the terrace.

It did not take long for Katie to approach him. "You are wasting your time with her," she said quite matter-of-factly. "She is the demanding sort and will expect a proposal of marriage out of you if you so much as kiss her."

Had he not been thinking this very thing? But he resented Katie's mention of it.

He arched an eyebrow. "And what have you to offer me?"

He knew he sounded surly and perhaps insulting, but what did she expect after decades of lies and not a single apology from her?

"I can offer you your heart's desire, Bromleigh. Anything you want. I am free now to give you all of myself." She drew close and held her perfumed body against him. Hers was a heavy scent, cloying and sweetly stale.

He eased away. "Out of curiosity, Katie, why did you marry Albin?"

"He was rich, titled, and doted on me. He was also my father's age, so I knew he was likely to pass on before I got too old to enjoy myself."

Gawain snorted. "That's touching."

"I loved you, not him. What do you want me to say? I saw the opportunity and took it for us."

"Us? I never asked this of you."

She sniffed. "No, you wanted me to be the wife of a soldier. How were we to live off your meager wages?"

"My father was the Duke of Bromleigh. He would have taken you in and looked after you. You could have made a comfortable life for yourself at Bromleigh Hall or in London if that was your preference. My father would not have stinted on your allowance. Nor would my brothers, had they survived to assume the title."

"A comfortable life? To be your proper and meek wife, left to sit about embroidering handkerchiefs for you while awaiting your return? To be dependent upon the largesse of your family and forced to behave as they saw fit? Never to rule a home of my own? No, this was never something I desired. Why should I be at their mercy if they disapproved of my friends or my style of life? And what if you had died in battle? What would have become of me then? You were third in line to succeed your father. What was the wife of a third son ever going to inherit?"

He said nothing, merely eyed her coldly.

She tipped her chin up in defiance. "Did you expect our *love* to provide all the nourishment I needed? You ought to appreciate the sacrifices I made for us."

"*Us* again? You keep dragging me into this decision completely of your own making. That's rich."

"But it is true."

"No, it was never true, and I don't appreciate your so-called sacrifice."

"Because you are still angry at the thought of losing me. You were never a good loser."

"That hasn't changed. Did it never occur to you to reach out to me and explain? I know I was away from England much of the time, but there were years when you could have contacted me.

Do you think I remain so besotted that I will once again fall for your lies?"

"Our hearts are bound to each other, Bromleigh. Why won't you admit it?"

"Yours was never bound to mine. Why have you come back, Katie? Is it because I am now a duke?"

"Will you pretend it is not an attractive quality? Every girl here is hoping to marry the Duke of Bromleigh." She moved closer to him again. "Marry me or don't. I do not care. Give us a chance, why don't you? I know we can rekindle the love we once had."

"No."

She sighed. "I am in Brighton until the end of August. I know you are here for another few days. Think about us. If you are not ready to come to me here in Brighton, then come to me in London. I'll be waiting for you."

He watched her walk away. She moved like a cat.

And just like a cat, she was now circling Cherish as though ready to spring upon an unwary mouse. He did not like that Katie had her eyes on Cherish.

Gawain rubbed a hand along the back of his neck. How much clearer did he have to be with Katie? Was an outright refusal not enough? There would be no rekindling of their relation. She was no longer the woman he wanted.

If anything, he was furiously kicking himself for being so dense about her for all these years. He'd held on to a dream of perfection that never existed and had only himself to blame for remaining so deluded. So many years lost by refusing to move on to seek his own happiness elsewhere. Well, he had not completely shut himself off. He would have married if someone special had come along. But no one ever had until now.

Cherish.

Yes, she was lovely in every way and could make him happy.

But he also had to think of Reggie. The lad needed a wife he could trust with his heart and with his life. A wife who thought of others rather than only of herself. If Cherish ever vowed to love Reggie, he could count on her to remain true to her word. If Reggie were ever to go into the army, she was the sort of girl who would wait faithfully for his return. Unlike Katie, she would not demand a fine home for herself or require an extravagant style of life.

Cherish was... Blast, she was perfect for *him*.

So what was he doing? Why was he trying to foist her on Reggie?

"Bah," he muttered, returning inside to watch Cherish and soak her in, because he could not seem to get his fill of the girl.

She danced almost every dance and had no shortage of admirers. Yet there was nothing haughty in her demeanor. If anything, she seemed uncomfortable by the compliments tossed at her.

However, she did enjoy dancing, and her smile was sheer radiance as she hopped and twirled in time to the music.

Gawain did not dance again, for the jaunty reels were more suited to the younger crowd, to Reggie and his friends, who were already in their cups and hopping about like frogs in a pond. Instead, he performed his duties to Fiona by wandering through the room and engaging her guests in conversation.

It was two o'clock in the morning by the time the dancing ended, and perhaps three o'clock by the time the last stragglers made their way to their bedchambers.

Gawain had not seen much of Katie after their discussion on the terrace, so he assumed she had climbed back in her coach and returned to Brighton.

Unfortunately, he was wrong.

He found her waiting for him in his bed.

Naked.

Bollocks. What was she scheming now?

"Katie, what are you doing? Put your clothes back on."

By the hard look in her eyes, Gawain knew she was not done with him yet. "Is this any way to greet the woman you once loved?"

"*Once* being the significant word in that sentence. Did you take nothing away from our earlier conversation? I told you, we are through. Our time has come and gone. In the past. Never to be resurrected. Done."

She sat up and positioned herself in what she thought was an enticing pose. "Come to me, Bromleigh."

He handed her the thin chemise she had tossed off and that was now dangling on the footboard. It was so sheer, he doubted it would hide anything of her body. She refused to put it on, but even if she had, it probably would not have done much good. Her bosom would have spilled out of it, for the material was so flimsy, little would be left to his imagination.

Not that he needed any imagination, since Katie was showing him everything. "Get dressed," he growled when she licked her lips in sultry promise and began to spread her legs. "I'll help you tie your laces."

She refused to budge. "You cannot send me home now. It is too late and much too dangerous for a lone carriage to be on the road at this hour."

He sighed. "Stay here, then."

"Now you are coming to your senses. Get out of your clothes and I shall have you com—"

"Gad, be quiet, Katie. I am not staying in here with you." He gathered some of his belongings and strode to the door.

"Bromleigh, where are you going?"

"To sleep in my nephew's room. He has two beds, and I shall manage quite well sleeping in the spare."

She scrambled off his bed. "You cannot be serious. Don't be a fool. Share yours with me."

Gawain knew this would be the most foolish thing he could ever do. "Goodnight, Lady Albin."

He shut the door behind him and strode down the hall to Reggie's bedchamber. His nephew's eyes widened as he opened his door to allow him in. "Uncle?"

Gawain strode past the lad and tossed his change of clothes onto one of the chairs. "Don't ask," he said, beginning to undress. "I am sleeping here tonight."

"Why?"

He said nothing as he stripped down to his trousers and then settled atop the mattress with a heavy sigh.

"Truly, Uncle. Talk to me. What is going on?"

"Lady Albin is sleeping in my chamber. I'll advise Fiona to send her packing in the morning."

Reggie chortled. "Ah, the Silver Duke has woman troubles. I thought something like this might happen. I'm glad you did not take her up on her offer. *Bloody hell.* You *didn't* take her up on it, did you? I mean, why leave afterward if the damage has already been done? Even if it was just a quick tumble. You know what I mean?"

"I did not touch her."

"Good."

"What business is it of yours whether I did or not?" Gawain glanced over at his nephew, who was gawking at him.

"Because you are my uncle and a man I admire. You ought to be setting the proper example for me."

"Reggie, you are giving me a headache."

"Hardly, it is that woman who is making your head pound. You seem to believe I am a young fool and always dismiss me."

"I'm sorry if I do." He groaned. "At the moment, you are a lot more clever than your fool of an uncle. I don't know how to shake her off."

Reggie stretched out in his own bed and propped himself up on one elbow. "She won't leave until she is good and ready. So you'll just have to make her ready."

"And how am I to do that?" What was wrong with him? Since when did he take advice from that young whelp?

"You ought to declare yourself in love with another woman."

Gawain laughed. "Oh, really?"

"Yes, really. And I know just the one."

"I am not going to pretend to be in love with any of those peahens Fiona invited here. They are for you and your friends."

"What about Lady Cherish?"

Gawain sat up. "Cherish?"

"Yes," Reggie said with a nod. "She is beautiful, kind. Intelligent. Charming. I saw how the two of you danced together. You are a perfect fit. And may I add, she knows how to make you smile. Oh, not that insincere smile you cast everyone. You have a soft one just for her. Lady Albin would believe you if you claimed to be in love with Cherish."

Gawain's teeth were clenched and he was now gnashing them. "Not her."

"Why ever not? She is perfect."

Yes, she was perfect. Which was why he intended her for his nephew. "Shut up, Reggie. Go to sleep."

"I can't. My head is still in a spin." His nephew had his eyes open and his hands casually propped behind his head, determined to hold a conversation. "Didn't Cherish look pretty tonight?"

Gawain sank back atop his mattress. "Yes, Reggie."

Lord, yes.

"Let's be serious now, Uncle. Is Cherish the reason why you would not spend the night with Lady Albin? You like her, don't you?"

Gawain rolled over to blow out the candle and fell heavily back onto the spare bed. "Stop asking questions."

"Why won't you admit you like Cherish?"

Gawain emitted a snore.

"Fine, don't answer me. I know you like her. So do I. If you won't court her, then perhaps I will. Actually, there is no perhaps about it. If you do not want her, then I am going to court her. What have you to say about that?"

"Not a thing, Reggie. Go to sleep."

Reggie sighed. "Fine, but this is not over. If you do not want that gem of a girl, then I shall have her. Goodnight, Uncle Gawain."

>>><<<

GAWAIN AWOKE EARLY the next morning after a troubled sleep that was all of his own making. His nephew had finally noticed Cherish and was ready to pursue her with the objective of marriage.

Why did this make him feel so wretched?

He quietly washed and dressed, then headed downstairs in the hope of finding himself alone in the breakfast room. After yesterday's activities, he expected everyone to sleep in late and was not pleased to find Katie waiting for him. Well, she knew his habits.

"Good morning, Lady Albin." He kept to formality as he went to the sideboard to fill his plate with kippers and eggs. What a nuisance to find her here. Was she going to follow him everywhere he went?

"Bromleigh, enough of your games. We need to talk."

"Not a chance." He intended to grab a quick bite then go for his usual morning ride. The sun was shining and it promised to be another fine day.

Indeed, it would have been perfect if not for the presence of his former love.

"I know you are still angry with me for what you think I did. But it is time you forgave me. I shall forgive you, too."

He glanced over at her. "What have I done that requires it?"

"You were beastly to me yesterday. It is time you realized your mistake and came back to me."

He sighed and took a seat across the table from her, motioning for a footman to bring him a cup of coffee. "Why are you here, Katie? What do you really want from me?"

She took a sip of her tea and then daintily set down the cup. "Is it not enough to simply want you?"

He laughed. "Yes, for some women. But never for you. Does Fiona know you are still here?" Someone must have helped her into her clothes and styled her hair this morning.

She arched a perfectly formed eyebrow. "I have no idea. One of Lady Shoreham's valets summoned the housekeeper when he found me in your bed. The poor man was quite shocked."

"Don't tell me—he found you naked."

She grinned. "Oops."

"I'm glad one of us finds humor in the situation."

"I assume Lady Shoreham has been told by now, since this is her house. Why are you so put out? I am a countess. She is not about to refuse me if I choose to remain."

Gawain held back a chuckle, for Fiona would toss the King of England out on his regal derriere if she were of a mind to do so.

He wanted Katie out of here. It was bad enough these footmen were listening in and now knew she had spent the night in his bedchamber. Naked. Hopefully, they also understood he had not remained with her.

Odd how her perfect hair and perfect smile, and every other detail of her perfect self, now irked him rather than tempted him.

He finished his breakfast, took a last sip of his coffee, and then rose. "I'm off."

Her eyes widened. "Where are you going?"

"Morning ride."

"I'll go with you. Give me a moment to change into my riding habit. Have the groom saddle a horse for me, as well."

"You came prepared, didn't you?"

"I always do."

"I prefer to ride alone." He strode out, his only concern being for Cherish, who had no idea of these goings-on and would take the brunt of Katie's anger if she wasn't warned. Even Reggie, as dense as that lad could sometimes be, had noticed his uncle's attraction to Cherish.

Gawain, of course, would always deny it. But it had to show, for what he felt was no mere passing fancy.

Was it possible he was in love with Cherish?

"Bah," he muttered, heading upstairs to knock at Cherish's

door and talk to her before he rode off.

He heard the soft pad of her bare feet as she scurried to answer the door, and then sucked in a breath at the sight of her. She looked adorably sleepy, her cheeks pink and her hair in a long, loose tumble over her shoulders.

Her big brandy eyes widened upon her finding him at the door. "Your Grace, what is the matter?"

Her nightgown and robe were of plain white cotton. No sultry silks for her. Yet she looked incredibly alluring.

"Cherish, you are going to hear a rumor that Lady Albin spent the night in my bedchamber."

Her eyes grew even wider, and she appeared shocked, as he knew she would be. But there was no other way to put it but to be direct. "Did she?"

Blast.

Her look more resembled hurt than shock. Perhaps he should have said nothing and just let her hear the gossip. But how would that have been any better? "Yes, she did. But I spent the night in Reggie's chamber. I want you to know that I was not in there with her."

"Why is it important for me to know this? You are unmarried and free to do as you please. Is this not what you Silver Dukes do? Take any woman you desire into your bed and then move on? No attachments. No responsibilities. No thought to the lady once you are done with her."

"Why are you making me out to be an ogre? I have never forced any woman into my bed or ever given false hope. I certainly did not invite Lady Albin into my bedchamber."

"How did she get in there then?" she asked, her small hand gripping the door so tightly, her knuckles turned white.

"Our doors are not locked. I suppose she assumed I would welcome her traipsing in, which I did not. Since she would not leave, I did."

"And slept in Reggie's room? Now that you have told me, what am I supposed to do about it?"

"Trust me."

Those warm eyes of hers, which so clearly expressed her displeasure a moment ago, now softened. "I do trust you, Your Grace. I'm sorry if I sounded surly. I am not always at my best in the morning, and your statement startled me."

"You, surly? You are a sweetheart, Cherish." He ached to kiss her, for her lips also had that rosy tinge of morning on them, and he could think of nothing nicer than sinking his mouth onto hers. "Well, I just wanted you to know the truth. Especially after our discussion last night. Yes, she was in my bedchamber, and I doubt I will be able to dislodge her. But I left and will remain in Reggie's room until she proceeds on her merry way."

She cast him a soft smile. "Thank you, Your Grace."

He sighed. "Call me Gawain. There's no need for formality between us."

"My goodness, you are very friendly this morning."

Not nearly as friendly as he would like to be, but he would talk to her about this later. He had a lot to think through before he said anything more to her. However, since he was a clot and unable to resist her, he leaned forward to kiss her lightly on the cheek. "I'll see you later."

He strode out of the house and went to the stable to saddle his mount, for he was eager to ride off before Katie followed him. For this reason, he attended to the saddle himself rather than wait for a groom's assistance.

The air was cool as he rode off on Odin. His horse enjoyed these morning runs as much as he did. A light mist still hovered over the waves that could be seen rolling to shore in the distance, but there was none on the land, since the sun had already burned through it save for a lingering tendril here and there.

The countryside was quite pretty around Shoreham Manor, consisting mostly of gently rolling hills, green meadows dotted with red and yellow flowers that grew in wild abundance, stone fences that proved easy for his horse to jump, tree-lined country lanes, and meandering streams that flowed into the English

Channel.

It was not long before he left Fiona's stretch of property and crossed onto the Northam estate. He was curious to see where Cherish was born and raised. She spoke of her home with love, but what was there for her to love about it now that she was confined to what amounted to indentured servitude because of her uncle's callousness?

He rode through an apple orchard, and then up a neatly maintained drive toward a big white house that was beginning to show signs of neglect. Whatever Cherish had poured of herself into this house would soon be lost because of her uncle's stinting nature.

Men such as Northam would never understand the devotion and effort it took to maintain one's properties. He was the sort to spend his generous inheritance indulgently on himself and then blame others when his well ran dry.

It bothered Gawain that the oaf could not spare even a shilling for Cherish's needs.

He dismounted and strode to the front door.

An elderly man, no doubt the head butler, opened it in response to his knock and immediately came forward to greet him. "Are you lost, sir?" he asked politely.

Gawain shook his head. "No, I am the Duke of Bromleigh. Your neighbor, Lady Shoreham, is my cousin."

"Ah, of course. Then you must be acquainted with our mistress, Lady Cherish. She is spending the week with Lady Shoreham."

Gawain smiled. "Yes, I am."

The butler's eyes immediately brightened. "A lovely girl, isn't she, Your Grace?"

"Yes, quite lovely. I did not mean to disturb anyone. Lady Cherish mentioned her uncle and his family were away, so I thought I would ride by and see if all was in order."

The old man, who now introduced himself as Potter, nodded. "The house is not quite as fit as it was under Lady Cherish's charge, but we are managing. I do hope she is having a pleasant time at the house party."

"She is the belle of the ball," Gawain said, truly meaning it. He had noticed glimmers of her radiance from the very first day, but it had taken until last night for her beautiful inner glow to shine through.

"I'm so glad, Your Grace. She is a lovely girl. We are all quite fond of her."

"It is easy to see why. She has charmed us all." He was not about to impose further, but changed his mind and decided to accept the invitation when Potter asked him in and gave him a quick tour of the house.

"You will notice Lady Cherish's touch throughout the home," the man said, pointing out feminine trappings here and there. However, they were not overdone. The house had an elegant look to it and was clearly decorated with a light, feminine hand.

"I'm surprised Lord Northam's wife hasn't made any changes," Gawain remarked.

Potter shook his head. "Oh, sir. Those are coming. Hideous redecorations, if you ask me. Poor Lady Cherish. It is as though they are purposely undoing everything beautiful she designed. Well, forgive me if I speak out of turn. Lady Cherish is well aware of my thoughts."

"Has she spoken to Lord and Lady Northam about their plans?"

"Yes, Your Grace. But she is helpless to stop them. Her father is no longer earl, and the new earl has no interest in what she says or thinks. It is very hard on her."

"I see." Gawain had now observed all he needed and bade Potter a good day. He rode back to Shoreham Manor at a lazy lope, since it was still fairly early and most guests would only now be waking.

As he rode his horse back to the stable, he noticed Reggie leading a docile mare out of a nearby stall. Lord Fellstone and

Lord Durham were following closely behind him with their own mounts, while Cherish, Fiona, and Lady Margaret, along with a few other early-rising guests, were gathered by the nearby meadow. Gawain realized they were there to cheer Cherish on as she attempted to overcome her fear of horses.

He was not needed, but had no intention of missing this moment. In truth, he wanted to be the one she turned to for assistance and support.

But it was too late to offer now. Reggie was proud as anything to help her.

Lord Fellstone also appeared interested, judging by the avid way he was eyeing her. The wretched fellow had claimed two dances from Cherish last night. Fiona had also partnered Fellstone with Cherish for supper, seating him to the left of her while Reggie had been seated on her right.

And here Fellstone was again today. Did the man have nothing better to do than fuss over Cherish?

A dismaying thought crossed Gawain's mind. Even more dismaying because he, with his Silver Duke high-handedness, had brought this upon himself.

Now that he had competition from these younger men, would Cherish want him?

CHAPTER NINE

G AWAIN FLINCHED AS he stood with the others watching Reggie assist Cherish onto her docile mare. Fiona must have loaned the girl one of her riding habits, because he did not think Cherish would have brought one with her for this house party. Also, the fabric was a bold maroon color, one he did not think Cherish would ever choose for herself. But that hue suited her complexion, bringing out the rose of her cheeks and warmth of her eyes. Not to mention it fit her glorious body to perfection. Well, perfect in his opinion, because it fit just a bit too tightly around the bodice and gave a hint of her spectacular attributes.

Cherish was about the same height as Fiona, but a little fuller in shape. Nicely full in the bosom, Gawain thought.

He frowned, for any pleasure he had felt a moment ago was now gone as he watched her struggle with her fear. She turned ashen as she mounted the horse and almost lost her balance when it took a slight, lurching step forward.

Gawain hopped the fence and strode forward to catch her before she slid off. Or was she purposely about to jump off? He did not want her to give up before taking even one turn around the meadow.

"Your Grace," she said with noticeable relief, and reached out for him to help her down.

He caught her by the waist and propped her back up. "You can do this, Cherish." He patted the docile mare who was growing agitated because she sensed Cherish's fear. "What's her name?"

"Sugar," Cherish said, her lips tensely pursed. "Please, help me down."

"Not yet," he insisted. "You've only just started. I know it is hard for you, but I have faith in you. Give it a try. Reggie and I will not leave your side."

His nephew, who had been holding on to Sugar's reins, nodded.

Gawain now turned to the mare and spoke to her in his most soothing voice. "There, there, Sugar. Behave yourself. That's a good girl."

Once he had calmed the mare, Gawain turned to Reggie. "I'll hold the reins while you climb on behind Cherish. Take a few turns around the meadow so that the horse feels comfortable with both of you in the saddle."

"I've got the mare, Uncle. You had better get on with Cherish, since you have a commanding way with people and horses that instills trust. I don't think she will trust anyone but you."

Gawain wasn't sure whether the *she* referred to Sugar or Cherish.

He studied Cherish. Her eyes had a wild look to them, wide and slightly glazed. He recognized this sign of panic, for he'd seen it in young soldiers their first time on a battlefield. Cherish was in no danger here, but she had been thrown off a horse once and probably suffered a more serious injury than she had let on. A sprained wrist and a bump on the head was what she had told him.

What he believed she had suffered was a serious concussion and an instinctive fear of horses no one had ever taught her to overcome.

Her lips remained tightly pursed and were as devoid of color as her ashen face. "Cherish, I am going to ride with you. Is that all right?"

She nodded.

He easily mounted behind her and wrapped her in his arms, encouraging her to lean back and hold on to his arms. As she did so, he felt her entire body tremble. He knew how to make a woman quiver with pleasure in the bedroom, and ached for this to happen with Cherish. But here and now, she was simply overwhelmed with fear.

He understood how difficult this was for her and admired her attempt to overcome a dread that stemmed from the darkest recesses of her memory.

"Reggie is going to lead your mare in a slow circle around the meadow. He will keep tight hold of her tether so she won't run off or do anything to frighten you. Once you are comfortable, he will let go, and then you and I will circle the meadow on our own. All right?"

"Sugar is a sweet horse, Cherish," Reggie assured her, careful to keep the docile mare to nothing faster than a walk. Any slower and the horse would fall asleep, Gawain thought.

But he was not going to remark on it because it would embarrass Cherish. Her fear was real and not to be taken lightly.

She kept her eyes closed all the while they rode around the meadow. Gawain wanted her to open them. "I have you, Cherish. I am not going to let you fall. Open your eyes now. You can do this."

She buried her head against his shoulder. "You must think I am so stupid."

"Not at all. You were a child when your accident happened, and that horse was probably too much for someone as little as you to handle. Tumbling out of the saddle was not your fault, nor did it show any lack in you."

He continued to speak to her calmly as Reggie led them around once again. This time, Cherish kept her eyes open. But he felt her tense every time Sugar took the tiniest misstep.

"The ground is uneven, that's all. Sugar is docile and will not bolt. You are in charge and she knows it. She will listen to your instructions."

Cherish turned slightly to stare up at him. "You are the one in charge. I am the coward she wants to throw off. Please don't be angry, but I don't think I can do this on my own."

"Yes, you can. Give it time. I'll stay on with you and we are going to take another turn, just us. Reggie, hand me Sugar's reins."

Cherish held her breath.

"You are going to pass out if you don't breathe," Gawain gently teased. "I will never let go of you until you tell me you are ready. I give you my word of honor."

"What if I am never ready?"

"Then I will hold you forever." The words rang surprisingly true as he spoke them, in so many ways other than merely riding. He could hold her throughout his life. Throughout marriage.

Their marriage.

Gawain was amazed the notion did not terrify him.

Still, it was ridiculous to think anyone could lose their heart to another upon a few days' acquaintance.

After completing several circles, he tugged on Sugar's reins to draw her up. They had gone in a slow circle and then a faster circle so that the horse had almost broken into a trot. They could have gone around a few more times, but Cherish was still fearful and trembled the moment he urged Sugar to speed up the littlest bit. And yet she was the one who now insisted on continuing because she was so determined to overcome her fear.

He thought she had done well for herself this first time out. "I'm proud of you, Cherish."

"Oh, dear heaven. I am so pathetic. Are we done for the morning?" she asked, sounding hopeful.

He nodded. "Yes, almost. I am going to get off now, but I want you to remain in the saddle a little while longer."

She gasped. "Without you?"

"Yes, you don't need me. Sugar is just going to stand in this spot with you in the saddle. I have her reins and will be right here with you."

"All right." She tried to sound brave, but those beautiful brandy eyes of hers were still wild, and her voice shook as she spoke. Her distress was evident to all.

"You can do this, Cherish." Reggie gave her an encouraging nod.

"I should be able to," she agreed. "I will. All you are asking me to do is sit on a horse. Even a child can do this. I don't know why I am so scared."

Because her last tumble off a horse almost killed her, Gawain knew. He took hold of her hand and gave it a light squeeze. "These things take time. No one expects you to overcome this in a day."

The onlookers had not walked away.

They were a nice group and were calling out encouragements to Cherish. Lady Margaret was particularly kind to her, and Gawain realized he might have been too harsh when first judging the little peahen. She lacked Cherish's intelligence, but was otherwise a pleasant and cheerful girl.

He noticed Reggie smiling at Lady Margaret. The girl blushed and smiled back.

What was Reggie doing? Had he not told Gawain just last night that he might court Cherish if he did not? So why was he tossing those grins at Margaret?

He would have a talk with the boy later. They would have plenty of time for heart-to-heart discussions if Katie would not leave and he were stuck sharing a bedchamber with Reggie for the rest of the week.

The annoying reminder made him think of Katie. Where was she?

Not that he cared to see her again, but he did not like the thought of her roaming around Fiona's house unchecked and thinking up mischief.

When Cherish asked again whether she could get down, Gawain nodded. "All right." He helped her to dismount.

She cast him a dismayed smile. "I thought I would do better.

Look at me—my hands won't stop shaking."

He took them in his once more. "You'll do better tomorrow. I promise you. Each day will get easier."

The others now joined him and Cherish while Reggie led Sugar back to her stall.

"You got back up on the horse, and that is enough success for today," Fiona insisted, and Lord Durham agreed.

"You were marvelous," Lord Fellstone said, and Gawain stifled the urge to punch him. Of course, this was the jealous ape in him coming out. Fellstone had done nothing untoward. No, all he had done was admire Cherish and... *Bollocks*, was he going to offer for her before the party ended?

Lady Margaret hopped up and down beside them and clapped her hands. "Cherish, you were brilliant."

Cherish laughed and gave the girl a hug. "Thank you, Margaret. But I was awful and cowardly, and utterly inept. Thank you all for being so kind to me as I struggled." She turned to Gawain. "I marvel at your patience. I am truly sorry if I disappointed you."

"You could never, Cherish. No apology required. And Lady Margaret is right, you were brilliant. Same time tomorrow?"

Her laughter was as soft as the breeze surrounding them. "Are you that much of a glutton for punishment to put yourself through this ordeal again?"

It struck him that he would do anything for this girl. "Yes. Let's just say I enjoy a good challenge, and you are certainly that."

While Fellstone, Reggie, and Durham now rode off for their quick jaunt in the surrounding countryside, Gawain returned to the house with the ladies.

He could have gone for another turn with the men, but preferred to see what Katie was doing. He spotted her seated in the parlor with a circle of friends and admirers. Most of Fiona's guests knew her, since she was popular among the *ton* elite. "How kind of you to assist that incompetent girl on her horse."

Of course, Gawain expected she had been watching and

probably seething at the sight of him holding Cherish. "It isn't incompetence, but something far more serious. Any man who has fought in battle will understand what I mean."

A few of the guests surrounding Katie nodded. Most had no idea what he was talking about.

He had no intention of elaborating, and walked on to see to the removal of the rest of his belongings out of the bedchamber Katie had now taken over. He had only brought clothes enough for the week, so it would not take long for Fiona's staff to transfer them to Reggie's quarters.

He felt mildly sorry for Reggie to now be stuck with him for the remainder of their stay. But this would also ensure the lad did not invite ladies into his bed, or sneak off into anyone else's bed, without Gawain knowing about it.

If Reggie seriously intended to court Cherish or that sweet but bubble-headed Margaret, then he should simply make his choice and not be dallying with anyone else.

By the time the switch in rooms had been made and Gawain had taken the time to wash up and change out of his riding clothes, luncheon was about to be served. He had hoped for casual seating arrangements, but Fiona planned a formal luncheon for them. He was not surprised to be assigned his usual seat at the head of the table, but cast Fiona a glower when he found Katie seated beside him again.

His cousin shot back a look that warned Katie was his problem, and he had better deal with her or Fiona would toss them both out. Well, he knew his cousin was not about to toss him out. Nor was she likely to do anything about his former love, who had already become a favorite at this house party.

Cherish was seated beside Reggie once again, and both were at the opposite end of the table along with Fiona, Durham, Margaret, and Fellstone. They seemed to be enthusiastically engaged in conversation and were all smiles.

One would think this merry little group had been friends forever.

Blast the girl.

Cherish was once again laughing at every one of Reggie's stupid jokes. When Reggie was not talking to her, then Fellstone had his turn regaling her with his witticisms.

Blast them both for being charming and attentive to her.

Gawain grumbled when Cherish laughed at *another* of Reggie's stories. He had not heard a single, stupid woodpecker laugh out of the lad. Yes, all was falling into place quite perfectly, and he could not feel worse about it. His stomach churned and he lost his appetite.

Katie leaned closer and cast him an insincere smile. "She is too young for you, Bromleigh. Is it not obvious she prefers Reggie over you? And if not Reggie, then Fellstone has this horse race won. You are completely out of the running."

"It is none of your concern, Lady Albin."

She sighed. "Ah, so formal with me? You are still angry with me. But I do not wish to see you hurt, Bromleigh. Lady Cherish is not for you."

"But you are?" He took a sip of his wine, and then set the glass down because he had no appetite for wine either. That she should refer to him as Bromleigh even in private conversation instead of merely as Gawain was also irksome and another indication of her admiration for his title and not *him*. "It is time you moved on and found yourself another duke who might be more receptive to your advances."

He noticed her composure slip the slightest bit. Was he finally getting through to her?

"You are serious about never forgiving me, aren't you?" Tears welled in her eyes, and her lips began to quiver so much he almost believed she was hurt by his remarks and might still hold feelings for him.

But he knew her very well, and was not surprised when he caught that flicker of triumph in her eyes when she thought he was softening toward her. Yes, it was all artifice and manipulation with her. Since she was so keen on titles, he used hers when addressing her now. "Lady Albin, you betrayed me and you know it. I may find it in my heart to forgive you someday, but I will never forget what you did."

"You are cruel, Bromleigh."

"I am just being honest." He sighed and shook his head. "Must we continue this farce? It is pointless. Please, stop wasting your time with me. Just go."

She called a footman over and held out her glass for more wine. Once he had filled her glass, she held it up in a mock toast. "My dear Bromleigh, I am not nearly ready to give up on you yet."

Were she a man, Gawain would have simply grabbed her and tossed her out. But he had never raised a hand to a woman and would not start now. Katie had to leave of her own accord or at Fiona's demand. She was never going to leave at *his* request.

However, he was not certain Fiona would confront Katie. His dear cousin seemed inclined at the moment to cause him misery.

Well, that would teach him to attend house parties.

If anything could be salvaged from this week, it would be Reggie's future. The lad seemed to be coming along nicely. In fact, he was showing more sense in these past few days than he ever had in the years since Gawain's sister had died. Having acquired this newfound maturity, would Reggie appreciate Cherish's worth and decide to marry her?

This had been Gawain's plan all along. He had thought it clever at the time. Now…not so much.

What would he do if Reggie proposed to Cherish?

CHAPTER TEN

G AWAIN STRODE TO the stable the following morning intending to take his usual ride and still return in time for Cherish's next lesson on overcoming her fear of horses. But he was dismayed to find Katie standing in wait for him. "What are you doing?" he grumbled, taking no pains to be polite to her.

Both of their horses had been saddled and were at the ready. Despite the early hour, Katie looked quite bright eyed and elegant in her riding habit. She wore one of those stylish riding hats with it, perched at a perfect slant atop her flawlessly coiffured head to show her off to best advantage. Of course, she knew how to make herself up splendidly, no doubt having sat in front of a mirror for hours, posing this way and that, until she got the look just right.

"We used to ride together in our younger days. I know you remember because we did more than ride our horses. You gave *me* a ride or two and enjoyed it immensely. Don't you dare deny it, Bromleigh."

He wanted to tell her to stop referring to him by his title, for it grated on his nerves. But he did not want her to call him Gawain, either.

Blast. He just wanted her gone. He had begged Fiona to toss her out already, but his stubborn cousin took his pleas as a lark and ignored him. "You are a big boy, Gawain. Can you not manage her yourself?"

No, he could not.

Oh, he was not concerned for himself but for Cherish. Why was Fiona being so dense? Katie had a vindictive side to her that she hid well from others. Had she not hidden this uglier side successfully from him when they were younger?

Well, he would keep close watch on her and hope nothing untoward happened.

He took the reins of his mount from the groom who had led the beast out. "I won't deny our past, Katie. But you do not seem to be listening to me when I tell you this is all we are to each other now, nothing more than two people who were friends years ago. I am never going to make the same mistake with you again."

"It was not a mistake, and I shall prove it to you." She called over one of the grooms to assist her in mounting.

Gawain had to admit she was an excellent rider and fearless in the saddle. In truth, she did many things well, in addition to having perfected the art of being charming.

While they cantered away from the stable and into the countryside, his thoughts strayed to Cherish and how lacking she was in horsemanship or *ton* elegance. Yet he far preferred her brand of charm, which was simple and honest. Therein lay the difference, for Cherish could tell him the moon was green and he would believe her. In contrast, Katie could tell him the sun rose in the east every morning—which it did—and he would question whether she was telling him the truth.

Trust was the issue, and he simply did not trust Katie. Nor did he like the pettiness he now saw in her behavior. He was used to people approaching him with the intent of getting something out of him, but was sincerely sorry that Katie could be counted among them. He had grown quite cynical over the years, and also quite adept at spotting those who sought to take advantage.

Katie fell into that category for certain. She was here and trying to cozy up to him because she wanted something out of him.

But what? He wished she would simply tell him straight out.

They raced across meadows and over hills, the wind biting as it struck Gawain's face. The day would warm eventually, but for now the overnight chill remained in the air and a morning mist lingered amid leafy copses and shallow dales.

Gawain did not particularly wish to speak to Katie, but their horses needed to rest after that run, so he drew his up beside a nearby stream. He dismounted and then walked over to assist Katie.

"What is it you really want from me?" he asked when she put her hands on his shoulders while he helped her down. But she held on to him when he tried to release her, lifting up on tiptoes to kiss him.

He pulled back and drew her off him as gently but firmly as he could manage. "Trying to kiss me will not work. Do you think you can find it in yourself to simply tell me the truth?"

"Here is the truth," she said, now rubbing herself against him. "You know we both want this."

He stepped back again. "How much clearer must I be? Stop trying to seduce me. It isn't going to work."

"Because you think I am too old now," she said, sounding quite wounded. Well, she was in her mid-thirties and probably worried about her looks fading. She was a woman who had done quite well for herself on looks alone. The possibility she was losing this advantage had to be an upsetting revelation.

"You are still beautiful, and I am sure most men think so. But what you also are is false, conniving, and selfish. Those are quite ugly traits. Stop trying to win me over, because I am long past caring for you. Why are you really here?"

"Because I want *us*. Isn't that enough truth for you?" Her cheeks turned pink as she appeared to struggle with her feelings, or perhaps it was merely irritation that he was being so difficult and thwarting her plans. "I know you don't believe me when I say that I married Albin for our sake, to give us the chance for a better life that we would not have had while you remained a third son. Had I known you were destined to be the duke, I would have married you and somehow managed to wait it out. But how could I possibly know such a thing would happen? I had no crystal ball."

"You don't get it, do you? Do you hear yourself? You only want me because I now have the title. Face it, Katie. You never really wanted *me*."

"But this is who you are…the Duke of Bromleigh. And do you forget that I gave myself to you when we were younger? What more proof do you need that I wanted you? And I still want you. Are you really so deluded as to believe the young ladies at Lady Shoreham's party care for you beyond your title? Do you think they want you in their bed?"

He knew quite well that most did not. Which was why he had no intention of offering for any of those little peahens.

"They flirt with you because they want to be your duchess," she said, not yet done with her little speech. "Why do you not ask *them* to tell you the truth? Or are you afraid of what they will say? Then I shall tell you what they are all thinking, even your precious Lady Cherish."

No, Cherish was different. She would melt at his touch, and lose her heart to him, if he kissed her.

"You are too old for them, and they will be repulsed by the intimacies you force on them, just as I was when my husband touched me. But I endured for *us*. I closed my eyes and pretended you were the one with me. After all I have been through, is this how I am to be rewarded for my sacrifice?"

"Rewarded?" He stared at her in disbelief. "You gave up on us building a life together, gave up on our happiness and our chance for children. You gave it all up without a thought for me, not even a letter of warning or a single conversation between us about your plans. You knew I would never agree, and you did not want me in a position to stop you."

As he spoke, he had been watching her shifting expressions and noticed her look of disdain at the mention of children. That look did something to his heart. She did not want to raise a family and would not have been a good mother to any sons or daughters they might have had.

This truly tore him apart. How had he been so blind? How did he not see what she was? A beautiful woman whose thoughts were centered only on herself.

He sighed, accepting the truth now and knowing he shared the blame for remaining oblivious. "You wanted your fine carriages and expensive jewelry above the love I was willing to give you. Well, now you have them. You have all the trappings of wealth, more than most ladies can ever dream of. This is what you chose, Katie. Do not expect me to accept it. I would not have done so then and will not do so now."

He had his failings as well, for he could have moved on and found someone else to marry. But he had used Katie's betrayal as an excuse to close himself off. That part wasn't her fault, only his.

Of course, he had not realized this was what he had been doing. All the while, he thought he had been searching for love.

He'd found it now with Cherish.

So why was he still playing matchmaker to her and Reggie? Or saying nothing as Fellstone hovered close?

He helped Katie back up on her horse and then mounted his own. Their ride back to Fiona's stable was as breakneck and reckless as their ride out. He supposed they both had anger and disappointment to work through. But their talk only firmed his resolve about Katie.

He wanted nothing to do with her.

There was not a chance in hell he would ever make her his duchess. She would think only of her own needs and never concern herself with the needs of others. This was not the sort of wife he wanted.

If ever he *were* to marry, it had to be someone like Cherish— someone whose heart was tender and whose instincts were kind.

Well, he did not know why his thoughts were even straying there, for had he not made a mess of that, too? He shook back to the present as they approached Fiona's manor.

Cherish was walking toward the stable as they rode up.

He immediately drew back on his reins to slow his mount, but Katie had no such intention. To his horror, she rode toward Cherish at full gallop and would have caused her serious injury if Cherish had not been alert and leaped out of the way in time.

But she fell backward and landed hard on the ground.

"Cherish!" He raced to her side, unable to restrain his fury, not only aimed at Katie but at himself for everything he had done wrong leading up to this moment.

He wrapped Cherish in his arms as she struggled to sit up. "Take another moment, love. You had the wind knocked out of you."

Love?

Had he just let that endearment slip?

She was shaking hard and too overset to notice. "She ran me down on purpose."

"I know. This is my fault."

She looked up at him in surprise. "How is it yours?"

"Long story. Let's get you back to the house," he said, stopping her as she struggled to rise and was obviously having difficulty. "I did not mean to have you walking on your own. I'll carry you back. Can you put your arms around my neck?"

"No, people will talk. Give me another moment to catch my breath and I'll manage on my own. I think I am all right." But she emitted a groaning laugh not a moment later and sagged against him. "This must be the Fates telling me I am not meant to be near horses."

He glanced around and saw none of the others who had been cheering her on yesterday. "You came out here alone?"

She nodded against his chest.

"Why, Cherish?" He was kneeling beside her and rather liked cradling her in his arms. She did not seem to mind, either, for she was comfortably nestled in them.

She placed her hand on his chest as she tried to get up again, but he stopped her once more. "Give it a moment longer. I wish you had waited for me. I would have accompanied you out here."

"No, I had to do this on my own. I felt so cowardly yesterday."

"Why? No one thought less of you for your struggles."

"I hate being this way, feeling so helpless and weak. I thought to approach Sugar and work my way up to riding her. Not that I consider myself brave enough to ride her yet," she said with a wincing laugh. "But I wanted to give her a little hay and have a talk with her. I even brought a few apples along for a special treat for her. It sounds ridiculous, I know."

"Not at all. I think it is quite admirable of you."

"Hardly. I was determined to have Sugar like me and was ready to bribe her to accomplish it. The apples spilled out of my basket. Oh, and the basket is crushed, too."

"Never mind about those. They are easily replaced. You are not."

She nodded. "You and Lady Albin ride so effortlessly. I wish I could do the same."

"It doesn't matter whether you ever do or not, Cherish. No one will like you any less for your lack of horsemanship. It is nothing compared to all your other fine qualities."

She snorted. "You needn't flatter me simply because I took a dive in the dirt."

"I'm not. Can you not see you are a favorite at this party? Those little peahens adore you, and several gentlemen of excellent character have also taken an interest in you."

"Oh, really?" She laughed.

"Yes, really. What about Reggie? Or Lord Fellstone? They have both been quite attentive to you."

"Perhaps." She gave a slight shrug, as though to dismiss his statement. "Are you ready to tell me your long story? How are you in any way to blame for Lady Albin's actions?"

"Is it so hard to figure out?"

"No, I suppose not. She wishes to revive your friendship and for some reason thinks I am standing in her way."

He lifted her in his arms to carry her to the manor house. "Do not protest. You were badly shaken, and I will not have you falling again."

She rested her head against his shoulder. To Gawain, it felt as though she belonged with him, her body soft and perfect as it molded to his. "Why does she think I am standing in her way?"

"In her mind, it is easier to blame you than admit to her own failings. She refuses to see that it is her own character I find unworthy. She was angry when I told her so. I spelled it out quite plainly."

"This is a reason to run *you* down with her horse, but why me? Lady Albin clearly does not like me. It is one thing to sneer at me, but quite another to put me in physical danger. Is there something more you are not telling me?"

He sighed. "I suppose she knows I admire you above any other young lady here. This is why she is worried you are her competition. It is beyond her abilities to accept that I will never have her under any circumstances. That door shut when she married Lord Albin. She refuses to admit any of the past is her fault and places the blame everywhere but on herself."

"Do you still love her?"

"No, Cherish. I meant it when I said that I stopped caring for her long ago. Even if I were still besotted—which I assure you, I am not—her behavior since arriving here, especially that dirty trick she pulled just now, would have opened my eyes to her petty nature. But I was already aware. A betrayal is a betrayal. Once trust is lost, there is no reclaiming it."

"You will never trust her again?"

He nodded. "How can I? This applies to anyone, not just Lady Albin. This is what I am trying to teach Reggie, to acquire that ability to sense a person's character. To know who will deceive him and who will not."

"And once deceived, teach him never to forgive?"

"Cherish, people don't change. If they lied to you once, they will do it again."

"But that is a little harsh, don't you think? Everyone makes mistakes."

"Yes," he said with a wry grin. "Even I am not perfect, as shocking as this may appear to you."

She laughed.

He loved the sweet quality of her voice, in addition to everything else he liked about her. "There is a difference between an honest mistake and outright deception. This is what I hope Reggie will learn in time."

Fiona rushed toward them as he reached the terrace and was about to carry Cherish into the parlor. "Gawain! What happened?"

"Accident by the stable," Cherish said, making no mention of Katie's running her down. Was she waiting for him to explain?

Reggie and Margaret also rushed forward. "Oh, Cherish!" Margaret cried with genuine concern. "We would have come with you. Why did you not tell us you were going to the stable?"

Gawain set her down on the settee in the parlor and called for one of the footmen to bring a glass of sherry. "It will help calm you down and ease your tense muscles," he explained when she eyed him dubiously. "How do you feel? Any sprains? Ankle? Wrist? Any bruises?"

"Just a few bruises, I think. Nothing more," she assured him, placing a hand lightly on her hip and wincing as she touched it. "I fell on it and on my arm. I may have scraped my elbow."

A crowd had now gathered around her. Gawain motioned them all away. "Give her some privacy. Go have your breakfast. This isn't a circus."

Most left as Fiona herded them out with the assistance of Lord Durham and Lord Fellstone. This left only Reggie and Margaret with Gawain as he began to run his hands along Cherish's nicely formed ankles. "Does it hurt when I press here?"

"No."

"Good." He moved to her wrists, taking them in his hands one at a time and pressing lightly. "Now?"

She emitted a soft cry. "The right one hurts a little. Hardly anything at all."

"You landed on it, and it took the brunt of your weight as you fell."

"What happened, Uncle Gawain? Did she trip?" Reggie asked.

Gawain shook his head. "No."

Katie walked in just then, looking smug as she slapped her riding crop against her gloved hand. She walked right by them with her head held high and no intention of issuing an apology.

Margaret gasped as she stared at Katie's retreating form. "Did she do something to hurt you, Cherish?"

Cherish pursed her lips, obviously uncertain what to say. "It isn't important. Just an accident."

"Accident, my arse," Reggie grumbled, and set an accusing eye on Gawain. "When are you going to get rid of that menace?"

Margaret nodded in agreement. "She is very mean."

Gawain frowned. "I would have tossed her out yesterday. But it isn't up to me. This is Fiona's house and her party."

"No," Reggie said, now sounding quite stern. "You are one to lecture me about my behavior. It is time you took responsibility for yours. That woman is here because of you. And she hurt Cherish because of you. So do not play your Silver Duke games and think to get away with them."

Gawain ought to have been angry with Reggie for such a display of insolence, but he was proud of him. Proud for standing up for Cherish and taking him on because none of this would have happened if not for his past actions. Perhaps he had been wrong to consider the lad soft and in need of toughening. Reggie was showing he had the makings of a man.

"You are right," Gawain admitted. "I have already asked her to leave...repeatedly. But she refuses. I cannot bodily toss her out while Fiona is permitting her to stay. That still does not excuse me. It never occurred to me that she would seek her vengeance on someone other than myself. Again, this does not excuse whatever part I played in it."

Now Cherish frowned. "How are you to blame? She is a grown woman and knew exactly what she was doing."

"Don't you dare absolve my uncle," Reggie said. "Everything he has done until this moment has led up to your injury. Thank goodness you were not hurt worse—not that Lady Albin would care. She is as obsessed with resuming her romance with my uncle as he is with avoiding it. But it cannot be overlooked that Lady Albin thought she had a chance with him because he has remained unmarried all these years."

He turned to Gawain before continuing. "Nor will she give up hope until you do marry, and you know it. But more important, what about Cherish?"

"What about me?" Cherish asked.

Reggie turned back to her, raking a hand through his hair in order to calm his own turmoil. "Lady Albin came at you because my uncle likes you. He likes you very much. Is it not obvious? In truth, I think he likes you so much it scares him."

"*Reggie*," Gawain said with a growl, having no desire for his feelings to be the subject of discussion.

His nephew ignored him. "You are more of a threat than you realize, Cherish. But will my uncle ever admit it? Will he ever follow his heart? No! He will let you go and pretend you are better off with me because this is what he does best, deny his feelings and lock everyone out. Those stone barricades around his heart are more precious to him than anything or anyone else. Do not fall in love with him, Cherish. He will only crush you."

He stormed off, and Margaret chased after him.

Gawain was now left alone to face this sweet girl who had done nothing to deserve any of the treatment she was receiving. Not from him. Nor from Katie. Nor from a vindictive uncle who meant to use her as a servant.

The footman returned just then with the glass of sherry he'd ordered.

Blast. How much had the man heard? Not that Gawain cared for himself, but he did not want Cherish tarnished in any way. He hoped Reggie's words would not be misconstrued to imply he and Cherish had done... No, they had to know she was respectable.

Her eyes began to water. "Cherish, here. Drink this." He meant to hold the glass to her lips, but she took it from his hand and took a sip on her own.

"I'll be all right," she said, trying to make light of her struggles. "You can leave me now."

"How can I leave you? Your hands are still shaking." He reached out to caress her cheek, but she turned her head away.

"I already knew this about you," she said, her throat so constricted, she could hardly get the words out. "For a moment, I thought perhaps you might open your heart to me...but no. It is as your nephew warned. You will never change."

Great, now she believed Reggie. Well, with good reason, he supposed.

"I wish my heart understood this about you," she continued in a voice so fragile, it sounded like delicate glass about to shatter.

He felt pain tear through him. The last thing he'd ever wanted to do was hurt her. "Cherish..."

"It is an awful situation, isn't it? I tried so hard not to let you in. But hearts are quite difficult to control, are they not? They set their own determined path and barrel straight on. It does not matter how hard we try to hold them back or try to guide them elsewhere. They will not be budged once they have set their course. Do not worry, I will force myself to forget you in time. In fact, I will start right now."

"Cherish, you are hurting and upset."

She took another sip of her sherry, grimacing as it slid down her throat. "Indeed, I am. But I will tell you this—if Lord Fellstone will have me, I will leap at his offer of marriage."

Her words were a solid punch to his heart. "Even if you do not love him?"

"Aren't you the very one who told me to start thinking of myself?" Tears formed in her eyes. "Well, this is me being mercenary…trying to be mercenary. Is this not what you want?"

"No, I did not mean—"

"Oh? Then what did you mean? Were you not encouraging me to turn greedy and grasping? Was I not directed to set my cap for Reggie? And failing that, find some other dupe like Lord Fellstone who might succumb to my captivating smiles and innocent blushes? Are you suggesting that now I should not grab what I can?"

He groaned. "I would not fault you for doing whatever you need to protect yourself. But the problem is, you are not at all hardhearted. You cannot fake your feelings, as you've just made clear."

"And now you know my feelings and do not care to reciprocate them. And why should you, when I have an uncle who is likely cheating me out of my inheritance and I cannot even ride a horse? Yes, you ought to distance yourself from me as soon as possible. In fact, I shall make it easy for you. Go away and do not speak to me again, for I do not wish to speak to you. Truly, I am so sorry I ever met you."

"Cherish, please—"

"No!" She drank the last of her sherry and obviously had no taste for it, if her expression was any indication. "Ugh, that is vile. I'll have another."

He sighed and set the glass aside. "I think you've had enough."

"Do I embarrass you because I am drunk before breakfast? I wouldn't worry about it if I were you. I am merely in pain, not yet drunk."

"I'll have Fiona's housekeeper fetch some bandages."

She shook her head. "A bandage won't fix my heart. There is only one thing that can fix what you have caused, and it is not something you will ever give me. So, here I sit, aching for the hope of love you brought to me…your love. Not Reggie's nor Fellstone's. I am so desperately sorry for ever letting my guard down around you. I should have been better prepared for the pain you were bound to cause. It was inevitable. This pain in my heart, I mean. These physical bruises," she said, glancing at her wrist and hip, "are nothing and will heal quickly."

"Speaking of those," he said with concern as blood began to seep through her sleeve, revealing yet another injury, "Cherish, your elbow is bleeding. Let me—"

"Stop pretending you care! It is nothing. I will deal with it. Can you not see the true cause of my anguish? I knew I was in danger of falling in love with you from the moment we met. I tried so hard to stop myself. I forced myself to list your faults." She sniffled. "But you have none."

He sighed. "Blessed saints, I have plenty."

"Well, I cannot seem to find them. You are irresistible, and I have been so foolish as to put my heart at risk. What a goose I am. I know I am nothing to you and will now be added to the pile of ladies you have cast aside. I wanted so much to be special to you." She hiccupped and held back a sob. "I am so angry...not with you, but with myself."

She reached for the bottle of sherry, but he moved it out of her reach. "This won't help."

"Oh, yes it will. Give it to me, or I shall become angry with you. In fact, I *am* angry with you. You know the effect you have on ladies. Why did you turn your charm on me? Why were you nice to me? You knew I would be defenseless."

"Cherish, I am taking you upstairs now and will have a doctor summoned to look at you. You've done more than merely scrape that elbow. The blood is oozing down your sleeve."

"I have told you, these physical injuries are nothing."

"They are *not* nothing." He attempted to assist her, but she rose from the settee on her own despite her noticeable pain.

"If you will not let me carry you, then at least take my arm to steady yourself."

"And rely on you once more? Lean against you and let you be my hero?" She slapped his hand away and then rushed out of the parlor.

Gawain was now left alone.

Was this not emblematic of his life? Alone. Not a single meaningful relation in his life.

No, that was not so. Cherish was that meaningful person, and he had just let her slip away.

What was wrong with him? Why had he not stopped her?

CHAPTER ELEVEN

C HERISH RETIRED TO her quarters to change out of her soiled gown and try to calm herself. Had she been too hard on this Silver Duke? She did not believe her injury was his fault. In truth, he had been sincerely concerned and rushed to help her.

But almost being trampled by Lady Albin's beast of a horse brought back terrors of that fall off her own horse all those years ago. She was shaken and overset, and her head was throbbing at the sensitive spot she'd hit when falling as a child. Then Reggie had lashed out at his uncle and set her off further.

She understood Reggie's concerns. What had started off as a fun bit of plotting between him and Fiona to match her to the Duke of Bromleigh had now gotten out of hand. Reggie did have the softest heart, and seeing her injured had upset him as much as it had upset her.

Everyone was now angry. Lady Albin, for one. The duke, for another. Reggie. Even sweet Margaret.

As for Fiona, Cherish expected to hear Lady Albin go flying out a window once her friend heard the full story of what had happened and got her hands on the woman.

It would be no less than that horrid countess deserved.

Cherish had just managed to remove her soiled gown and was standing in nothing but her chemise when she heard a knock at her door. "Who is it?"

"It's Fiona. Let me in." She opened the door a crack to make sure no one else was with her, then nodded and stepped aside as Fiona marched past her in a huff. "I cannot believe that woman!"

Cherish sighed. "I gather you heard what happened by the stable. Who told you, Gawain or Reggie?"

"Reggie told me. The witch might have killed you." Fiona's eyes were blazing, and she began to pace across Cherish's room, but paused to stare at her when she saw that Cherish had a handkerchief pressed to her elbow and it was stained with blood. "Should I summon a doctor for you?"

"No, I am more shaken than seriously harmed. Truly, I can take care of this scrape myself."

Fiona continued to stare at her, an eyebrow raised in question. "Will you help me bury her body after I strangle her?"

Cherish laughed. "Sure, why not? I keep a shovel at hand by my bedside for just such a purpose."

They both had a chuckle.

"But seriously, Fiona. I am all right. Do stop pacing. You seem to be more upset about the incident than I am." This wasn't quite true, because Cherish was very much outraged and had unfairly taken her frustration out on the duke. "I promise you, I am just a little bruised, that's all."

"A little bruised? Cherish, will you listen to yourself? Your wrist is swelling...and there is blood pouring from your elbow."

"It is not pouring. It is hardly worth noticing." She had stopped most of the bleeding by now, she hoped. It still required proper tending, but Fiona was already seething over the incident and Cherish did not wish to add more reasons to inflame her.

"My head groom saw it all and confirmed what happened. I confronted that witch before coming to see you. I told her if she is not out of my house within the hour I shall burn all her belongings, and her along with them."

Cherish grinned. "I'll help you light the bonfire."

Fiona laughed as she sank onto Cherish's bed. "I am so sorry for my part in it. Gawain begged me to toss her out before she caused trouble, but I was enjoying watching him squirm and thought it would help our matchmaking cause to keep her here. I thought it would push him toward you that much faster."

"It hasn't. If anything, it has turned him off to any serious relations with women." She sank onto the bed beside her friend. "I did not help matters either. I was so upset, I told him I never wished to speak to him again." She flopped on her back atop the mattress. "Oh, Fiona! I said terrible things to him. He will never have me now. Perhaps it is for the best. He was never going to propose to me. We were all wrong to hope he would. And now I've fallen in love with him."

"You have?" Fiona's eyes widened, and she cast Cherish a smile of pure delight. "I'm so glad. He is not immune to your charms. In fact, I have never seen him so taken with anyone as he is with you. I cannot say for certain, but I think he may be falling in love with you, too."

"No, he isn't, and will never be." Cherish sighed and sat up again. "I told him that if Lord Fellstone proposed to me, I would accept his offer. What a stupid thing for me to say. But I was overset."

Fiona patted her hand. "I am sure he realizes it. He will not allow matters to remain this way. I would not be surprised if he sought you out within a few hours. He does not dare do it now while you are still riled."

"He won't ever." Cherish took several deep breaths to keep from crying. "I've ruined my chances with him, assuming I ever had any in the first place."

"Well, there's always Reggie."

She laughed. "Oh, the poor fellow. No, not Reggie. He likes Margaret, and she adores him. I will do all I can to encourage that match. She is a sweet girl, and I hope Reggie's feelings for her turn into love. But I'm not sure he takes her seriously yet. He has been quite attentive to her recently, have you noticed? And do you know what Margaret asked me?"

Fiona shook her head. "No, what?"

"She asked if I would help make her smarter. Being deprived

of an education, even the most rudimentary knowledge of history, politics, the arts and sciences, has left her ignorant and feeling stupid. Are we not guilty of dismissing her for this very reason? But she is aware of her limitations and is afraid Reggie will never propose to her while he considers her nothing more than a charming peahen."

"Oh, the poor thing."

Cherish nodded. "I said I would help her out."

"Good, I will do the same. She has a kind and compassionate heart, and I am so sorry we may have hurt her feelings."

"She is too sweet ever to blame us. Well, I hope one of us ends up happily matched by the end of this week, and I would not mind at all if it were Margaret."

Fiona patted her hand again and then rose. "I agree. But if it is to be only one of us, then I would rather it be you. Well, I had better see what Lady Albin is up to now. Hopefully, she is packing and will soon be on her way. She certainly came prepared with a complete change of wardrobe for every occasion. I never saw anyone bring so many clothes for what should have been a mere dinner party and a possible overnight stay. I feel as though I allowed in the Trojan Horse. It was a completely calculated ambush on her part."

"Fiona, do you think she truly loves him?"

"Who, Gawain? Honestly, I don't know. In my opinion, she does not. I am not sure she ever loved him or was ever capable of loving anyone other than herself. Are her actions not revealing enough? She could not have married Lord Albin and abandoned Gawain the way she did if she was a girl in love. No one coerced her, and her family was not in dire straits."

"I see."

"Cherish, she did not even approach Gawain after Albin's death. So why is she suddenly desperate to do so now? No, the lady is a schemer and wants something from him."

"I suppose we'll never find out the reason now that you've kicked her out."

"Well, the *ton* is rife with gossip. I may hear something within the next few months."

"I suppose it does not matter. Come knock at my door once she is gone. Not that I am afraid of confronting her, but I dare not risk another outburst from her that spoils your party. Besides, I think I need to clean out my scraped elbow and see just how badly the rest of my body is bruised."

"I knew you were hurt worse than you let on. Why won't you admit it?"

Cherish pursed her lips, knowing she was being stubborn. But everyone already knew she was afraid of horses, and to now make a scene of having to leap out of the way as one bore down on her... Well, she did not want them to think she was a helpless weakling.

Fiona sighed. "I'll send my housekeeper up to you with clean cloths and brandy for those wounds. But have her fetch me if it turns out to be something more serious than a few bruises and scrapes."

Cherish shut the door after Fiona and then sat at the edge of the bed to steady herself, for she was feeling a little dizzy. The pins holding her chignon in place had loosened and her hair was looking quite a mess. Since she did not care to lie down with pins poking her head, she took them all out and let her hair tumble loosely about her shoulders.

She worked out a few knots with careful strokes of her brush, then set the brush aside and stretched out on the bed. Suddenly feeling exhausted and quite deflated, she saw no harm in closing her eyes for a minute or two in order to ease the throbbing in her head.

Her elbow had stopped bleeding, too. She did not need to keep a handkerchief pressed against it.

Perhaps her loss of blood was contributing to her headache. The best cure for that was simply to rest.

She must have fallen asleep atop the covers much longer than a few minutes, for the next thing she knew, someone was lightly shaking her awake.

She ignored the first few attempts, but this person was persistent. She grumbled as she opened her eyes, surprised to find the Duke of Bromleigh in her bedchamber. "Your Grace?"

"Cherish," he said in that deep, rumbling voice of his that shot tingles through her, "I need to cleanse that nasty scrape at your elbow. I'm sorry I woke you. Fiona's housekeeper was in here earlier to tend to you, but you were so lost in sleep, she was reluctant to disturb you. I felt treating your injury was too important to delay. Let me have a look at your elbow first, for it was bleeding and there's dirt ground into it."

She slowly sat up, her head still reeling a little. "I'll take care of it."

He frowned. "Look at me, Cherish. Why do your eyes look unfocused?"

"It is nothing. I fell asleep and am just waking up."

He tucked a finger under her chin and gently tilted her head up so that their gazes met. "You hit your head when Lady Albin knocked you over, didn't you? Tell me where it hurts."

She tried not to wince as he ran his fingers lightly across her brow and delicately touched each temple. "Stop! I shall recover with a little rest. You needn't poke and prod me."

"That glaze in your eyes advises otherwise. Try to stay awake, for I fear you might have suffered a concussion."

"No, it is nothing more than a little bump. I'll be all right once you go away. Your Grace, you—"

"Call me Gawain, will you?"

"Why?"

"Because you are dear to me," he said with such depth of feeling, she almost believed him.

"Me? Dear to you? How can you not despise me after those horrible things I said to you? I did not mean them."

"I know." He caressed her cheek. "Besides, I am quite thick-skinned. You weren't saying anything I did not deserve."

Her cheeks warmed to his touch, which was exquisitely gentle and quite dangerous to her composure. But in the next moment, she realized they were alone in her bedchamber.

Was there no chaperone? Where was Fiona? Or her housekeeper, the reliable Mrs. Harris? Her situation was already intolerable and would only get worse if he was found in here. "Oh dear. You must go. I cannot be alone with you."

"Fiona will be up here shortly. Cherish, I am not going to compromise you."

She laughed in disbelief. "What do you call this?" She groaned and glanced down at herself. How could he overlook her bosom practically spilling out of her chemise? If that flicker of heat in his eyes as she sat up was any indication, he had definitely taken notice. "I am not even dressed."

He strode to her armoire and took out her robe. "Here, let me help you put it on."

"No, I can do it myself," she insisted, knowing she would melt in his arms if he touched her.

"All right." He sank his muscled frame into the chair beside her bed and watched as she struggled to don the garment by herself. It pained her to raise her arm, but she was not going to admit it to him. He sighed, probably knowing it had to hurt. "For what it's worth," he said, his voice gentle, "I have already seen whatever there is to be seen of you, so it matters little how thoroughly you now choose to cover yourself up."

She frowned at him. "A gentleman would not have come in here."

He trained his dark emerald gaze on her, his look as hot as it was determined. In this moment, Cherish felt the full extent of his power and the granite resolve behind it. "I am no gentleman. And I still need to cleanse that wound."

"Fiona will do it."

He cast her a wry smile. "But I am here now, and Fiona and her staff are still busy tossing out Lady Albin."

"Good grief. How long does it take?"

"Quite a while, apparently, since she is reluctant to go. I have no idea what she wants of me, or why she refuses to be honest with me. But it seems being truthful is no longer in her repertoire, assuming it ever was. This makes me all the more determined to thwart her objective."

"She wants to marry you. That is her objective."

"If so, it is not for any reason other than she wants something from me."

She nodded. "I am constantly amazed by the stupid things people do. Whatever her motives, she is better served by simply telling you the truth. Well, I am one to talk, since I have made an utter mess of my own situation. How long was I asleep?"

"No more than half an hour, I expect."

"That long?"

He arched an eyebrow and grinned. "Yes, that long. And Lady Albin is still here. She is a leech who will suck the blood out of anyone foolish enough to draw close. As we are all finding out, she is hard to dislodge once she sets herself in a place. But this is Fiona's home, and Fiona has finally had enough of her. She'll have Lady Albin out within a few minutes, I'm sure. It cannot be long now. I would assist, but I think my presence will only inflame the situation. Reggie is taking charge."

"Good for him." Cherish studied his expressively handsome face and the frown now on it, which was quite severe. "You were once in love with her. What are you feeling now?"

He shrugged. "I suppose if I feel anything, it is relief. I cannot help thinking what my life would have been like if she and I had married. Ours would never have been a happy union. You saw her behavior. Is this how a duchess conducts herself?"

"For the most part, those of your rank can do whatever they want."

"You are an earl's daughter, born just as entitled as she was. Yet there is only caring and compassion in you despite your difficult circumstances. She has everything and tramples on it. Perhaps I ought to thank her for marrying Albin and setting me free. She did me a great favor in spurning me."

He poured brandy onto one of the clean cloths the house-keeper must have brought in while she was sleeping, and doused it so that it was thoroughly soaked. "This will sting, Cherish. I'm sorry, but it cannot be helped."

She closed her eyes and emitted a yelp when he applied the cloth to her elbow. "Is this revenge for the horrid way I spoke to you earlier?"

"Never. You are too sweet for me ever to hurt you." His voice softened to a silky rumble that shot more tingles through her. "You had every right to be angry with me. Did you mean it when you said I had claimed your heart?"

"What do you think?"

He cut a strip of bandage and tied it around her elbow. "I think you see me clearly for who I am, not a duke but a man who is quite a bit bullheaded and cynical, and who trusts few people. I'm glad I have stolen your heart despite my faults, and I would still like to hear the confirmation from your lips."

"Why must you hear it again? Are you not tired of hearing constant love declarations from the women you have spurned? I think you are sufficiently filled with conceit and do not need my admission of love to further inflate your already swelled head."

"Ah, Cherish. You certainly know how to flatter a man," he said, chuckling at her sarcasm.

She sighed. "Is it any wonder I am still a spinster? The women all flock to you like moths drawn to firelight, and it galls me that I am no different."

To repeat her hopeless declaration of love would only serve to further humiliate her. Oh, how she wished to feel nothing for him.

But she adored everything about him.

"I'm glad you care for me, Cherish." His gaze was still fixed on her, the smoldering heat in his eyes completely unraveling her resolve. But she had to be strong and not succumb to him.

Why was he here? What did he want of her?

And why was Fiona taking so long to join them?

She shook her head, trying not to wince. "I won't say it again to you. I have made enough of a fool of myself. It is your turn next."

"To pour my heart out to you?"

He did not look in the least inclined, but she ought to have expected no less from this Silver Duke. Still, it wounded her to know she was not at all special to him, even though he made her feel that way. "Do you have any feelings for me?"

"Of course I do. You are lovely."

"Lovely enough to marry?" She wiped away the tears that had formed when feeling the sting of the brandy applied to her elbow, although some of those tears were for herself and her hopeless situation.

Why did she have to fall desperately in love with him?

In a matter of days, no less.

"Never mind, that is just my misery talking," she said. "You've known me less than a week. Even I think it is too much to ask of you in this short time."

He reached out his hand and lightly touched it to her hip. "You struggled when walking earlier. Let me see your hip. I need to make sure it is merely bruised and nothing worse."

She gave a mirthless laugh and skittered back a little on her bed. "No! That is indecent."

"Keep the rest of your body covered up, but I must look at you, Cherish. You might have fractured it when you fell backward. You took a bad spill, much worse than you are letting on."

"The hip is just bruised."

"Cherish, you are hurting all over."

"I am not," she insisted, which did not sound convincing at all, since she was now sniffling and wincing every time she moved.

He cast her a look of exasperation. "Stop being stubborn, will you? You are incapable of hiding your feelings from me...or anyone, for that matter. I am not going to look at your rump. I give you my word of honor."

"You have already seen too much of my heart and probably too much of my body. It is more than I can bear just now. Please, go away."

"No. We need to talk and you need to stop scowling at me." He rose and crossed the room to close the door, an outrageous act that would certainly seal her ruination.

She frowned at him. "Open it at once. Are you mad?"

"Possibly, but we still must talk, and I do not wish us to be disturbed."

"What sort of a conversation are we going to have while I am half naked and we are alone in my room?" She curled her hands into fists, determined to punch him if he thought to take advantage of their situation. "Being in love with you does not mean I will allow you to take liberties. Go downstairs. I will be along in a few minutes."

Whatever he meant to say to her next was drowned out by a sudden commotion downstairs. The shouts filtering up from the entry hall were loud enough to reach their ears despite the door being closed. "What in blazes?" the duke muttered, striding to the door he had just closed and flinging it open. "Stay here, Cherish. Let me see what is going on."

Fiona's housekeeper rushed in just as he was about to step into the hall to investigate. "Your Grace," she said, emitting a soft cry. "Oh, this is simply awful." Her face was ashen as she stared in dismay at Cherish.

Cherish's breath caught. "What is it, Mrs. Harris?"

"Your uncle... He is here."

Her stomach churned. "What? But he isn't due back for another week yet."

"I'm so sorry, m'lady. But he's here, quite angry, and charging through the house in search of you. The footmen are trying to restrain him, but he is in quite a temper. Oh, Lady Cherish, you mustn't come downstairs. Your Grace, keep her safe. Don't let that ogre get his hands on her. There's no telling what he will do if he finds her."

Cherish scrambled off the bed and stood shakily. "I am not going to hide like a coward and allow him to ruin Fiona's party. I had better—"

The duke growled, interrupting her. "Are you mad? Did you not hear what Mrs. Harris just said? You are to do nothing at all."

"How can you expect me to sit here like a helpless lump while he storms through Fiona's house?"

"You were almost trampled by a horse not an hour ago. Is this not enough excitement for you in a day? I will deal with him."

"You? No, I must take care of this." She cast him a look of defiance that he promptly ignored while he peered down the hall again to make certain her uncle was not approaching. But she could hear the horrid man still bellowing and slamming doors downstairs, creating chaos while on his rampage. Fortunately, the hour was early, so most guests were still safely tucked in their rooms, although his noisy presence must have awakened them all by now.

"Cherish, do not argue with me. Promise me you will stay here while I deal with him."

"No. If you go downstairs, then so will I."

He strode back to her side and gently nudged her onto the bed. "Don't you dare. Why are you being so stubborn? Don't you realize you are in danger?" He put an arm around her waist when she shot back up and tried to dart past him.

She frowned at him. "I am not a child who needs to be coddled. Let me go!"

"No." This time, he drew her up against his body and held her fast when she tried to escape his grasp. "Do you hear me, Cherish? You are not to go to him. Nor will I allow that man anywhere near you."

Her uncle was now shouting for Fiona.

"Am I to hide in here while he goes after Fiona next? She already has her hands full getting rid of *your* Lady Albin."

"She is not my… Never mind. I am not going to stand here and argue with you. Cherish, look at you. Your hair is undone and you are barefoot, not to mention you are not even dressed."

He stroked a hand through her hair that had fallen in a loose tumble down her back and was not even drawn back by a hair ribbon. Well, perhaps he was right. She could not walk out of her bedchamber clad only in her undergarments and robe without causing more scandal.

He stared at her toes peeking out from under the hem of her robe.

She emitted a deflated breath. "Mrs. Harris, will you help me dress?"

"No, Mrs. Harris," the duke cut in, overriding her request. "You are to stay here and make certain Lady Cherish does not leave her room. Tie her down, if you must." He now released Cherish with the intention of handing her over to Mrs. Harris's care, and then raked his fingers through his dark mane of hair. "Gad, what a morning this is turning out to be."

"Indeed, a horrible morning," Cherish muttered, intent on ignoring his orders. As soon as he turned to leave, she went to her armoire and withdrew a gown. "I am not having you deal with my uncle on your own," she muttered. "He is my problem. My responsibility. Block his path, Mrs. Harris. Throw your body across the door."

"Lady Cherish!"

"Oh, never mind. Your Grace, just wait for me while I dress and we shall confront him together. It is the only way. You do not know him as I do. He will not budge from here without me."

She removed her robe, shocking the housekeeper because the duke was still in her bedchamber and about to argue some more about her remaining in hiding. But his mouth gaped open before he managed to speak a word.

Drat, the chemise was sliding off her shoulders.

He was now staring at her with fiery eyes as she donned the gown. Fiona and Reggie claimed he felt more for her than he was letting on. Perhaps they were right, and his smoldering gaze proved it.

But so what? He was never going to admit it.

"Mrs. Harris, will you help me tie the laces?"

"Yes, Lady Cherish." The obviously rattled housekeeper hastened to assist her.

Only afterward did Cherish realize what she had done, disrobing in front of the duke as though he had every right to be in here with her and belonged by her side. However, he certainly did not belong here, and she had to rectify her mistake at once. "Your Grace, kindly stand outside and wait for me."

He laughed. "Did you not think to ask me that before you undressed in front of me? There is no point in my leaving now, since I have already seen everything there is to see of you."

She gasped. "You have not! Of all the effrontery."

"Blessed saints," he muttered. "I'll strike a deal with you—promise me you will stay up here at least until I calm your uncle down. Will you do this? Then you can join me downstairs and we shall deal with him together."

"I cannot promise any such thing. You are wasting your time and do not know him as I do. He will not be calmed until he confronts me. How many times must you hear this before you will believe me?"

"Put this out of your head at once. I am not letting him anywhere near you while he is so enraged. Cherish, for pity's sake. Stop being stubborn and just let me deal with him without having to worry about you."

"No, and you really ought to stop telling me what to do. This is my family mess and my responsibility to handle. He is always unpleasant, that's just his nature. Although I will admit, he is exceptionally loud this time." She sank onto her bed and reached down to put on her shoes. She decided not to bother fixing her hair, since her uncle was bellowing again, and she dared not waste any more time in doing it up properly.

The duke had remarked on what a horrible morning this was

turning out to be, and she heartily agreed. If only she could go back to sleep and pretend none of this was happening. But her wretched uncle was intent on causing trouble. That Lady Albin was still here and would be witness to their inevitable confrontation also irked her to no end.

"I am ready, Your Grace." Her head was now in a spin and the duke was watching her quite intently. She placed her arm in his and smiled up at him, but she could see he was not fooled at all and knew she needed to hold on to him to steady herself.

He cast her a concerned look. "Cherish—"

"*No.* I do not need you to act like a protective ape over me."

"Who is to protect you, if not me?"

"You? Ha! That is a jest. I am going downstairs with you and that's an end to our discussion. I have to face him now or my life will be intolerable once I am back at Northam Hall." She emitted a soft breath. "However, I am glad you are by my side. He can be quite a boor, and I think he is angrier than he has ever been with me at the moment."

"Does this not trouble you, Cherish? It certainly worries me. Why should he be so enraged merely because you are attending a neighbor's party?" He frowned pensively. "This does not feel right. Something is decidedly rotten about this entire situation."

She nodded. "Is it not obvious? My uncle has been cheating me, although I do not know exactly what he's taken from me because no one will tell me. It is becoming clear to me that they have all been in on it. My father's solicitor, his banker, and my toad of an uncle and his ogress wife. This is why my uncle thinks to keep me confined to our home while his two accomplices will not respond to my letters."

"They'll respond to me, that's for certain. Stay here while I wring his bloody neck and get the truth out of him."

"You? But you are a Silver Duke."

"So what?"

"You are not going to be around to protect me beyond these next few days. So kindly do not stick your nose in this and let me deal with him on my own."

"No," he muttered, disengaging himself from her and giving her another useless warning glower to stay put. "Do you think I will ever allow anyone to hurt you, whether now, or a year from now, or a decade from now?" That said, he turned and strode down the hall, looking as marvelously fierce as any warrior of legend. All he lacked was a suit of shining armor.

But Cherish did not think he needed one as he marched off to slay her evil dragon.

Was it any wonder she loved this Silver Duke?

CHAPTER TWELVE

A S GAWAIN MARCHED out of Cherish's bedchamber, he heard Cherish's uncle start up the stairs in search of her. The oaf's heavy footfalls clomped on each step as he continued to shout her name. "Cherish! Where are you? Do not make this worse for yourself!"

Gawain was not a praying man, but he was now feverishly praying Cherish would use some sense and let him handle this matter while she remained safely hidden in her bedchamber. He came face to face with her uncle just in time to prevent him from advancing beyond the stairs. They'd reached the landing at the same moment, but Gawain was a big man and easily able to block this oaf's path.

"Take another step, Northam, and I shall toss you down the stairs headfirst." He folded his arms over his chest and positioned himself at the top step in order to pose an impenetrable barrier between Northam and his niece.

"You had better do as he says, Uncle," Cherish said, softly padding up behind Gawain as she clearly ignored all his warnings to keep herself safely tucked away.

Blast the girl. He ought to be angry. He *was* angry. But he also wanted to hold Cherish in his arms and protect her with his life.

Not that he felt either of them were presently in serious danger of losing their lives at the hands of her bellowing uncle. The man was big, but out of shape and no match for Gawain.

However, Cherish was little and did not stand a chance of defending herself.

He had no idea what Northam might do to her once he got her back home. He fully expected the cur would beat her for defying him. Surely Cherish had to know this.

Gawain would kill him if he ever raised a hand to her.

He nudged her firmly behind him. "That is far enough. You can talk to him from there."

She sighed, but did not try to skirt around him again. "Uncle, why don't we all go into Lady Shoreham's study and discuss this misunderstanding like reasonable adults?"

"You defied me!"

"How? I am a grown woman capable of making my own decisions. I have every right to choose my own friends, and I resent your coming here and upsetting us all by howling like a banshee at this hour of the morning. I am no runaway child. Nor am I an idiot, so do not insult my intelligence by pretending you care whether I live or die."

"Your father left me in charge of you," Northam growled as he lunged for her.

Gawain held him off and ordered Fiona's footmen, who had been chasing her uncle and now stood just behind him on the stairs, to restrain him. "Take him into Lady Shoreham's study and hold him there until I arrive. If he struggles, you have my permission to toss him headfirst over the railing."

That quieted the man. He gave no struggle as they marched him away.

Gawain turned to Cherish. "Why must you be so contrary? I am trying to protect you. Stay up here until further notice."

"Why must you be so pigheaded? You have no right to order me about. I am coming with you."

"No, you are not."

Her eyes widened and she clenched her fists. "You really are being insufferable, you know."

"Me? I seem to be the only one using any common sense. Can

you not see he is dangerous to you?"

She cast him a pained look. "Of course I see it. This is precisely why it is important for me to hold my ground now."

He held her back when she tried to descend the stairs.

"Why won't you allow me to confront my uncle?"

"Do you really need to ask? Do you still not get it? He may have quieted for the moment, but he is a raging bull and you are a…" He groaned. "You are a kitten."

Her mouth dropped open to form a perfect *O*, and she let out a soft breath. "Is this what you think of me? A helpless kitten? I resent that! I can fight my own battles."

"Blessed saints, you are a stubborn thing. You cannot even ride a horse, and you think to take on a raging bull?" He wanted to howl in frustration. Could anything more go wrong this morning?

Her expression turned pained once again. "That is not fair."

"I know. Forgive me, Cherish. But I am so worried about what he might do to you. Knowing when to retreat is just as important as knowing when to march forward and fight. But this is something you do not seem to comprehend. If I had a key to your room, I would hide you inside and keep you safely locked away until I am finished with your uncle. Why are you meddling when I am trying to get rid of the fool on your behalf?"

Her uncle was just the sort to fight dirty, too. The churl would not hesitate to hurt Cherish. Why did she refuse to see this?

"Stop treating this as a lark," Gawain continued. "Can you not see he is too incensed to be reasonable?"

"Of course I can. But I am outraged, too. What right does he have to tell me who to see or where to go or what to do? I have no intention of confronting him alone. I want you with me. I am delighted to have you by my side, especially now that you are so puffed up like an enormous bullfrog."

"A bullfrog?" Was this what she thought he was doing? Croaking warnings at her?

She sighed. "If you must know, you make my insides melt."

He groaned.

"I'll be all right," she said softly. "He won't dare put a hand on me while you are standing beside me."

"Which entirely begs the point—what will he do to you when I am not around to protect you?"

"This is precisely the reason why I must take the lead in confronting him. If you do it, he will walk all over me once I am back at Northam Hall." She pursed her lips, obviously concerned about what might happen to her once she returned home.

They were such sweet lips, and all he wanted to do was kiss them. Well, that would have to wait until the danger to her had passed.

Yes, he was going to kiss her. So much for his brilliant matchmaking plans. That scheme had completely blown up in his face. He wanted this girl and was not about to let anyone else have her. More important, he could never allow anyone to hurt her.

"I am not going to fight with you, Cherish."

She nodded. "Good, let's go. Fiona's footmen ought to have him tied down by now."

"No one has tied him down. Stay behind me and do not utter another word." If she thought this meant he was about to let her have her way, she was mistaken. He marched downstairs, intending to confront Northam in the privacy of Fiona's study. However, guests were already gathered in the entry hall, curious as to what was happening.

He was certainly providing plenty of entertainment fodder. Two circuses going on at once. Had Fiona sent Lady Albin packing yet?

He ignored everyone's questions as he made his way to the study. Northam's bellows carried beyond closed doors.

To Gawain's dismay, the footmen were once again wrestling with Cherish's uncle. Gawain motioned for the hapless footmen to release Northam. "But do not leave. Remain behind me and do not allow that cur anywhere near Lady Cherish."

The door remained open once he walked in, because all the onlookers now crowded the doorway and spilled into the entry hall. Those in the back now craned their necks, eager to hear what was about to be discussed.

So much for privacy or discretion. The London gossip rags would have to print double editions to fit all the scandals happening at Fiona's house party.

"You ought to be ashamed of yourself," Cherish chided her uncle as the crowd parted for her, allowing her to follow Gawain into the study.

Gawain nudged her behind him. "Quiet."

"Of all the gall," she muttered, and was about to pop around him again, but he held her firmly back in place. It was easy to do, since she was little and his hands were big enough that he only needed one to keep her pinned against him. As he did so, he grazed her arm and felt moisture on the fabric of her sleeve.

Her elbow was bleeding again. *Bollocks.* He wanted to get this scene over with so he could tend to her properly and make certain she rested.

"Oh, drat," she said, also noticing the blood.

Gawain passed her his handkerchief. "Keep it pressed to your elbow."

"Thank you, but I am still irritated with you for—"

"Cherish!" Gad, they would have lost the war to Napoleon in two days if all his soldiers behaved as unreasonably as she did. "Enough, love. Do as I say."

Did he just call her *love*?

Bollocks again.

How had that slipped out? Had she even heard him? Everyone else surely had, and now there would be another scandal tossed into the pot.

Cherish was still muttering about his apishly protective instincts and how annoying they were.

He was a duke. A Silver Duke. Not some great mountain ape

running amok in Fiona's study.

Perhaps he was not as calm or rational as he thought, for he wanted to pound Cherish's uncle to dust. "Why are you here, Northam?"

The look of loathing Northam cast Cherish did not bode well for the girl. What was going on?

"She's coming back with me," Northam spat out. "I'll send for her things later."

Gawain planted his legs wide and crossed his arms over his chest. "No. Cherish stays here."

He wished more footmen were on hand to grab this man and toss him out, but most were already occupied assisting Fiona and Reggie in sending Lady Albin packing. Another unwanted guest who would not leave.

Well, it was of no moment. He would handle Northam by himself. He only needed the footmen to keep Cherish from meddling.

Where was Durham? Or Fellstone? He would not mind their assistance, too. They would be better able to keep Cherish safe if a fight broke out and fists flew. Not that he intended to instigate a fight or ever strike the first blow. But Northam had his hands curled into fists and was obviously contemplating taking a swing at him.

"Let's sit like gentlemen and discuss this peacefully," Gawain suggested to Northam as they stared each other down.

"She's my niece. No discussion. I'll give *you* peaceful," her uncle growled, and threw a punch. Gawain easily sidestepped him. The howling clod tripped over his own feet and wound up sprawled on the floor. The onlookers laughed, but this only served to further infuriate him. "I'll get you for this, Cherish!"

Gawain planted a boot firmly on his back, preventing him from getting up. "Northam, stop making a nuisance of yourself and go home," he said in his authoritative voice normally reserved for soldiers serving under his battle command.

Her uncle's expression turned menacing when he saw Cherish now standing beside Gawain. "You little witch!"

"Oh, a witch, am I? Put a hand on me and I will come at you with my broomstick, you odious man. I'll turn you into a newt and your odious wife into mare's sweat. How dare you threaten me!"

Gawain sighed. Was no one capable of behaving?

"Indeed, Northam. That is no way to speak to a lady. Apologize to your niece or I will not let you up."

Her uncle began to curse at him instead.

Was the man daft, speaking so disrespectfully to him or his niece? But he was obviously a low creature, not the sort anyone of stature would ever allow into their drawing room. "You have embarrassed your niece enough. Since you refuse to behave like a gentleman, you and I shall step outside and deal with each other accordingly."

"And I shall have your guts for garters!" Northam howled, then cursed the moment Gawain shoved him to his feet.

He had barely regained his footing before he lashed out at Cherish again. "You'll feel the back of my hand the moment I get you home. As for Lady Shoreham—"

"Shut up, Northam," Gawain warned. "It is one thing to insult me, but I will not have you threatening the ladies."

"That's right," Cherish said, also determined to come to the defense of Fiona. "Lady Shoreham is blameless. I alone defied you, and I shall do it again and again. You have no hold over me."

To Gawain's dismay, more onlookers had gathered in the entry hall. They ambled in from all over the house. Some from the dining room, some still in their bedclothes, having just come out of their bedchambers, all of them eager to witness the scene unfold. Adding to Gawain's irritation was the presence of his one-time love, Lady Albin. Had she not been put in her carriage and driven off yet?

Blessed saints.

Would this woman never leave? She stood before him with a condescending smirk on her face. "What a happy little scene," she

160

tossed out with a bitter laugh.

None of Fiona's other guests were laughing now, for they understood the seriousness of Cherish's situation.

He spared a glance at Cherish, who was still steaming over her uncle's behavior and probably had not heard Lady Albin's snide remark because she was too busy threatening to ram a broomstick up his arse, though she used a more polite word to describe Northam's rear.

And now she was threatening to turn him into a turnip and bury him in a turnip patch. "And do not think the Northam Hall servants will ever allow you to beat me or lock me away. They will leap to my defense."

Gawain would talk to her later. He was glad she had the spine to hold her ground with her uncle, and perhaps he had underestimated her resolve. Or overestimated the threat behind her uncle's bluster. That Cherish did not appear afraid of his physical threats probably meant he had not struck her before. But that did not mean she was safe from a beating. There was always a first time.

Right now, he meant to remain an impenetrable barrier between these two Northams. Why was the vile earl here? What was really going on that he had to tear home a week early and drag his niece away from Fiona's party?

As the oaf spouted more threats against Cherish, Gawain knew what he had to do. She was no prisoner, nor would she ever be any man's drudge. She could not remain under that man's roof a single night longer.

Cherish must have decided this same thing, for she took a deep breath and then tried to speak over her uncle's ranting. "Stop shouting at me. You can scream until you are blue in the face, but I am never going back with you."

"Think again, you useless, deceitful chit!"

"Whatever I must face next, it shall be better than spending another moment under your roof. Get out of this house and never come near me again. The next time you approach me, I shall shoot you."

"With what, you stupid girl?"

"With the weapon I shall personally hand her," Gawain said, seriously tempted to withdraw his pistol at this very moment and aim it at Northam's gut. But he did not wish to escalate this matter, so he made no move to reach into the boot where he kept the weapon holstered. "You heard the lady. She told you to get out. If you refuse, I will toss you out myself."

"And he has the muscle to do it, too," Cherish interjected with an air of satisfaction.

"Where will you go, Cherish?" her uncle said. "Into this man's arms? Has he already had you?"

"This man?" She gasped and skittered forward once more, too irate to keep a safe distance from this oaf.

Gawain drew her back to keep her out of her uncle's reach. Gad, these Northams did not take kindly to orders.

She cast him a look of irritation before addressing her uncle. "Do you not know who he is? This is the Duke of Bromleigh. *The* duke. And you were foolish enough to insult him and then try to strike him."

"What do I care, you insolent girl? I demand you come back with me now. How else are you to keep a respectable roof over your head? Or have you already decided to go with the duke and become his mistress? How long do you think it will take him to tire of you and leave you destitute? Will you slink back to Lady Shoreham then? And hope she will take a ruined girl like you on as her scullery maid, for that is all you will be good for?"

"Enough, Northam," Gawain said, knowing it was long past time to take proper charge. He ought to have hauled the bounder out immediately and kicked him into the mud. But Cherish had needed to confront him, as misguided as her reasoning was.

Well, she had told him off sufficiently, and nothing more needed to be said.

He stared down the unpleasant man. "You have now insulted your niece, Lady Shoreham, and myself. It is time for you to go.

Lady Cherish will not be returning with you, just so we are clear about this."

"Then I shall be clear about my position as well. If she defies me, I shall not allow her back into my home to retrieve any of her belongings, not even a single stitch of clothing. What do you say to that?"

"Lady Shoreham will help her out with any clothes she needs. So will I, if it becomes necessary. It is pocket change for me."

Cherish frowned at him. He ignored her. He knew she had pride and would not sponge off her best friend beyond accepting a gown or two, but that was irrelevant at the moment.

Nor would she take so much as a ha'penny from him. Also irrelevant at the moment.

He meant to marry her and make her his duchess.

She tipped her chin in the air. "I shall find myself a *respectable* position as companion or governess. I am not afraid to work, nor am I so deluded as to believe His Grace will rush forward and offer something beyond a new wardrobe, which I will refuse from him because it is unseemly for a bachelor to offer such a thing to me. He is a Silver Duke. They do not marry."

Gawain frowned. "Cherish—"

"Please, Your Grace. I know you cannot offer me anything more. I will manage on my own."

It tore at him that she dared not count on him beyond an insignificant wardrobe. Did she think he would simply abandon her?

Blessed saints, he wanted her in his life forever. She was nothing like Lady Albin. That woman was maliciously smug and enjoying Cherish's downfall.

Reggie stepped forward. "I could marry you, Cherish."

She gasped and glanced in dismay at Margaret, who now looked as though someone had shoved a sword through her heart. The poor girl was about to burst into tears. "Yes," Margaret said, her lips quivering and tears forming in her eyes, "it is right that you must. Cherish is our friend and needs to be protected."

"No, Reggie," Cherish said with determination. "You deserve someone whose heart lights up for you." She gave Margaret a hug. "I will not marry him when it is obvious he deserves someone as fine as you."

Gawain sighed. Yes, that little peahen, Margaret, truly adored his nephew. Even he, as thickheaded as he was and resistant to matters of love and marriage, had noticed how much the sweet girl cared for Reggie. Nor had it escaped his notice that Reggie was growing to care for her. Perhaps it was not an all-consuming love yet, but Margaret's genuine adulation was bringing out the better part of his nephew, and Gawain liked what he had been seeing these past few days.

To his dismay, Fellstone stepped forward next. "Lady Cherish…"

"Oh, no. You too?" She shook her head with vehemence, then winced and put a hand to her temple. "You cannot want me when you have no idea what sort of dowry I will bring to our marriage or whether my toad of an uncle will ever release it without a legal battle. And honestly, do you really want to be connected in any way to him and his equally wretched wife?"

Fellstone grimaced and stepped back into the crowd.

Gawain knew Fellstone was not a bad sort, but he was in need of a wife with substantial funds and could not afford the luxury of falling in love with someone who might turn out to be poor.

Lord Northam's mouth curled into an ugly sneer. Unable to get at Cherish, since Gawain still blocked him, the fool attempted to punch Gawain again. He easily avoided the blow and twisted Northam's arm behind his back with enough force to bring the wretched fellow to his knees again. "Stay down," he commanded, angry with himself for making a bungle of the entire incident.

He should have gone downstairs upon first hearing Northam's bellows, grabbed him by the scruff of his neck, and hauled him out of the house before allowing him to utter another word. But Cherish would have come down with him, barefoot and indecently dressed, for everyone to ogle.

Now, they were surrounded by every last one of Fiona's guests, who had listened in as Northam debased and utterly humiliated Cherish. "Stay down or I will beat you senseless. Your brains will make quite a splat on Lady Shoreham's lovely Florentine marble floor."

Her uncle began to squeal like a pig as he squirmed and yelped and tried to escape his grasp, but Gawain was stronger and would not let him up, for he had reached his limit of patience.

Fiona's guests began to laugh and cheer, for the vile creature was finally getting his due.

But Cherish was not laughing. In truth, she appeared on the verge of tears.

It was bad enough Margaret was crying, but did Cherish have to cry, too?

Someone in the crowd urged Gawain to beat up her uncle. Cherish's eyes rounded in alarm as others began to urge the same. "Your Grace, you must not!"

He glanced at her. "Why not? Does he not deserve it? Are you sure you do not want me to do it and rid you of this pesky problem?"

She gasped. "Perhaps I dream of it, but only in jest. You cannot harm him."

"Even after he spoke to you the way he did?" He cast Northam a lethal glance, eager to tear this man apart limb from limb. "Cherish, no one has the right to treat you in this manner."

"I know, but you will only have trouble piled on you if you hurt him."

"If you think I am going to stand by while he mistreats you, then you had better think again. Is this how he always talks to you?"

"No, he's never bellowed at me like this before. Truly, this is something new." She inched closer to stand by his side. "But he's… I don't know why he is behaving this way, quite frankly. One would think he was afraid to have me leave him. But I assure you, he and his wife would not care if I dropped dead in front of them tomorrow."

"But they would care if you married tomorrow. Is that not so, Northam? I saw how you blanched when my nephew and Lord Fellstone stepped forward."

Her uncle attempted to grab her again, but Gawain still had him pinned and merely jerked on his arm to keep him down. He then ordered Fiona's footmen to take him and hold him, which they did with renewed zeal. "Northam, Lady Cherish is no longer yours. You are never to touch her or come near her without her permission, or you shall find yourself dealing with me."

"Who are you to stop me?" her uncle hissed. "I am her guardian."

"And I am Bromleigh. *Bromleigh*," Gawain said in a roar, as though his name alone could send a shiver through the loathsome man.

"You shall never have her," he hissed again. "I will never give my consent to a marriage."

Cherish laughed. "He is a Silver Duke. They do not marry."

"First of all," Gawain said, barely containing his rage, which was mostly directed at himself for having everyone believe he was cold as ice and his heart could never thaw to accept another person into his life, "she is beyond the age of consent and free to marry whomever she wishes. Second, I do not need your consent to question your solicitor about the old earl's bequests to his daughter. In fact, I shall order an accounting done this very day on her behalf."

"You have no right!"

"How much did you pay his solicitor to collude with you in cheating your niece? You do not fool me for a moment, Northam. I know what you are doing to her, as does she. The difference is that she is powerless against you, but I am not. You shall not get away with stealing her inheritance."

"You cannot threaten me! I am her guardian. You are nobody to her. I shall bring you up on charges in the House of Lords!"

"Cherish, please…let my uncle beat him unconscious," Reggie called out.

"I'll assist," Fiona added.

Durham, Fellstone, and several other guests insisted on joining in.

Cherish's uncle turned his rage on all around them. "You shall all be brought up on charges if you dare set a hand on me!"

"Enough of this farce," Gawain said, the glint in his eyes now revealing the depth of his own fury. "I assure you, Lord Northam, your actions today will reach royal ears. When I am through with you, you will be on your knees groveling at my feet and begging for mercy."

"You are bluffing."

"I never bluff." He turned back to Cherish. "Tell me what the Northam staff ought to pack for you. Reggie, Durham, and I will ride over with your uncle to see that it is properly done. And I believe there is jewelry of yours he and his wife have taken. Write down which pieces, and I shall personally take them into my custody."

By this time, most of the house party guests were making quiet bets among themselves as to what was going to happen next. Would Gawain punch her uncle? Would her uncle attempt to punch Gawain again? Would Cherish leave with her uncle?

The one thing not wagered on was whether Gawain would marry her. It was not in consideration, of course. As everyone was eager to point out, he was a Silver Duke and marriage was out of the question. And why would Cherish think any differently? After all, he had rejected Lady Albin, so what chance did Cherish ever have of gaining an offer from him?

But they were all wrong.

He wanted her more than he had ever wanted anything or anyone in his life. He wanted her even though she was irksome and stubborn, and had not listened to a word he said while he had been trying to protect her.

In truth, he was proud of her for wanting to stand up to her uncle. At the same time, he was frustrated and mad as blazes that she wanted to do it on her own.

He would have turned into a veritable beast if her uncle had set a hand on her.

"Cherish," he said softly, running his fingers through her hair to lightly brush the strands behind her little, curled ears, "there is one more thing we need to clarify before I leave to collect your things."

She nodded. "I'll make my list right away. There isn't much I want from that house. He's already ruined most of it."

"No, you mistake my meaning."

She looked up at him, truly having no idea what he was asking. "My list is short and I will prepare it quickly. Is this not what we are talking about?"

"No." Gawain shook his head and cleared his throat.

"Oh, then what do you need me to do?"

Bollocks.

He so badly wanted to kiss this girl.

"Cherish," he said with a soft ache to his voice, running his knuckle lightly along the line of her jaw, "I need you to marry me. This is what I need you to do and what I am asking with all sincerity."

She blinked. "What?"

A collective gasp rose from the crowd, after which they all turned silent so that one could hear a pin drop.

Cherish blinked again. "Are you serious?"

"Never more serious or determined about anything in my life." He heard more gasps as he bent on one knee before her.

"Oh, dear heaven," she said in a whisper.

He took her hand in his. "Cherish Northam, will you marry me?"

CHAPTER THIRTEEN

G AWAIN ROSE AND held his breath while awaiting Cherish's answer, although he knew she was going to accept.

She loved him and had already told him so. And he surely had to be in love with her if her irritating insistence on facing her uncle had only made him more determined to protect her.

Indeed, it seemed everyone was holding their breath while awaiting her answer, even her toad of an uncle, whose face had gone from apoplectic purple to ashen gray.

Ah, yes. This confirmed to Gawain the man had been stealing from his niece and was now about to be found out. Not only found out, but about to face the wrath of a Silver Duke who would soon be married to his niece.

Stupidly, if Northam had simply left matters alone and allowed Cherish to remain at the party, Gawain might not have been pushed to propose.

No, that was not quite right. He might not have been pushed to propose at this very moment, but his heart had known Cherish was the one for him the moment he set eyes on her. He had been too stubborn to acknowledge it and instead continued the farce of matching her to his nephew, when all along he knew he could never let this precious girl belong to anyone but him.

Well, they belonged to each other now. They both knew it and felt it, only he had been an idiot to resist the obvious.

"Cherish?"

Why was she taking so long to accept him?

Did she need reminding that marriage to him would make her a duchess and untouchable by her uncle? He also suspected that an accounting would reveal she had independent means, perhaps was even an heiress. He could not imagine her loving father ever purposely leaving her destitute. Of course, he could not pass on the entailed properties to her, but there had to be sufficient assets outside of the entailment that would have been left in trust for her.

Not that Gawain cared what she brought into their marriage beyond herself, but he was not about to let anyone steal what was rightfully hers.

"Do you remember the question?" He arched an eyebrow and grinned, for she looked deliciously bemused, and he did not want her thinking he was in jest.

She let out a breath and smiled up at him. "My head is still a bit foggy, but I do remember the question. It is not something I ever expected to hear from you."

He nodded. "I know. I'm sorry I ever left you in doubt."

"Oh, do not keep him waiting," Margaret said with an impatient squeal. "Cherish, you must tell him what is in your heart."

"He knows it already, Margaret." But Cherish nodded. "Your Grace, there is no one for me but you, for it is *you* that I love. Not your title. Nor your wealth. Just you. I shall be delighted to be your wife."

Cheers broke out all around them, and cheering loudest were Fiona, Reggie, and Margaret, who was hopping up and down and clapping. "I knew it! It had to be love, for you are the kindest and loveliest person, Cherish. I am so happy for you."

"Thank you, Margaret." Cherish gave the girl another heartfelt hug.

"Do I get one, too?" Gawain asked, his chuckle deep and resonant.

She nodded and rushed into his outstretched arms. "Thank you," she whispered with a shudder of relief that coursed through her lithe body as he wrapped his arms around her. "We shall work it out later."

Work out what? Did she believe he was merely pretending? That it was only a ruse to protect her from her uncle and he would beg out once the danger to her had passed?

He intended to disabuse her of the notion as soon as they had a quiet moment.

"This calls for champagne!" Fiona pushed forward to hug him. "Smartest thing you've done in your life, Gawain."

Lady Albin stormed off. Reggie cast him a knowing look, for he had been the one to insist Lady Albin would never give up on him until he married.

Gawain was relieved to be done with her. But he felt no joy in seeing her brought down. For all her faults, they had a history, and he did not wish her ill. She had gone off in a huff, but he'd seen into her heart for just a moment, and she had looked defeated as well as angry.

What was going on with her? He might have helped her out had she told him the truth instead of resorting to mean tricks and selfish ploys. Perhaps he would seek her out at some point over the next few days to question her before she returned to London.

But his priority was now Cherish.

After all, it was not as though his proposing to Cherish had shattered his former beloved's soul. If she felt devastated, it was only because she had failed in her objective, whatever that objective was. It had nothing to do with losing him.

But that glimpse of her with her defenses down concerned him.

However, his greatest worry was for Cherish, since she would remain vulnerable until he married her.

Her uncle was standing quietly for the moment, no doubt thinking hard about how to thwart Gawain. But it was never going to happen. He meant to obtain the license this very day and marry Cherish tomorrow morning.

He turned to Cherish, who appeared quite pensive, and

placed a hand gently on her shoulder. "Having second thoughts already?"

She looked up at him, her eyes dancing with mirth. "Not about you. I have done nothing but dream of you since the moment we met. I am so filled with happiness, my heart is about to burst. But did you see that look on Lady Albin's face as she ran off just now?"

"You noticed?"

She nodded.

"Do not be fooled by her, Cherish. She never loved me. However, I sense she is in serious trouble. I wish she had confided the problem to me. I would have helped." He shook his head and sighed. "You are the immediate concern, and I mean to fix your situation as soon as possible."

Her smile slipped a little. "Is this why you proposed to me? Out of a sense of duty to protect me?"

"No, Cherish. I'm sorry. That did not sound very romantic, did it? Let me get rid of your uncle first, and then I shall do better."

Everyone marched into the dining room as Fiona's footmen set out the glasses filled with champagne atop the buffet. Northam refused to raise a glass in toast. Gawain ordered him carted outside and held by two of Fiona's burliest footmen. He understood the man was in no humor to celebrate an engagement that would soon lead to his demise, but the oaf was not going to ruin his and Cherish's special moment.

Gawain waited until her uncle was hauled off. Only then did he turn to Cherish. Her eyes sparkled as she took a sip of champagne, and she looked lighter and more carefree than he had ever seen her. Not that he had seen much of her, for they had only met a few days ago.

This fact ought to have frightened him, but it did not. As foolish as it seemed, his heart had recognized her importance at once. In that moment, all his impenetrable walls had come down for her.

He joined in the cheering when several guests offered up a toast to their happiness.

Reggie's turn came, and the boy had a wicked smirk. "The tables are turned, Uncle."

Gawain grinned at his nephew. "Watch what you say, Reggie."

"And lose this precious opportunity? Not on your life." Reggie downed his champagne and then held out his glass for another serving. "You see, my friends, this Silver Duke came to Shoreham Manor determined to have me betrothed to a young woman of his choosing. That young woman was Lady Cherish. But it seems his plans went awry, because she stole his heart instead of mine."

A collective chuckle ran through the crowd.

Reggie raised his glass again. "I wish you every happiness, Uncle Gawain. I know you shall have it with Cherish, for you chose wisely, even if it was unexpectedly for yourself."

Gawain allowed a few more toasts and a few more jests, but put an end to this distraction as the well wishes got bawdier. "Reggie, Durham, I think it is time for us to escort Lord Northam home."

The two set aside their glasses and marched Cherish's uncle to the stable to retrieve their horses.

Before following them, Gawain planted a kiss on Cherish's forehead. "I will see you later."

"Oh, but my list! Well, it does not matter. Take anything you find in my bedchamber. I do not care about anything else."

"Not even the sentimental pieces of jewelry?"

She shook her head. "No, the cameo brooch you gave me is more than enough, and I will treasure it always. I do not want anything Lord Northam and his wife have touched."

"All right," he said, pleased that she thought so highly of the brooch he had bought her the other day. But this was among the reasons he had fallen in love with her—for her sense of what was valuable and what was not.

Well, he'd loved everything about her from the moment they

met. Perhaps this explained why he had yet to be hit by a sense of dread at the prospect of marrying Cherish. What would his fellow Silver Dukes say to this surprising turn of events? He would see them soon enough and find out, although he was sorry indeed they would not be here for the wedding.

He, Lynton, and Camborne had been friends a long time and close as any brothers. He knew they would wish him well, but not before giving him a hard time for breaking their bachelor bonds. However, he would wish them the same good fortune were they ever to find their right match.

It did not take him, Reggie, and Durham long to ride over to Northam Hall along with a wagon in which to load Cherish's belongings. He doubted she would have much, since her uncle had been going out of his way to deprive her of all the trappings of her status ever since he took over responsibility for her.

Cherish had not cared about these slights nearly as much as she ought to have done. It simply was not in her nature to take offense or hold grudges. However, Gawain was not nearly as nice as she was and felt nothing but outrage on her behalf. He was not about to let her uncle's cruel attempts to deprive her of her dignity and worth go unpunished.

As for that punishment, he would take his cues from Cherish, for he did not wish to overset her. Still, he would go after that oaf even if it was not done as thoroughly as he truly wished. He understood that Northam was her only family, and Gawain had to respect her feelings even if he considered her too softhearted.

He would not be happy, but Cherish's happiness was more important.

He smiled thinking of her. Despite her quiet manner, there was an air of confidence about her, a spirit that her uncle had not been able to destroy. She had a sweet nature, but was no little mouse to be pushed around. He liked that unmistakable confidence in herself. As irritated as he was with her lack of fear for her own safety, he was also greatly relieved to see this spark of determination shine from within her.

Her uncle looked sallow and deflated as they rode to North-am Hall, obviously contemplating his mistake in coming after his niece and dreading what would transpire next.

Good. It was time the tables were turned and this man paid for his wrongdoing.

Gawain had met the Northam Hall butler and several others on the Northam staff when he stopped in the other day. "Good morning, Potter. We have come for Lady Cherish's belongings."

The man's eyes rounded in surprise, but he hesitated not a moment before nodding. "At once, Your Grace."

Lord Northam was not pleased by his own head butler's compliance. "Anyone who assists Bromleigh shall be sacked on the spot. Not a thing is to be touched. She owns nothing. Not a gown or a shoe buckle. It all belongs to me!"

Gawain frowned. "Be quiet, Northam. I am keeping count of every petty, vindictive word out of your foul mouth. If you think this will not come back to bite you in the arse, then you had better think again."

He turned to the butler. "Get her things packed at once, Potter. Ignore your master's threats. I shall hire anyone he sacks for doing the right thing."

Upon hearing those words, the Northam servants came out of the woodwork like ants. They ignored their master while he ranted and raved, and paid no heed to the equally unlikable Lady Northam when she lumbered down the stairs and began to shriek at them in outrage.

The servants took care as they packed Cherish's possessions. The Northam footmen then loaded them onto the wagon Gawain had brought along for this purpose. "Well, Northam? Are you going to discharge your entire household? Even your cook and scullery maids came out of the kitchen to assist me. It will serve you right if you and your wife are abandoned entirely and left to fend for yourselves."

"Blast you, Bromleigh," Northam grumbled, and stormed back inside without a word to his staff, for it was obvious he dared not lose any of them.

Potter looked back at Northam's retreating form and then turned to Gawain in dismay. "Too bad he kept silent. There is not one of us who wishes to serve him. Lady Cherish is another matter. We would lay down our lives for her. Your Grace, may I be so bold as to ask what is to become of her?"

Gawain smiled. "She is to become my wife."

"Your wife?" The old butler's eyes turned moist, and he cracked a broad grin. "I speak for the entire Northam staff when I say that we wish her every happiness and know she will have it with you. This is excellent news. You will not find a finer lady."

Gawain nodded. "I shall convey your regards to her. Send word to Lady Shoreham if Northam dares to mistreat any of you after I've gone. She will let me know."

"Thank you, Your Grace. That is very generous and much appreciated. Alas, I fear he is too enamored of his comforts to risk an uprising from his staff. I expect we are safe enough from his threats and bluster. Unfortunate, but there it is."

Gawain and his companions made it back to Shoreham Manor in time for lunch. He was ravenous, but had to attend to a delicate matter with Cherish first.

She must have been fretting as she watched for his return. Gawain's heart melted when he saw her standing on the front steps with her hands clasped in front of her and a worried look on her face. He noticed that she had changed out of her gown into a fresh one, for there was no bloodstain on the sleeve.

Good, for that scrape had concerned him. He'd thoroughly cleansed it, but did not like that it had bled again during her confrontation with Northam.

She lit up upon noticing his smile of conquest. He pointed to the wagon, which was filled with her belongings.

Fiona, Margaret, and a dozen other guests hurried out to greet them, but Gawain had eyes only for Cherish. Lord, would he always turn soft as pudding at the sight of her? Was this what love did to a man? This was something new for him, a feeling he'd never experienced in the forty years of his life.

Upon reflection, he had never once felt this way with his first love, Lady Albin. That youthful affair could best be described as passionate, intense, too often volatile, but certainly not a mature love to last a lifetime.

Gawain dismounted, handed Odin to one of the grooms, and then strode to Cherish. "Come with me," he said, taking her hand to lead her into the garden, where they might have some privacy.

She felt so right walking beside him, her hand soft and little as it was swallowed in his. He felt good just being with her.

In addition to changing out of her bloodied gown into a finer one, she had attended to her hair. No doubt Fiona had sent her maid to Cherish with specific instructions. Her hair was stylishly drawn back in a ribbon, but left long and loose to cascade down her back. Not at all proper for going about London, but perfect for a country house party.

Especially practical if he wished to untie the ribbon and slide his hands through those silken strands as he kissed her.

Yes, Fiona was sharp and did not miss a trick. Cherish looked beautiful and suitably prepared for that first kiss he now intended to give her.

"Did my uncle cause any further trouble?" she asked, having no idea about his purpose as he led her away from the others.

"No, love."

She laughed and looked up at him. "Did you meet my ogress of an aunt?"

"Yes, *love*. And she was every bit the ogress you warned she would be. But I easily handled her and her equally unpleasant husband."

"I knew you would. You are simply marvelous." She cast him a breathtaking smile. "Did she attempt to give you trouble?"

"Of course, but her own staff quickly shut her up. They did the same to her husband, too."

"Truly? Oh, dear old Potter. I'm sure he led the way. What did he say to them?" She suddenly gasped. "Did he put himself at risk? They are a vindictive pair. I cannot—"

"All's well." Gawain shook his head and laughed. "I told your staff that if Northam sacked any of them, they were to come to me and I would provide work for them. Every last one of them came forward to help gather your belongings, even down to the scullery maids."

Cherish cast him another of her radiant smiles. "You are brilliant! But Northam Hall has a staff of twenty-five who will now all need jobs."

"No, love. Northam may be furious with them, but he and his wife value their comforts beyond anything else. He quickly realized that no one would be left to attend them, nor would anyone reliable come forward to replace those he had discharged once word got around about what he did. Everyone is safe, at least for now. But I did tell Potter to let Fiona know if Northam makes any trouble. What do you think of that, *love*?"

"I think you are a chess master and checkmated him brilliantly."

He sighed. "Are you not going to remark on my endearment for you?"

She gave a merry laugh. "I was wondering what that was about. Am I truly your love? I dared not hope, because I love you so very much and was worried you had only proposed to me in order to save me from a dismal fate. But you seem content with our situation. Are you, Gawain?"

"I am." He drew her into his arms as they reached a private spot in Fiona's garden, one that was hidden by a copse of trees and also provided a lovely overlook to the cove and its glistening waters in the distance.

A gentle sea breeze wafted around them, causing the branches to bow and sway with a soft rustle of leaves. "I had already made up my mind to marry you, Cherish. I was going to find the right moment to tell you how I felt before your idiot uncle ever came along and forced my hand."

Her eyes widened. "You were?"

He nodded as he held her in his embrace, for he was in no hurry to let her go. "Yes."

"Why? What made me different from the other women in your life?"

"I'm not sure I can describe it. I think it was the sum of you. Your warmth, your honesty. Your beautiful smile and beautiful eyes. It was in the way you made me feel whenever I was around you. I liked having you beside me. I liked talking to you. Whenever you walked into a room, everything suddenly felt good and right."

She nodded. "This is very much how I felt whenever around you. Safe. Wonderful. Meant to be. I love you, Gawain. But you know this. I'll do my best to make you happy. But what shall I call you? Bromleigh or Duke is too formal. Sir? That also seems too formal."

"I agree, it denotes someone subservient addressing me, and you shall never be that. As my wife you shall stand as my equal."

"That is quite forward thinking of you," she remarked, obviously pleased.

"I am not so old yet as to be stuck in my ways."

"Nor am I," she said, then reminded him that she was old enough to be considered a spinster. "Gawain is a wonderful name, but your friends and family also call you that. I ought to call you something special for your ears alone. *My dearest.* Yes, that might do if you don't mind, for this is how I feel about you, and will do so forever."

"My dearest," he said in a whisper and caressed her cheek. "I like it. I'm sorry I did not think of it first, for this is what you are to me as well. But there is one more thing we must do to seal this betrothal."

She looked up at him, her smile more radiant than the sunshine surrounding them. Her hair shone a lovely molten gold as she stood in the dappled light, looking so achingly beautiful he could barely catch his breath.

The breeze off the water delicately mussed her lively curls as she stood gazing up at him. "There is a *thing* to do? What have I forgotten?"

"You haven't forgotten anything," he said, watching her purse her lovely lips. "But I have yet to kiss you."

She inhaled lightly. "No one ever has done that before. Is it not the saddest commentary on my life? You'll be my first kiss."

"All the better, and I am determined to make it special for you." The surf below crashed against the rocky outcropping as he spoke, reflecting the turbulence of his feelings. It struck him just how deep and powerful their love could grow over time.

Poets spoke of love eternal. Gawain could see himself feeling this way about Cherish.

"Ready?"

She nodded. "I have been waiting for you all of my life."

CHAPTER FOURTEEN

G AWAIN BENT HIS head and closed his mouth over Cherish's beautifully shaped lips with a heartfelt urgency and deep sense of satisfaction. He kissed her with possessive hunger, for he had finally found the one person who would always share his heart.

The one person he could always *trust* with his heart.

Cherish lifted on tiptoes and wrapped her arms around his neck, sighing as she surrendered herself to him. He deepened the kiss as she responded with warmth to the pressure of his mouth on hers.

Her lips were soft, and they tasted so sweet.

She moaned and melted against him, pressing her body to his with innocent urgency. He'd ached to feel her against him, to breathe in her intoxicating scent, that delicate hint of rose blossoms as their petals unfurled in sunlight. The roses in Fiona's garden held a fragrant trace of lemon, which he also inhaled on Cherish's warm skin.

This was what she was—a beautiful garden rose.

She leaned into him, the soft pillow of her breasts molding to his chest and setting his blood on fire. She fit so perfectly against Gawain, as though she were made just for him. He slipped the ribbon out of her hair and buried his fingers in her silken strands, aching for the moment he would see their golden shimmer against his pillows.

He felt a satisfaction he had never known before, a peace that had eluded him for all of his life until now. It had taken him all these years to understand what those romantic poets were going on about, this matching of one soul to another.

Truly, theirs had to be a love eternal, one that could not be measured merely by time. He had never believed such a thing possible. And yet here was Cherish Northam. Perfect, beautiful. *His.*

He ran his hands along her body, allowing no more than a graze of her full breasts despite the urge to explore them with his hands and lips. Cherish had a woman's body, and he looked forward to drawing out her hidden inner passion in the privacy of their bedchamber.

He knew she would not hold back, either. She was inexperienced but also a woman full grown and ready to be a wife. He could tell by the way she held on to him and arched against him that she was eager to embark on this journey of intimate discovery. He hadn't a doubt they would suit each other in bed as well as in life.

One more night and he would claim her for his own.

Not that he wished to wait even another hour, but it did not feel right to take her outside of the bonds of marriage when he would have the lawful right to do so within a day.

Although she was not resisting his advances, he gently broke off their kiss when he heard others approaching. He wanted to do more than run his hands over the curves of her body, but an innocent first kiss would have to be enough for now. He had a marriage license to obtain still.

"This is what I hope for us, Cherish," he said, his voice rasping as he ended the kiss. "To live truly as husband and wife."

She nodded. "Perhaps in time a love match for us both. I know my feelings for you run deeper than those you have for me."

He should have denied it, for he had known he was going to marry her from the moment they first met. It was sheer stubbornness on his part that delayed his admitting the inevitable. Well, it was also the brevity of their acquaintance.

Even though he felt as though they had known each other all of their lives, in fact it had only been a few days. What duke in his right mind would ever propose on such short acquaintance? Perhaps it helped that Fiona knew her so well and liked her as well as she would a sister. Indeed, Cherish fit in splendidly with his family.

Her smile shone in her eyes, revealing she was well pleased by their first kiss. "This has been quite a day, but all worth it for this happy end. I hope you shall kiss me often. This first was very nice."

She had a way of looking at him that lightened his heart. He grinned, for he was quite willing to accommodate her request. "There shall be more, if you wish them."

"Oh, I do wish them." She laughed, but then turned serious a moment later. "Thank you for this. I am still worried this is a dream and I will soon wake up."

"You did receive a bump on the head," he said with a frown. "But your eyes look clear and you do not appear to be unsteady."

"I am floating on a cloud, Gawain. Nothing can ruin this day for me now. Not a jealous countess or a cheating, scheming toad of an uncle. Are you sure this is not a dream?"

"No dream, Cherish. Nor do I need you to thank me for something I did as much for myself as I did for you. I'm sorry it was not more of a courtship."

She shook her head. "A Silver Duke courting a young lady? Chaos would have erupted. To even hint at an interest in me would have caused a riot in *ton* circles."

"Perhaps, but we seem to have caused quite a stir anyway." Between Katie's mischief and Northam's rants, plenty of entertainment had been provided for Fiona's guests. There would be plenty of gossip fodder for the London papers, too.

"That is true. No proper courtship, but it shall still be a fun tale to regale our children. *My little imps, if ever I told you of your father's...*" She gasped. "Oh, but you do not wish to have children. I...I did not mean..."

He took her hands in his. "Cherish, forget every stupid thing I've said or have been rumored to say. It is all different with you. If you wish to have children, then we shall have them. With you as their mother, I know they will be cared for and loved whether or not I am around to see them grow up."

She regarded him in dismay. "Do not say that. You must be with me into our dotage."

"I hope to be," he assured her, "for I am not keen to depart this world so soon. Especially while you are in it. But you know our lives will not necessarily turn out as we hope. Things happen. Whether I live or die is not in my control. So, let us take one day at a time and be grateful for every moment we have together."

"All right. But I will not let you go without a fight," she said, closing her eyes and leaning into him as he dipped his head to hers for another kiss, this one scorching and ravenous, for he wanted her to feel the heat between them and know he was going to bring out all her fiery passion in their marriage bed.

She sighed when he eased his lips off hers.

"You taste as sweet as honeysuckle," he said.

She nestled in his arms, each of them content as they stood beneath the summer sun and soaked in the warmth of their future life together.

Most of the guests had gathered in the dining room by the time they made their way back to Fiona's house. They entered through the parlor only to encounter Fiona, Reggie, and Margaret waiting for them.

Fiona smiled. "I knew he would kiss you. I hope you liked it."

"Oh, dear heaven," Cherish muttered as a blush crawled up her neck and into her cheeks. "Am I that obvious?"

Gawain merely arched an eyebrow. He loved his cousin, but she could be irritating at times.

"I cannot wait to be kissed." Margaret sighed and set her gaze on Reggie, who grinned at her wickedly.

"That can be arranged," Reggie said.

Gawain groaned. "Come on, whelp, I'll need that license if I am to get married tomorrow."

"I'll unpack my things while you're gone," Cherish said as she let go of Gawain's arm.

"I'll help you, Cherish," Margaret squealed, and walked out with her, leaving Gawain alone with his cousin and his nephew.

Fiona cleared her throat.

Gawain sighed. "What? All I did was kiss her, I promise. Reggie, care to join me while I obtain the license?"

His nephew threw his arms around him and gave him an enormous hug. "With greatest pleasure, Uncle Gawain."

Gawain laughed and hugged him back.

"Will you not join us for a meal first?" Fiona asked. "Or I can have my cook pack up something for you."

Gawain shook his head. "Reggie and I will grab a bite in town. I want that license. I mean to marry Cherish at the parish church tomorrow morning. Would you mind turning tomorrow's breakfast into a wedding breakfast? I know it is very short notice, Fiona. But I dare not put this off for even a day. I don't trust Northam."

"It is disheartening how many bad men like him exist," Reggie muttered.

Gawain nodded. "Which is why it is important that good men always step forward to counter them."

"I'm glad you are marrying Cherish, Uncle Gawain."

Fiona nodded. "I have already put my kitchen staff to the task. After all my meddling and plotting to put you two together, did you even need to ask?"

CHAPTER FIFTEEN

T HE PARLOR GAMES were quite merry that night, but Fiona was still bent on torturing Gawain by pairing him with the worst teammates. Lord Pershing was still drunk, still useless, and still on his team. Sweet Margaret was newly added to his team in place of Lady Eugenia, who had set her cap for Fellstone and maneuvered to be on his team.

Gawain did not mind, for Fellstone was a decent chap and in need of an heiress. Lady Eugenie surely was that, and would bring quite a fortune to their marriage, assuming Fellstone married her. She was still a peahen with not a brain cell to be found between her ears.

Margaret was different, he was coming to realize. The girl was not dim-witted at all, just held back by her family when it came to education. What the girl lacked in knowledge, she made up for in enthusiasm. She might come around and turn out to be quite clever once Cherish and Fiona tutored her.

Lady Yvonne had also been placed on his team once more. She was another one with not much brain matter between her ears, so he knew their team would finish last in every game.

Fiona had fixed her team with the best players, so it came as no surprise when hers won every round. She had selected Cherish, Reggie, and Durham. They were easily the smartest competitors.

Charades was a disaster. This time, Gawain did not mind.

Margaret was giving the clues for his team.

Gawain could not make heads or tails of what she was trying to convey. "Dear heaven," he muttered, "is it even an English word?"

Cherish was seated beside him and trying her best not to laugh. He loved her smile, and loved how kindly she treated Margaret, who really was still a little peahen and clueless, but had a good heart.

Margaret was spinning in a circle and patting her back.

"Time's up," Fiona said. "What was your phrase, Margaret?"

"Shark fin soup."

Huh?

"I was pointing to a fin on my back," she explained proudly. "A shark fin."

"Ah, well done," Reggie said, casting her a besotted smile. "That was very clever of you."

She sparkled like a little star. "Thank you, Lord Burton. That is very kind of you to say. But I think it wasn't really very clever, because no one on my team guessed it."

"They were not paying close enough attention. I would have guessed it," Reggie assured her.

Gawain sighed.

He was getting married tomorrow, but would wager his estate that it would be Reggie's turn before the year was out. He would approve, of course. Cherish liked the girl and thought she was a good influence on Reggie. He agreed, for Margaret was never going to manipulate or take advantage of his nephew. The girl did not know the meaning of malice. She probably couldn't spell it either, but the point was that she would make a happy home for Reggie. There would be no one like Lady Albin stepping in to ruin his nephew's life.

While the others remained in the parlor to continue the games, Gawain excused himself and Cherish. After all, Cherish had been run down by Lady Albin's horse this morning. Even though she appeared to be fine, she did have some bruising on her hip and wrist, not to mention the scraped elbow and the small bump on her head, which was hidden by her hair but could be felt.

He held out his arm to her. "Ready, love?"

She nodded.

Margaret heard the endearment and cooed.

"The day started miserably for you," Gawain said as they climbed the stairs together, his arm protectively around her waist.

Cherish paused in front of her bedroom door and leaned lightly against it as she regarded him. "I am not complaining."

"You never do, I am discovering."

"I have no reason for it." She cast him a weary smile. "I look forward to living under *your* roof instead of my toad of an uncle's roof. Although I will miss Northam Hall itself. It is such a lovely home, and I was always happy there until the new earl and his wife moved in."

Music drifted toward them from downstairs, where the other guests were now moving on to dancing. Well, those like Pershing would head to the study to drink themselves into a stupor. A few others would settle in for games of cards. Others for billiards. Some would disappear into the garden for a quick tryst behind some shrubbery. Such were the activities at these ever-popular house parties. No one needed a reason to drink, gamble, dance, or dally.

Often the dalliances were continued in the wee hours of the morning with gentlemen sneaking into ladies' bedchambers. He contemplated doing the same with Cherish, for her luscious body had him in a roil. But he decided against it.

Tomorrow night, once they were husband and wife, would do.

Fiona's guests had been present when he proposed to Cherish this morning. It was a coup for them to be present to witness the fall of a Silver Duke. They were going to relate their firsthand account to their *ton* friends and the gossip rags. He did not want it also said that he had taken Lady Cherish Northam to his bed before exchanging vows of marriage.

"I am sorry your friends, Lynton and Camborne, will not be here to see us married. Well, I suppose they would not approve."

"On the contrary, they would heartily approve."

Cherish's eyes widened in surprise. "They would?"

"Absolutely." He placed his hands on either side of her body and leaned in to lightly trap her against the door. "Everyone assumed we were averse to marriage, but it was never so. None of us meant to avoid it. The years rolled on and we never found that one special lady to our liking."

"It is said you sampled many."

"An exaggeration, Cherish. Women tossed themselves at us, and on occasion we were receptive to their advances. Never anything serious." He gave her a rakish grin. "Occasionally depraved."

"Gawain!"

"Teasing you, love. We were fairly tame by rakehell standards. That's all it ever was. But now I have found you, and you are the wife I want." He was not ancient by any means, but forty years old was a long time to wait to experience love. He had pretty much given up hope of ever finding the right woman.

So had his friends. Lynton had been married, but the union between him and his late wife was by no means a love match. They had barely spoken to each other, although she had done her duty and given him children. In some ways, Lynton was the most cynical of the Silver Dukes, and most reluctant ever to marry again because his first experience had been such a disappointment.

However, Gawain truly wished this same happiness he had found with Cherish for them both.

Cherish cast him that magical smile of hers as she looked up at him. "Reggie seems quite taken with Margaret. I wonder if Fiona would ever consider remarrying. She had a good marriage with Albert, but..."

"He did not leave her breathless."

"Well, he was no Silver Duke. Should I allow you to come into my bedchamber? After all, you have the marriage license, and we are to be wed first thing tomorrow."

He dropped his hands to his sides and studied the soft angles of her face. "Don't tempt me with your big brandy eyes. No, we've given everyone enough fodder for gossip."

"I am sorry for those two."

He furrowed his brow. "Who? My friends?"

"No, my uncle and Lady Albin. She might have won you back had she just been honest with you."

"No, Cherish. She had no chance once I met you. I was already smitten from the letters Fiona wrote to me about you. All I needed was a first glimpse of you to know I was about to fall madly, deeply, and wildly in love with you."

She inhaled. "You truly love me?"

Bollocks.

He had not meant for it to slip out that way, although it seemed cowardly and petty to deny it now. In truth, he had no wish to deny his feelings for her. Cherish had been nothing but honest with him. It was not fair to let her go on believing he had offered to marry her merely in order to protect her.

He had used endearments when referring to her, but she obviously needed more convincing. "Yes, Cherish. My heart was lost to you the moment I saw you beside Fiona that first day. You were standing in a circle of sunlight in the parlor, trying to pull your hand out of hers so that you could run off before we were ever introduced."

Cherish nodded. "She wouldn't let me go."

"I'm glad. Your hair shone gold and your dark eyes sparkled. I had never seen a more beautiful woman in my life."

"And still you wanted to match me with Reggie?"

"It was a halfhearted attempt at best," he said with a groan. "Was it not obvious? I could not take my eyes off you. Nor can I now." He drew her back into his arms and crushed his mouth to hers, kissing her with every ounce of longing and every promise of building a life together.

He kissed her as he knew she had always yearned to be kissed. Deeply. With enough heat to make her swoon.

With fire in his soul.

She responded in a similar manner, as he knew she would, because she was honest about her feelings and he had easily been able to read them from the start.

"Answer me this, Cherish," he said with a chuckle after ending the kiss, but keeping her in his arms since he could not seem to draw away from her, even though it was only a matter of a day before they would be together always. "Did Fiona ever intend to help me match you with Reggie? Or was I doomed from the very start?"

Her eyes were beautifully alight as she grinned. "You were doomed, I think. Although she did not let me in on her plan immediately. However, she always thought I was perfect for you. Now looking back, it ought to have been obvious to me. She went on and on about you for months before we had ever met, and had built you up so much, that I was in dread fear of meeting this paragon cousin of hers."

"Yes, Fiona is prone to exaggeration."

Cherish laughed. "No, you were all that and more. I am certain she contrived this house party to lure you here specifically to meet me. I also expect she embellished her concerns about Reggie to ensure you would accept the invitation. So you never had a chance. She had no intention of allowing your scheme for Reggie to succeed."

"I'm not sure I like the way she manipulated me."

Cherish cast him a mild look of reproof. "You were trying to do the same to Reggie, so you must not be angry with her. As for Reggie, did you notice how he and Margaret behave around each other? She adores him. I think they are a good fit for each other. Well, I hope he comes around and marries her. Will you take issue with him if he chooses her?"

"No, I will give my consent."

"Thank you." She sighed. "That is a relief."

"Why do you think I would give him a hard time if he chose her? I may be dense for myself, but I am fairly clear sighted when it comes to others. Yes, I would prefer if she were a bit more clever. But her heart is good. In her own peahen way, Margaret makes him feel like a hero and brings out his noblest instincts. Just as you do for me."

He bent his head to kiss her again, covering her mouth with a soft but possessive kiss. "I had better leave you now, or I will not have the strength to leave you at all."

She looked up at him in that starry-eyed way he was getting to like immensely. It felt good to have a woman look at him in this way instead of with cold calculation. "Nor shall I encourage you to go."

"I'll come in with you, but only to make certain nothing is amiss. Your uncle is now a desperate man, and I dare not leave you unprotected for a single moment."

"You have posted two footmen beneath my window and another who will be patrolling along the hallway overnight. I think I shall be safe enough." But her smile faded a little. "I am going to miss being in your arms tonight."

Most betrothed couples would not think twice about taking liberties, but he could not do this to Cherish. It had all been so rushed. It had all been so surprising. "I think there will be more pleasure in it for you in coming to me for your first time as my wife. However, there is something more we must take care of as soon as we are married."

She eyed him quizzically. "What is that?"

"A marriage contract drawn up between us."

"To protect your interests?" She nodded. "I understand."

"No, it is quite the opposite. I mean to protect you. We will attend to the formality immediately upon our return to London. I need to make certain you are never left vulnerable to anyone's greed."

"Do you mean your nephew? Reggie is as honorable as you

are. He would never treat me as my uncle has."

"I was not thinking of Reggie, for I trust him too," he said, musing aloud as he led her into her bedchamber. "But there are no guarantees about what may happen in life, and I need to be certain you are left secure."

"Especially since my father saw fit to leave me with almost nothing," she said with a grunt. "You are kinder to me than he was."

"Cherish, I don't think your father overlooked you. In fact, I think you have an inheritance, perhaps a sizeable one, that your uncle has been hiding from you. You already sensed something was wrong but did not know where to turn for help, since every one of your father's people were in collusion with him."

She nodded. "Now I have you to help me reclaim it."

"And it shall remain yours, whatever there is. I do not want any of it, but will do whatever I can to make certain no one ever steals it from you again. In fact, I have already sent off a message to my man of affairs in London. I have instructed him to pay a call on your father's solicitor and demand to see documents, for I want all involved to know we are watching them closely and will be coming for them next."

"His solicitor is a horrid little man," she muttered, giving a nod of approval. "That ought to scare him into compliance. But what if it does not?"

Gawain arched an eyebrow. "It will. This is the beauty of the slightly terrifying aura surrounding Lynton, Camborne, and myself. No one dares to cross a Silver Duke."

Her eyes shimmered with mirth. "Ah, this is the bit of ruthless determination you were hoping to instill in Reggie. Good thing you like me."

"It is scary how much I like you," he said with a laughing groan. "Well, being an old man and having experienced probably too much of life has also given me the confidence to know the right thing when it comes along."

"This spinster has seen almost nothing of the world, but I also know what feels right, and everything about you felt right from the moment I set eyes on you, too."

He turned serious for a moment. Despite how confident both of them were of this decision to marry, there were important issues still to be discussed. He was always thorough in his dealings, and during his years in military service had always gone over battle plans in careful detail. With their marriage ceremony mere hours away, should they not have some discussion on the terms?

She seemed to know his thoughts and put a finger to his lips. "We are both sensible."

He shook his head. "Quite the opposite. We've led with our hearts since meeting each other."

"Does it feel odd to you? It does a little to me," she admitted. "But whatever problems come up, we shall work them out. For me, there can be no problem too great to solve between us. I do not see how anything can be more important than spending my life with you."

He nodded and kissed her on the nose, then took a moment to check her room to make certain nothing was amiss. "I'll see you bright and early in the morning."

She cast him an endearing smile. "Pleasant dreams, Gawain."

"Same to you, love."

Cherish, for all her common sense and shy demeanor, sparkled at the endearment. Yes, they would figure out the living arrangements and sleeping arrangements without difficulty once they settled into married life.

GAWAIN'S SLEEP WAS calmer than it had been in years, obviously Cherish's influence. He awoke the following morning to an incredibly beautiful day, the sky a deep and striking azure blue. A cool breeze off the misty waters also cooled his skin as it wrapped around his body.

He had returned to his bedchamber now that Lady Albin had vacated it. No doubt Reggie was thrilled to no longer have his ogre uncle sharing his quarters and ensuring he remained celibate.

Well, Reggie was not going to stray, since he appeared to have settled on Margaret. Her parents were with her at this party and no doubt closely watching their precious dove. Even if they were not, Margaret was another innocent like Cherish. Reggie would not visit her and soil her before they were betrothed.

Gawain usually took care of grooming and dressing himself, never particularly liking to be fussed over by a valet. But he did not protest when Fiona sent her late husband's valet to him with the express direction that he look his best for his wedding day.

He allowed the valet to take extra care in his grooming. The man checked on his bathwater, and also took over the task of shaving him. He made certain Gawain's suit was freshly pressed and in perfect condition. Tied his cravat.

Dear heaven. Gawain had been doing this for himself since he was the age of six.

The man even measured precisely how much shirt cuff to show beyond the sleeve of his jacket. After what seemed an eternity, Gawain was pronounced ready.

He strode down the hall to make certain Cherish was awake and getting ready herself. He needn't have worried about her oversleeping this morning, for the entire household appeared to be up and already stirring like bees about a hive.

Fiona's maids looked quite harried as they bustled up and down the hall to attend to everyone who would join them at the parish church within a few hours.

Cherish's door was open, and he could hear her chattering with several ladies. But as he was about to stride in, Fiona and Margaret, obviously the ladies she had been talking to, came down on him like a pair of shrieking banshees and pushed him away. "Stay out!" they cried, slamming the door in his face.

"Blessed saints," he muttered, and stalked away.

So what if he wanted to look in on Cherish? Was it not right that he should see to her care? They would be husband and wife within two hours. Would the sky fall in if he happened to catch a glimpse of ankle or a hint of creamy flesh?

With a shake of his head, he marched to Reggie's quarters and was pleased to receive a warmer greeting from his nephew. "Uncle, isn't this a marvelous day for a wedding?"

He smiled at the lad. "Yes, Reggie. Are you almost ready?"

"Another moment and I'll be done." Reggie's valet was just straightening his cuffs when Gawain strode in. "How is Cherish?"

"I'm not sure," Gawain said with a grunt. "I almost had my head lopped off when I tried to see her. Fiona and Margaret are standing guard and allowing no one in. I assume they will have her ready shortly."

Reggie had a mirthful gleam in his eyes. "I love Fiona, but she can be irritatingly headstrong when it comes to having her way. She was determined to match you with Cherish, so I have no doubt she will get Cherish to the church on time, even if she has to carry her on her back."

Gawain grinned.

Reggie's gaze turned affectionate. "Any second thoughts, Uncle?"

Gawain shook his head. "Not a one, incredible as it seems considering my marriage-averse reputation. I am amazed how easily everything falls into place when one has found the right person to share one's life."

"I'm sorry it took you so long to meet her. But the important thing is that you recognized her worth and did not let her slip away."

"Thanks to Fiona's prodding. I suppose I needed to be set up. You took on your role with much enthusiasm."

"Uncle, please know I was not aware of her game until it was well underway. But I will admit to heartily joining in once I learned of it. Am I forgiven?"

"I am the one who owes you the apology."

"Whatever for?" Reggie asked, sounding quite surprised.

"I behaved like an insufferable arse, coming at you with all my demands. I am truly sorry for that, Reggie. You are a far better man than I was at your age. It was not right of me to expect perfection out of you when I had set a terrible example for you to follow."

"Not at all. You have always been good to me. I needed a bit of a kick in the backside to grow up and prove my worth to you."

"You have, Reggie. I ought to have recognized your abilities sooner." Gawain shook his head. "Had our situations been reversed, you in charge and demanding I marry, I would have been an utter arse about it. Rebellious. Angry. Insolent. You are a lot nicer than I ever was."

"I have no complaints about you," Reggie assured him, his expression now serious. "I think you do not realize how much I love you. No one was kinder or more attentive to my mother as we realized she was dying. No one could have taken better care of me than you did. In all the months of her illness, you were there and made sure we lacked for nothing."

Gawain shrugged off the compliment. "We are family. This is what we do for each other."

"I want you to know that I will do the same for Cherish if ever it becomes necessary. Obviously, she can never rely on the Northam family. I have never seen lower forms of life than her uncle and his wife. Well, she will have all of us now to protect her from that odious pair. She and Fiona are already close as sisters."

They marched out together and waited downstairs for the ladies to join them. As the minutes passed, Gawain began to pace.

"Uncle," Reggie said, casually resting a hip against the ornate entry hall table and appearing far too relaxed, "you'll wear a hole in the marble floor if you do not stop prowling."

"What's taking them so long?" Gawain muttered. "Cherish should have been down here by now."

"I'm sure she would have been were it a normal day, but it is not. Everyone is fussing over her, making certain she looks her best."

"She is already beautiful. I cannot look at her without her leaving me breathless," he admitted, feeling particularly close to Reggie after their brief talk. "What more needs to be done? And what is so complicated about putting on a gown? Or sticking one's feet into slippers?"

Reggie chuckled. "For someone with your reputation when it comes to seducing women, you surely do not know much about them. But I suppose you know more about removing their clothes than helping to put them back on. Uncle, one must respect the ritual. It isn't every day a young lady marries a duke. I'm sure there were scented bath oils involved, a relaxing soak in a tub. Not to mention Fiona will have her maid attend to Cherish's hair so that it is styled to perfection."

Gawain emitted a strangled sound somewhere between a curse and a grumble. "I'm going to take out every last pin from her hair the moment I get her alone."

Reggie laughed again. "We all noticed how pretty she looked when confronting her uncle yesterday, that silky mane tumbling down her back in a riot of golden curls. I don't blame you for having itchy fingers and wanting to plunge your hands in that glorious mass."

"Reggie, good grief." But Gawain grinned and gave a reluctant nod. "Despite my aged eyes, how could I overlook that?"

"You have the eyes of a hawk and very little ever escapes your notice." Reggie suddenly straightened up and turned toward the staircase. "Look, here they come."

Gawain's breath caught in his throat.

Blessed saints.

He did not know what had been done to Cherish, but she looked like a princess gliding down those steps. Her gown was a mix of russet and gold that seemed to shimmer and float around her exquisite body. Her hair had been done up in an elegant twist and drawn back off her face, save for a few golden curls that lightly framed her graceful features.

Her smile upon noticing him shot straight to his heart. "What do you think, Your Grace?"

"You look beautiful." He held out his arm. "Ready?"

She nodded as she walked to him. "Yes, although I still feel as though I am walking in a dream. You look so handsome."

"Silver hair and all?" He knew Cherish did not see him as old and failing. He was hardly that. Nor was he a vain peacock to deny his age or fret about his scars and the care-worn lines on his face. Those were earned over years on the battlefield. He was proud of every scar and furrow. Still, there was no overlooking the fact he was not young.

Apparently love had a way of erasing flaws, because he did not think Cherish saw a single one of his.

As for Cherish, she was perfect for him in every way possible.

During his war years in Spain, he had come across a fortune teller who had set up a tent beside their encampment and offered to tell fortunes for a small fee. He had refused to allow his men to partake because he feared the old hag would give them false hope of survival and make them reckless in the throes of battle.

He was surprised when she did not get angry or put a hex on him. In truth, she took it in stride and offered him a bit of advice before she moved on. "Yours is a young and tempestuous soul," she had warned him. "Your true happiness lies in finding the right complement to it."

"What? An old soul?" he had shot back in all his arrogance.

"No, a wise soul. You are fire and she must be water." What she really meant was that he was an idiot and needed someone smart to guide him.

Still, he had liked that description. Fire and water. He had scoffed at the fortune teller's words at the time, but he understood them now. Cherish was clearly that perfect match for him. She was gentleness and calming waters. He was too often arrogant and demanding, although he tried his best not to be this way. But it was easy to fall into this sort of behavior when everyone fawned over him and kissed his arse even when he was being unreasonable. No one wanted to tell a duke the truth for fear of offending him. Cherish would always rein him in and speak to him with honesty.

"You suddenly seem far away," she said, taking his arm.

"No, Cherish. For once, I am ever present."

"And ready to marry me?"

He smiled. "Ridiculously eager."

Her step was light and agile as they walked to the waiting carriage. She had a serene confidence about her, and although she looked younger than her twenty-four—almost twenty-five—years, she had likely exhibited this same serenity as a girl looking after her ailing parents. He did not think there was a moment in her life when she could have been described as inconsiderate or rebellious, or had ever behaved like a frivolous peahen.

Perhaps this was why they were destined to be a good fit for each other. She would ground him with her common sense and he would push her to be more daring.

He breathed a sigh of relief when she hopped into the carriage without difficulty, showing no lasting effects from yesterday's tumble other than a scrape to her elbow that was presently bandaged and covered by her long glove. The slight swelling in her wrist had already subsided by the time he inspected it last night. As for her hip, she was no longer wincing with each step. The discomfort was not something she could easily hide. He would have spotted it had she been in pain.

Of course, he would take a closer look tonight. She could not hide her scrapes and bruises once she had her clothes off.

They settled in Fiona's carriage, just the four of them, since Margaret was to ride in the carriage immediately behind theirs with her parents. Other conveyances stood in readiness for the rest of Fiona's guests, who would follow shortly behind them.

Gawain was sorry Cherish had no family to stand beside her, but she did not appear to be suffering for the lack. He gave no further thought to the matter, since Fiona had taken on the role of clucking mother hen and beloved sister to Cherish.

Within the hour, they were at St. Paul's Church, the small, but splendid, stone church nestled between lush, rolling hills not far from the sea. Nothing was far from the water here in the country outside of Brighton.

By the time the last guests arrived, he and Cherish had signed the required ledgers and were standing in front of the altar, merely waiting for the stragglers to enter and settle in the pews before the vicar proceeded with the ceremony.

Cherish was incandescent as the vicar began his sermon.

As for him, he was on alert for her uncle and any last-minute tricks the oaf might try to pull. But he needn't have worried, for all went smoothly. There was no sign of the man or his ogress wife.

Before he knew it, the vicar was leading them through the recitation of their vows.

"I do," Cherish said a moment later, her voice echoing sweetly around him.

"Gawain, Duke of Bromleigh, Marquess of..." The vicar listed his titles, a list that ran ridiculously long when one added the knighthoods, too.

Cherish's eyes rounded in surprise.

He arched an eyebrow, silently conveying that he was just a man, no matter how many honors were accorded him. He had been no more than a soldier until his father's and brothers' untimely passing. Just a soldier and nothing more. He did not want Cherish to get caught up in his supposedly elevated status.

But as the vicar read off the last of his titles, Cherish grinned and rolled her eyes at him. He grinned back, knowing she would never become full of herself now that her status was raised to duchess. "I do," he replied, his voice ringing loud.

A cheer rose from the crowd as the vicar declared them man and wife.

He kissed Cherish lightly on the lips.

"I love you," she whispered.

"Same here," he replied, not certain that she heard him, as everyone now rushed forward and surrounded them with cheers and well wishes.

Shortly thereafter, everyone returned to Fiona's manor for the wedding breakfast. Gawain noted the flicker of surprise in Cherish's eyes when Fiona's staff greeted her as Your Grace. After a moment, it sank in. Her smile broadened and she accepted their good wishes with all the graciousness of a true duchess.

"How does it feel, Cherish?" he asked when they sat down to enjoy the elaborate repast organized by Fiona's cook on a mere day's notice.

"To be your wife?" She took his hand under the table and cast him an affectionate smile. "Vastly different from my quiet existence. It is amazing how quickly one becomes the center of attention merely because of one's title. But I shall enjoy being your wife immensely, especially in our private hours together."

The rest of the day passed in a blur, and yet also felt interminable. Gawain hardly had a moment alone with Cherish. Finally, as the evening wore on, he took her hand in his and bade all the revelers a good night.

They retired to her bedchamber because he did not want their first night spent in the bed Lady Albin had commandeered from him and been sleeping in as recently as two nights ago. Her heavily perfumed scent still permeated the drapes and bedcovers, as though she had purposely sprayed her scent around his room, like a jungle cat marking its territory.

He breathed a sigh of relief once inside Cherish's small-but-elegant chamber, and lit a candle or two now that the sun began to fade. "Glad that's over."

Cherish nodded. "My stomach is aflutter. It is hitting me now that I am your wife. I'm not sure I will pass this first test."

He frowned, taking a moment to understand her meaning. "Cherish, there is no test. There is just us getting to know each other at our own pace. Nor are there any rules on how quickly we must get to…ah, to…"

She smiled at him. "Get to the good parts?"

He chuckled. "Yes, how quickly we get to the good parts."

Cherish's hair shone a molten gold in the soft candlelight, and she looked incredibly beautiful. He could tell she was worried about disappointing him, but she need not have been. His blood was already on fire, and he did not even have her out of her gown yet.

However, he did not want to rush their *moment*, even if his body had other ideas. "My only concern is to make certain this marriage cannot be annulled, should your uncle ever try to cause trouble. Beyond that, we can enjoy each other at our leisure."

Of course, this assumed his body did not betray him and have him behaving like an untried schoolboy bedding a woman for the first time.

Cherish was lost in her own concerns as she stared at the bed. "I must warn you, I am woefully ignorant."

"You are clever and will catch on fast, I assure you." He kept his gaze on her as he removed his jacket and then his cravat. "Besides, do you think this does not please me? You must know you married a possessive ape."

She laughed and regarded him avidly as he removed his waistcoat. "Your apish tendencies are to be protective, not possessive. You would not have been able to push me at Reggie if you were truly possessive."

"It was a close thing. Every time I saw you, I wanted to pound my chest and chase away all rivals. I wanted to make you mine. I must have confused the blazes out of Reggie and put the devil's fear into poor Fellstone."

She laughed and shook her head. "You hid your turmoil well. Truly, I had no idea."

"I could not hide these apish feelings from myself. I was in agony. Served me right for coming up with the stupid scheme to match you and Reggie. I suppose I even owe your toad of an uncle a debt of gratitude for pushing me toward the right decision. Will you help me with the cuffs, Cherish?"

She nodded and immediately scampered to his side.

He could have arranged for a valet to attend him and a maid to attend her, but he did not want others in here with them tonight, even if it was merely to assist them in preparing for bed. He wanted Cherish all to himself.

But this was a flaw he needed to work on. *Does not share well with others.* Not that there would be others in his life or hers from now on. Theirs was already an unbreakable love match, whether Cherish realized it or not. He had no intention of ever straying. Why should he when he had the best woman beside him?

Cherish's fingers were nimble, and she had little trouble assisting him with the task of removing his cuff links. "Where shall I put them? Atop my bureau for now?"

He nodded. "That will do just fine. Thank you." He settled on the bed, sitting on the mattress while he removed his boots.

She offered to help, but he shook his head. "No, Cherish. I will manage it. My boots are dirty and might accidentally stain your gown. It's a lovely gown, by the way. Or perhaps you just make everything you wear look better because you are so pretty."

She laughed and blushed. "Perhaps it is time for you to get spectacles."

"No, my eyesight is perfect. I see you very clearly." After this, he removed his shirt. Since the sight of him bare chested heightened her blush and appeared to disconcert her, he kept his trousers on for now. "Your turn, Cherish," he said softly, taking her by the shoulders to turn her away from him so that he could get at the buttons, tapes, and laces down her back.

What a body on this girl. She was full in all the right places, and soft wherever she ought to be. He meant to explore every inch of her tonight.

He kissed her neck, knowing exactly where to find the most sensitive spot. She gasped and turned to him. "How did you do that?"

"Do what, Cherish?"

"Make me tingle."

He smiled. "I should hope I learned something over the years."

She nodded. "Yes, your experience. I suppose all the ladies respond to you this way."

"No," he said with a light frown. "Everything changes when two people are committed to each other. What will pass between us is something special, shared only by us, and will strengthen our bonds. I did not marry you because you were like everyone else. Do not worry about doing something wrong or right—just be you."

Having said that, and not certain he had convinced her to simply relax and enjoy the moment, he pressed his lips to the graceful curve of her neck and suckled lightly.

He smiled when she sighed and leaned against him. "That feels good, too."

Her eyes were closed as she allowed herself to succumb to these new sensations. That she seemed to enjoy them and want more was a promising sign. He took his time untying the last of her laces, liking the way she seemed to trust him and respond to his touch.

Her skin was warm and her scent was a delicious mix of floral and fruity. He gave her neck a final, soft kiss as he slipped the gown off her shoulders and allowed it to slide with a silky *whoosh* onto the carpeted floor. After carefully setting the gown over one of the chairs, he then began to undo her corset. Flames shot through him as he turned her to face him and took in her delectable body that was barely hidden beneath her sheer chemise.

"Don't, love," he said when she tried to turn away and cover herself up. "You are beautiful. Let me look at you."

She nodded and set her hands to her sides, not certain what to do next. "All right."

The little control he had left disappeared once he took the pins from her hair and watched the mountain of curls tumble down her back in a now-familiar golden cascade.

How had no one claimed her hand in marriage before this?

Not that it mattered, for she was his now, and he meant to introduce her to the pleasures of the bedchamber. More important, he hoped to show her how love between two people could flourish. Everything already felt sweeter to him because they were husband and wife.

He lifted her in his arms and carried her to bed, searing her with his kisses as he set her down in the center of it and removed the last of their clothing with as much prowess as one could muster while in hot, inglorious haste.

Both now bared, he covered her with his big body and began to lightly run his hands along her curves. He started innocently at first, merely running his fingers along her arms and then down her legs. Along her sweet, nicely rounded bottom. But it was not long before he dipped his head and took the tip of her breast in his mouth to gently suckle it. By the time he moved on to the other, she was breathing heavily and clutching his shoulders.

He slid his hand between her legs, pleased to find her ready for him.

Well, was this not his reputation? He knew how to arouse a woman's passion. Cherish, although outwardly serene, did feel things strongly. He had little trouble evoking the desired responses from her, and he took delight in watching her changing expressions. Wonder. Shyness. Eagerness. Willingness.

Heat.

She wanted to experience whatever he had in mind for her this wedding night.

He took his time because she was innocent and everything was new to her. Her delicate hands gripped his shoulders as she sighed and purred, and then arched beneath him as he licked and stroked her. She readily took him in when he entered her.

Lord, she was so exquisitely slick and tight.

He took care to be as gentle as possible, but she quickly became accustomed to him and wanted more.

He was already on fire and hot with need. *Blessed saints,* she felt good.

It did not take long for her to fall into his rhythm and begin to lose herself in the heightened sensations. Soon, restraint and caution fled them both, and flames of passion consumed them.

They shattered together, she soaring and he spilling himself into her with a satisfied growl and a splendid release that felt better than anything he could ever recall. It took a long moment for them to regain their senses amid laughing grunts, joyful groans, and a messy tangle of limbs.

He rested his forehead lightly against hers, satiated and breathing heavily as they simply absorbed each other. He drew his head up slightly to watch her still floating amid the pleasurable sensations that were so new to her. Finally, she opened her eyes and smiled at him. "That was very nice."

He chuckled. "I would say so. How do you feel, love?"

Her smile was radiant. "Very much adored."

Gawain lifted onto his elbows so as not to crush her. "You are, Cherish. You are."

He had been with many women, had his pick of the prettiest. But none came close to Cherish. She was a mix of innocence and sensuality. Everything about her stirred him, from the cream of her skin to the rose tips of her breasts. From the lushness of that golden mane atop her head to the triangle of gold between her legs. She was softness and silk.

He meant to roll onto his back, not wanting to keep the bulk of his weight atop her. He was a big man and his muscled body was hard in comparison to her softness. She did not appear to mind his weight at all, and emitted a mew of protest when he started to shift his body. "Cherish, how will you breathe if I stay atop you?"

"I can breathe just fine. This feels so nice. I never knew it could be like this between us."

He planted a kiss on her forehead, and then did move onto his back, but brought her along with him.

"What we did just now... That was wonderful," she said, nestling in his arms.

"It certainly was." He was inordinately pleased with himself and still reveling in her passionate response. Some men bedded their wives purely for the purpose of begetting children and used mistresses for the earthier pleasures of making love. But it sat ill with him, and he had no wish to be such a man. He had pledged to be faithful in his marriage vows and meant to keep to his pledge.

But Cherish made it easy for him.

Beauty and brains. Kindness. Passion.

He was giving up nothing in remaining faithful, for there could be no finer bed partner for him than his own beautiful wife. It pleased him that she would be his beloved mate in every sense.

"Gawain..."

"Yes, love?"

She looked up at him with those heart-melting brandy eyes. "How long before we can do this again?"

CHAPTER SIXTEEN

C HERISH REALIZED SHE must have asked a stupid question when Gawain sank back against his pillow and laughed heartily. "Give me a moment to recover and I'll have at your luscious body again."

"Be patient with me. I didn't mean to sound so foolish."

He caressed her cheek. "No, sweetheart. It wasn't foolish at all. How could you know? My laughter was because of my own relief that you enjoyed it. I hoped you would."

"I did." Cherish snuggled against him, loving that his muscled arms were wrapped around her. He seemed very well pleased, if that affectionate, slightly possessive smirk still playing on his lips was any indication.

She had never thought of herself as wanton, but he had evoked more passion in her than she thought possible. In truth, she had no idea that she possessed any. It left her stunned that such depth of feeling had been hidden within her all this time.

Only for him, of course. She could not imagine herself responding to another man's touch in this way.

For all his jests about being a Silver Duke, he had a wonderfully fit body. A fully matured man's body. Firm and muscled, but also slightly marred by battle scars. He was broad in the shoulders. She liked the mix of salt and pepper in his hair along his temples and the breadth of his chest. She also liked that he was not a *ton* ideal of elegantly thin.

His muscles had been honed by years of physical labor and exertion. He also had the scent of a man. Clean, of course. But hot, earthy, and with a hint of spice that made her want to inhale him deeply and run her tongue along his skin.

He might like it.

Should she try it?

She was not quite so bold yet, which seemed ridiculous, since they had discarded their clothing and she was enjoying the sight of his naked splendor as much as he was obviously enjoying the sight of her in all her glory.

She tried to tuck the sheet around her for the sake of modesty. He grinned and did not stop her, but he remained stretched out atop the bed covers, not caring that she had grabbed the lion's share of them. Well, why should he be shy about his spectacular body? Her heart had yet to stop fluttering wildly. His arms fascinated her, the way his muscles rippled when he lifted her or put his weight on his forearms.

Dear heaven.

He was all hers to enjoy for the rest of her life.

She tried to be discreet, but he had to know she was looking her fill and enjoying all of him immensely.

He made a joke about his age and the gray in his hair, though she had not noticed more than mere traces. "Does the difference in our ages bother you, Gawain? It is not all that uncommon for a man to be significantly older than his wife. And need I remind you that most men would consider me old and firmly on the shelf."

"Then they are fools."

"I'm glad you think so." In her opinion, he would look equally handsome with a full head of silver hair. She only hoped hers would look as good when she got older. "What happens next?" she asked.

Despite his assurances, she still wondered whether he only meant to protect her from her uncle but did not really wish to change his Silver Duke ways. He seemed sincere in making this a true marriage, and had even said he loved her. But how much did they truly know about each other? Even if all he said was true now, would it change within a month?

A kernel of doubt remained within her heart.

Perhaps it was foolish to worry about such a thing. He had said he loved her, and treated her as though he did. Nor was he the sort to make a statement merely to mollify her.

But surely he must have uttered words of love to other women he had bedded. Had he held them as sweetly as he held her now?

She hoped his love for her was no passing whim. It *felt* everlasting.

But dukes were different from other people.

Even if he did hold her in his heart, what would happen next?

"What do you mean, Cherish? Are you asking what happens next in our lovemaking?"

"Well, that too. You know I enjoyed it. But I meant our future. Do you truly intend for us to stay together? Please, I would rather have the truth."

He gave her cheek a light caress. "I gave you my solemn marriage vow, and I aim to keep it. The only way we shall not be together is if you wish us to part ways."

She gasped. "Did I not give you this same vow? I have no desire to live apart from you. But I would not presume to make such demands on you. No matter your assurances, I cannot overlook that you were pushed into marrying me to save me from my uncle."

"No, Cherish. Let us put this to rest once and for all. I know my reputation is not an easy one to overcome. But I was not coerced, or made to feel guilty, or ever pushed into marrying you. I am here and will always be with you because I am in love with you."

She sat up and stared at him, and then shook her head and blinked several times, as though fearing the dutiful husband might disappear and the cold-hearted duke he was reputed to be stepped back in his place.

He reached out his arms to take her back in them. "Do you have any idea how truly lovely you are?"

She cast him the sweetest smile. "Apparently not. You've caught me by surprise."

"I know. I should have been more romantic with you. There wasn't much time, and it turns out I'm not really very good at expressing love."

She leaned over and kissed him. "Gawain, do you think it is possible for someone to fall in love before ever meeting the person of their dreams? I tingled the very first time Fiona mentioned your name. It was as though my heart already knew I was meant to fall in love with you. I was in a tizzy for days before you arrived, and almost fell into a swoon when I finally did meet you."

"I kept all of Fiona's letters about you. I've read every single one many times over. I would have recognized you the moment I walked in even if you weren't standing right beside Fiona. I knew you would be beautiful, but not even her glowing description could do you justice."

"How was I this first time...you know, our coupling?"

He cast her an irreverent smile. "Do you see me complaining?"

"Well, I did not think that you would."

He shook his head. "Are you asking me to compare your performance to others?"

"Yes, I suppose I am," she said with a wince. "Your reputation precedes you. Your prowess with women is legendary."

He groaned. "Oh, bollocks. It isn't."

"Any lady would feel loved in your arms. But were you at all disappointed?"

"No, Cherish." He rolled onto his side, propping himself on one elbow as he leaned slightly over her. "It was extraordinary. *You* were extraordinary. Nothing to do with experience or practiced tricks—which, by the way, I look forward to teaching you," he said with another naughty grin. "What I loved was how genuine your pleasure was, and I know it was genuine because you are honest in your feelings."

"I could never hide them from you. I think I was half out of control before you even touched me."

"So was I, love. We have a very deep connection, something we each felt from the very start."

She sighed. "Yes, it's true. I'm sorry I am asking so many questions. It isn't you I doubt, but myself. This is nice, you and me together. I feel so at peace beside you."

"And you are worried we will not have this once we return to London?"

"Yes, this friendship and this intimacy."

"Are you wondering about our sleeping arrangements?"

She nodded. "I know it's common practice for dukes and duchesses to have their own separate quarters even if we do remain living under one roof."

"I was never trained to be a duke and do not particularly care for this common practice of separate quarters, but what do you prefer? The choice is yours, Cherish."

"Goodness, am I not obvious? I want to be with you." She placed a hand on his cheek. "I thought I would finish out my days as a spinster, alone and not particularly loved, since my own relatives cannot seem to abide me. So, to find you and win your heart... It is not something I could ever take for granted. I would like us to share a bedchamber, if that is all right with you."

"More than all right." He kissed her lightly on the lips. "I hope you will let me know if there is anything else you would like to put into effect. You have a very easy nature, and I can be bullheaded. I don't want you to hesitate in telling me if something is not to your liking."

"I think you are going to spoil me as I have never been spoiled in all my life, even by my loving parents. I will have to think hard to find something to complain about. If I do find fault, it will likely be that you spoil me too much."

"Do not deprive me of that joy," he said with a laugh. "I can well afford it. And do not forget that you are not the only one saved by this marriage. I never thought it would happen. Not that I blamed anyone but myself, for I am hardheaded and insufferable. I had resigned myself to living out the rest of my days alone, an old goat fumbling around a ridiculously large manor on an enormous estate. I am delighted this will not be my fate after all."

She burrowed against him, wrapping herself in his warmth. "Oh, how wonderful! We shall be two old goats rattling about your ridiculously large estate together."

"Unless we are blessed with children. Cherish, I meant it when I said all my rules and plans were tossed out the window once I met you. If you desire children, then we shall have them."

She nodded against his chest. "I ache for them, especially because they will be ours. I cannot imagine anything more wonderful than having a son like you. And a daughter, too. I hope they will have your zeal for life and are fighters. I know I am too complacent."

"I will put a little fire in you."

She laughed. "You already have."

"As for our children, I hope their hearts are as kind and compassionate as yours. But we shall not have any offspring if all we do is spend the night talking." He settled over her once again.

She liked the heat of his big, roughened hands on her skin, and the light crush of his body weighing down on hers. Then his mouth pressed down on hers and he cupped one of her breasts in the palm of his hand, running his thumb lightly across the tip.

Oh my.

She was lost to all sensibility as fire swept through her veins, and she soon shattered, leaving nothing of herself but glitters of starlight.

Had she responded too quickly? Did he feel cheated?

She had not mastered this art of love yet, but Gawain did not seem to mind at all. Indeed, he attained his own release shortly after hers and had a conquering smile when he took her back in his arms.

He seemed quite pleased with the progress of this night.

As the hour grew late, Cherish thought she would have trouble falling asleep after Gawain had claimed her this second time. So much was new to her, and her senses were excited. The intensity of their coupling had opened her heart and changed how she viewed herself, no longer ignored and unwanted.

Gawain had called her a temptress and proclaimed she had wrung every last drop out of him. She thought it was the most amusing thing she had ever heard. She? A temptress? Not in this lifetime. But she was glad he thought of her in this way.

She fell asleep nestled in his arms, and must not have moved a muscle the entire night, because she awoke in the same position come morning. She smiled, trying not to wake Gawain as she slipped out of his hold and stretched the ache out of her bones.

"Now that is a sight to wake up to," he said with an appealingly husky growl, and arched an eyebrow as he studied her.

"Oh." She drew the sheet around her bosom, knowing it was foolish of her to blush after what the two of them had done last night. "I did not realize you were awake."

"I'm usually up at dawn, but did not want to disturb you." He slipped the sheet off her and sat up to kiss the swell of her breasts. "You are the most beautiful woman I have ever beheld...clothed or unclothed, Cherish."

"I suppose you have seen many." She thought about him and Lady Albin, but was not going to mention her. She would rather undergo the labors of Hercules than ever bring up that woman's name again. Not that she was jealous or particularly worried. After all, he had rejected his first love, as well as all the other beauties who had shared his bed in the intervening years.

"Gad, I said that awkwardly." He shook his head and groaned. "My reputation as a hound is all in the past now. What I meant to convey, rather awkwardly, is that I am glad you are my wife. Last night was a pleasure beyond all my expectations."

She nodded. "Same for me."

He nudged her back into his arms. "I love you, Cherish."

She thought he meant to couple with her again, but they quickly sat up when they heard a quiet knock at their door.

"That will be Fiona's maid sent to attend to you." Gawain rolled out of bed and hastily donned his shirt and trousers. "My valet is probably waiting for me in my old quarters."

He handed Cherish her night rail and then crossed to the door, waiting a moment for her to don it before he opened up. "Your Grace, I was sent to see to Her Grace. Shall I order a bath for her?"

He nodded. "And have another sent up for me in my quarters." He then turned back to smile at Cherish. "I'll knock at your door within the hour. Take your time. Let Fiona's staff spoil you."

She wished they could have remained in bed all day. But they were at a house party. Even though they were newly wed, it would have been embarrassing not to make an appearance.

And yet her face would turn to fire the moment anyone looked at her. They would all know what had gone on last night, and—

Dear heaven.

Had any of them heard her soft cries? These walls were not particularly thick.

Her cheeks heated at the mere thought.

Fiona's maid scurried off to order their baths and returned in short order. It was not long before several footmen came in rolling a tub and carrying buckets of heated water. Cherish stood quietly off to the corner, doing her best to keep out of the way. She let out the breath she had been holding once the footmen left her bedchamber and Fiona's maid shut the door. "Your Grace, is something the matter?"

"No, just a little overwhelmed."

The maid nodded. "Who wouldn't be if married to that stunning man? A Silver Duke, no less. But anyone can see how much he cares for you. I'm sure he did not hesitate to show you, either.

Quite fit, he is. If you take my meaning, Your Grace."

Cherish stepped into the now-filled tub, relaxing as she eased into the warm water. "Do you know what Lady Shoreham has in mind for her guests today?" she asked, eager to change the topic because she did not want to discuss her wedding night with anyone, even if it was the best night of her life.

"A ride in the countryside for those who wish it and archery for those who prefer to remain behind. Then a picnic by the folly for all at midday. Then more lawn games for those who wish it or another shopping excursion into town. Of course, tonight will be more music and dancing."

Cherish encouraged the girl to chatter, anything to deflect the talk from her extraordinary night with Gawain. "Do you have a beau, Molly?"

"Oh, yes, Your Grace. He's a bit of a lump, but he's a good fellow. Doesn't drink too much, nor does he chase the ladies, although he isn't much to look at, so I doubt he'd have much luck even if he were a bit of a rake. And no one's ever going to look as good as those Silver Dukes, are they? But my Harry is quite a catch. He has all his hair and most of his teeth, and his family runs a thriving farm."

Within the hour, Cherish was washed and dressed, but her hair was still damp from its washing. Molly had done up her hair in a soft bun at the nape of her neck. She would undo it and leave it long and loose to dry as soon as most of the guests rode off on their morning trot. There would not be many left behind, since this was an avid horse crowd.

She would enjoy the solitude, perhaps grab a book to read in the sunshine, and then ask Molly to do up her hair again once it had fully dried.

Her stomach went into a mad flutter when Gawain returned to escort her downstairs. He looked big and splendid, and she caught the fresh scent of lather on his skin when he bent to kiss her. It was merely a polite kiss on the cheek, but he had that appealingly naughty grin that had her heart melting and Molly giggling. "You are not dressed for riding," she said with some surprise, knowing how much he enjoyed his early morning jaunts and was quite disciplined when it came to his routine.

"I've asked Fiona's head groom to take Odin through his paces today. It is only our second day married and I did not want to abandon you, even if only for an hour or two."

She shook her head. "I am holding you back. You needn't worry about me. I'll have plenty to occupy my time while you exercise Odin."

"Tomorrow, love. I haven't had nearly enough of you yet."

Molly *eeped* and scurried out of Cherish's chamber.

Cherish groaned. "My face is going to burst into flames the moment anyone looks at me, especially if you keep that wicked grin on your face."

He laughed. "I'll try to look grim and serious, but can you blame me for smiling? It's all your fault, you know. You are delectable. How about we take a stroll on the beach once the riders head off?"

"That would be lovely."

They walked downstairs, and Cherish was surprised to see Northam Hall's butler standing in the entry hall, looking quite perplexed. "Potter, is everything all right? What are you doing here? Oh no! Did my ogre of an uncle sack you?"

"No, it is more that he has abandoned us." He raked a hand through his hair. "He and your aunt had us pack up all their belongings and the family silver, which struck me as most odd, and then they took off before the crack of dawn for Goswell Hall in the north country."

"But they hate it in the north. They were most vocal about never setting foot back there again, weren't they, Potter?" The rambling estate known as Goswell Hall was the seat of the earls of Northam, and much of it was crumbling. Not even her father had had the wherewithal to save this drafty fortification built of ancient stone. The walls around the medieval keep were full of cracks and in danger of falling down.

"Yes, Your Grace. They were quite vocal in their dislike of it."

"That is truly odd." Cherish turned to Gawain. "Goswell Hall is the Yorkshire seat of the Northam earls. It is one of several entailed properties. But what would make them sneak off like thieves in the night to a place they have always detested? With the silver, no less. Potter, did my uncle say when they are coming back?"

"No, but I do not think they ever plan to return. When I dared ask Lady Northam, she cursed us all and muttered *good riddance.*"

Gawain's expression turned dark as thunder.

Cherish looked up at him in surprise. "What does it all mean?"

"Can you not guess, Cherish?" he asked with furrowed brow.

"No. What are you suggesting?"

He gave her cheek a light caress. "We are married. He knows I will be coming after him shortly demanding a full account of your inheritance. Why would he leave a place that he rightfully owns?"

She inhaled lightly, and then gaped at him. "Are you suggesting Northam Hall has been mine all along? I know it was not part of the entailment, but I just assumed when they moved in and took it over that... Dear heaven. Is it possible it has been mine all along? Those despicable cheats!"

"I will have to check the deed records to make certain they did not attempt to convey the property to themselves. Even if they did, I will quickly get it straightened out. I have no doubt in my mind that your uncle and his witch of a wife were the usurpers. They are now fleeing like rats abandoning a sinking ship, but they will be made to pay. Same for everyone else involved in this larceny."

Potter nodded. "Their plan to keep you isolated and unmarried has fallen apart now that you are Duchess of Bromleigh. Rest assured, I will order the staff to shoot them on sight if they ever attempt to return. We'll show them no mercy for what they tried to do to you. Loathsome people. We shall gladly assist you in any way possible, Your Grace."

Cherish regarded Gawain. "It is frightening how complete their betrayal was, and that they might have gotten away with it had you not married me."

"You were catching on to their thievery and would have done so sooner had your father shared his intentions with you," Gawain muttered. "It cannot be overlooked that he enabled them to act this boldly. It is a lesson for me, as well. You are smart and capable, Cherish. I will make certain you are aware of all my holdings and know exactly what my plans are for them."

She nodded. "I am also to blame for not being more insistent. The few times I tried to talk to my father, he dismissed my concerns, claiming it was not a woman's place to deal with these legal headaches."

"Backward and stupid," Gawain said with a growl. "But all too common. All this could have been avoided had he shown you his testamentary documents or even once discussed them with you."

Cherish tried not to get angry about this, since it would all be put back in order shortly. "He patted my head and told me not to worry about anything. He assured me that he had left me in good hands."

Potter snorted.

So did she. "He was so fond of his younger brother and completely taken in by him."

Gawain appeared to be getting angrier as he gave the situation more thought. "I'll make certain everything your father left you is rightfully transferred to you and fully accounted for before the end of summer. I think I must ride to London this very day, Cherish. I need to stop that unholy alliance of uncle, banker, and solicitor before they can cover up their misdeeds."

Cherish's heart ached. "You would leave me?"

"Only with the greatest reluctance," he assured her.

Potter cleared his throat. "There is more, Your Grace. They

are gone now, but not before ransacking Northam Hall. They must have done it during the night when we were all asleep in our quarters and could not hear them moving around. I shudder to relay the news. But you will soon see for yourself. It is a terrible sight."

Cherish gasped. "Those vile villains!"

Gawain raked a hand through his hair. "Is this not more proof that they must be stopped before more harm is done?"

She hated to admit that he was right. "I'll ask Mrs. Harris to help us pack right now."

He took her hand. "No, Cherish. Not us, just me. You cannot ride a horse. We'll lose precious days if we go by carriage. Odin is a beast and can fly over the terrain. I already have my solicitor at work on the matter of your inheritance, but my letter must have reached him only today. He could not have gotten anything done yet. I will engage a good Bow Street man to follow those curs and investigate them thoroughly. He'll ferret out whatever those thieves are trying to hide. If I leave now, I can reach London hours before Northam and his wife arrive to plot their next mischief."

Reggie had come down while they stood in the entry hall discussing what was to be done. He must have overheard most of the conversation. "Let me attend to it," he insisted, tossing his uncle a pleading look. "This is my chance to prove myself to you. Give me a letter authorizing me to act on behalf of the Duke of Bromleigh and his wife. As for the Bow Street runner, I know you use Homer Barrow. Give me the authority to engage his services and we'll get the old earl's solicitor and banker hauled into prison so fast, their heads will not stop spinning for a week."

Cherish readily agreed to the plan, for being apart from Gawain after a single day of marriage was no way to start their lives together. "I like the idea, Reggie. Can you ride out immediately? There is everything to be gained by reaching London ahead of my uncle. You'll be able to cut him off from his fellow conspirators before they can do more damage."

She had come into the marriage with nothing. Gawain had not cared, but it still wounded her pride. He was now trying to make things right for her, but was it not just as important for Reggie to prove his worth?

"Gawain, we can follow in a day or two. But I would like to assess the damage to Northam Hall first, and make certain the farms have not been touched. We'll then take up the fight wherever Reggie left off."

He sighed, contemplated the suggestion, and then nodded. "Potter, alert the staff that we will arrive within the hour. I'll be seeing my nephew off first."

"Very good, Your Grace," Potter said, and returned in haste to Northam Hall.

"Cherish, I'll do as you wish and remain here with you. But it is important for us to get to London quickly afterward."

She nodded. "We will. I promise."

He now turned to Reggie. "You had better ride like the wind. There's to be no straying from your mission. Take Durham with you. He has connections to those in power that you don't have yet."

Reggie appeared eager to embrace the task as he ran off to find Durham.

Gawain then strode to Fiona's study to write the necessary authorization letters while Cherish went in search of Fiona. She found her in the dining room having breakfast with several of her other guests.

Cherish drew her aside and quickly explained what had happened.

"Those beasts! I hope their carriage rolls off a cliff with them in it," Fiona said, outraged on Cherish's behalf. She then gave Cherish a fierce hug. "What a way to start your marriage. Are you all right?"

Cherish nodded. "Yes, truly. I am angry, of course. But I am not dealing with this on my own any longer. I now have a true family to support me, and it is a great weight lifted off my shoulders. Those two will get their comeuppance."

She knew Gawain was even more incensed over their actions than she was. Being a Silver Duke, he was going to act immediately and fiercely. Was this not part of his appeal?

He strode out of the study with a frown on his handsome face. "These are done," he said, indicating the letters he held. "Are Reggie and Durham ready yet?"

Cherish nodded. "They're grabbing a quick breakfast while waiting for you. Gawain, I see you are champing at the bit to go with them, but they will get the job done. Neither my father's solicitor nor banker will get away with their crimes. I am most concerned with the Northam Hall farms, for those are the profitable properties. I have no idea what he has done to them, and those need to be restored as fast as possible."

He had to be thinking of her as weak and ineffectual in some respects, for she was afraid of horses, had allowed her father to dismiss her as a helpless female even though she had run Northam Hall on her own for several years, and then allowed her father's half-brother to make a servant of her and almost steal her property. But she also knew how to manage an estate and make best use of its potential. She hoped he saw her as something more than incompetent.

Well, she knew he did, for he had never once looked at her in a condescending way. In truth, he looked at her with love in his eyes. It was very nice to feel the warmth of his gaze now that they were married and he was no longer hiding his feelings.

Fiona was fussing over Reggie and Durham as they marched out of the dining room and met them in the entry hall. "I'll have my cook put together food and ale for your journey," she insisted. "What about your clothes, Reggie? Shall I help you pack?"

"Gad, Fiona," he said with a grunt. "All done. I am a grown man, not a six-year-old boy."

Durham grinned. "Me too. All done. But you are welcome to burrow through my unmentionables if it pleases you."

Fiona pinched his shoulder. "Do not make fun of me."

"Ouch!" He gave his shoulder a rub. "Who's making fun? You've known me most of my life. If not you, then what other woman would I trust with my unmentionables? There comes a point in a man's life when he begins to think about such things."

"Oh, really? Stop grinning at me in that simpering way. It is most unattractive. And do not lump me in with your sordid conquests. I've seen the sort you escort about London. Your taste in women is execrable, Durham."

"Did you ever consider I might have someone perfect in mind?" Durham maintained his irreverent grin as he stared at her.

She pinched his shoulder again. "Get to the stable and stop leering at me. I powdered your bottom when you were but a babe, you insolent clot."

Margaret and a few other guests joined them as they all shuttled to the stable.

Cherish ought to have felt miserable, but she could not summon any bad feeling when she had Gawain by her side, a new friend in Margaret, and just realized Durham was in love with Fiona. Maybe—just maybe—Fiona cared for him, too. So what about the difference in their ages? If it did not bother Durham that she was older, why should it bother Fiona? There could not be more than six or seven years between them.

Fiona was still fussing over Durham and Reggie. "Don't forget to stop at coaching inns along the way for some proper, hearty meals. The fare at those inns is usually quite good. You'll have to stop at regular intervals, since your mounts will need rest and tending. And be careful. These are wicked, wicked people you are dealing with."

Cherish stepped forward to thank them, and Gawain did the same. "The Bromleigh townhouse is fully staffed and all is at your disposal."

"Thank you, Uncle." Reggie cast Gawain an impertinent grin. "I intend to make full use of your excellent stock of brandy once our assignment is done."

Their little group now circled Reggie and Durham as they all stood beside the stable.

Cherish tried not to be obvious about keeping well away from their enormous beasts who were as big as Gawain's horse, Odin.

Gawain was ever aware of her fear and did not make a point of it. He led her aside and took her in his arms. "You're shivering, Cherish."

"I'm trying very hard not to, but my body doesn't seem ready to cooperate. I must be such a disappointment to you."

"A disappointment?" He turned her to face him and kissed her until her legs turned to water.

It was a thoroughly inappropriate and wonderful kiss.

Fiona, Margaret, Durham, and the houseful of guests at the stable with them were watching and cheered Gawain on. That kiss would have thoroughly compromised her had they not already been married.

The man certainly did know how to kiss.

Reggie cleared his throat. "Great idea. I think I need to bid Margaret a proper farewell."

Gawain growled. "Reggie! Don't—"

But his nephew had taken Margaret in his arms and was kissing her with shocking heat.

Cherish exchanged a delighted glance with Fiona. There would be another wedding in the works.

Gawain growled.

Cherish laughed as she placed a restraining hand on Gawain's arm. "You have only yourself to blame. You really are setting a terrible example for him."

"Because I love my wife and wish to kiss her?"

He'd said it aloud, proclaimed his love in front of Fiona, Reggie, Durham, and everyone present, including Margaret and her parents. Margaret's father appeared livid until Reggie approached him and asked to speak to him upon his return from London. "I love your daughter," he said, and then turned to Gawain. "You're not the only one who found love this weekend."

Lord Durham was a very good sort and would not gossip about what he had just seen and heard. But Fiona? The news would be all over Brighton within minutes. If gossip could fly, the news of this Silver Duke being in love with his wife would reach London within the hour. That his nephew had also fallen in love was perhaps less interesting, but that news would also travel fast because Margaret's family was not without prominence.

Gawain stole another scorching kiss from Cherish.

"Are you trying to outdo your nephew?" she teased, her cheeks turning to fire.

"No, sweetheart. Just kissing the woman I love."

Fiona and Lord Durham were grinning at her. Had they heard this, too?

Of course, everyone heard. Gawain had made certain of it.

She wanted to berate him, then stopped herself. How foolish was she to rebuke a husband who showed affection for his new wife? Yes, he was being apish about it in order to make certain everyone understood theirs was a love match and not him stepping in to save her from her wretched uncle because he pitied her.

She did not think it was necessary, for who would ever dare touch her now that she was his wife? No one was ever going to challenge the Duke of Bromleigh or dare take anything that was his.

Everyone knew Silver Dukes protected what was theirs. And after last night, was there any doubt she was his?

CHAPTER SEVENTEEN

C HERISH STOOD AT the edge of the stable, watching from a safe distance as Reggie and Durham rode off. She was standing by the fence near the spot where Lady Albin had tried to run her down, and still felt uncomfortable being so close to all these horses. Fiona's other guests were now gathering to fetch their mounts for their morning ride. They rode massive, snorting beasts, and she was trying hard not to tremble.

But standing out here with Gawain was more important than her stupid fear.

Her cheeks were on fire and would not stop burning because Gawain had made an embarrassingly ardent show of kissing her earlier. Several of Fiona's guests made bawdy quips, which she endured with good nature.

After all, he had a rakish reputation to uphold. But Cherish understood Gawain's true purpose in putting on this show. If he decided to ride off for London tomorrow—because it was not in his nature to sit back while others took on Northam and his lackeys—others might view it as a husband abandoning his wife immediately after their wedding. This would have spawned the vilest gossip, and he meant to stamp out those nasty fires of innuendo before they ever blazed.

She remained standing by the fence, as far out of the way of pounding hooves as possible while the other riders rode past her. Margaret, who was proving to be a good friend, came up to her and took her hand. "Archery targets are being set up on the lawn, Cherish. Do you want to shoot a few? We can pretend those targets are Lady Albin's rump."

Cherish laughed. "Margaret! That sounds perfect, but Gawain and I need to ride over to Northam Hall." She quickly related what her uncle and his wife had done to the manor house, as reported by her butler.

"Oh, what a wretched pair they are. I'm so sorry. How do you feel? Are you all right?"

She nodded. "I will be now that they are gone. But there is work to do in assessing the extent of the damage and deciding what needs to be done. Next, Gawain and I will go to Brighton to check on the land records and see what shows up in the deed registry. I think it might show that Northam Hall is mine, or else why would those two have run off so fast?"

Margaret nodded. "Or destroyed any of the house if they were the rightful owners."

"Ready, love?" Gawain asked, returning to her side now that he had procured Fiona's rig so they might ride straight to Northam Hall.

Margaret giggled and ran off.

Gawain shook his head and sighed. "Are you the only woman in Creation who does not titter inanely and coo like a peahen?"

"Well, you did have me cooing quite a bit last night and again this morning," Cherish reminded him.

He grinned wickedly. "Yes, I did."

They gave their apologies to Fiona for missing the midday picnic she had planned for her guests, and then drove off in the borrowed rig. Cherish did not think it would take her long to assess the damage her oafish relatives had caused, since she had already seen much of their dereliction transpire over these past months.

But to her dismay, what she encountered was beyond comprehension. Potter had not exaggerated the wreckage done overnight by Northam and his wife to her childhood home.

"They will pay for this," Gawain said with a growl, and Cherish knew he did not merely mean monetary reimbursement.

He wanted revenge.

Cherish was in a daze as she walked from room to room and took in the slashed furniture, smashed vases, and curtains that had been pulled down.

Potter was quite glum as he escorted them from room to room. "I'm so sorry, Your Grace. I blame myself for not being more vigilant."

"No," Cherish said with a shake of her head. "How could anyone have foreseen such madness?"

"We stopped them after one of the footmen heard vases smashing and went to inspect the noise. Only then did we realize what they were doing, but it was too late to prevent all this damage. They are a vile pair, and they've stolen the family silver, too. I hope they choke on their silver spoons."

"We shall redecorate," Cherish said with determination. "Do we not need to get their stench out of this house?" She tried to make a jest of it, for Gawain was obviously fuming and mad enough to ride off to London this very day.

She did not want him going without her, and she was not ready to leave yet. She still had to assess the damage to the Northam farms and set about making repairs. In truth, she did not think those had been touched last night, because it would have required the evil pair to ride an hour in the dark just to reach the closest farm. The true damage to the farms had occurred over the months of their neglect. For her own pride, Cherish wanted to secure the income flow they had provided as recently as last year, when she had been in charge and the new earl had not gotten his hands on them.

Gawain did not care about her inheritance, and had never made her feel lesser for coming to him with nothing. But it irked her, especially now that she knew her father had not forgotten her.

"I doubt they set foot on any of the farms last night," Potter remarked. "There wasn't time. Thank goodness for small favors."

They took inventory of the rest of the house, Cherish's dismay increasing as not a single room had been left untouched. "Potter, have the staff continue to clean up this mess as best as they can. I doubt anything can be salvaged. Perhaps the torn canvas on the portraits of my parents can be repaired. I suppose this was done to purposely hurt me. They will have to be sent to a London art specialist for this task. Fortunately, they did not bother to slash any of the other paintings. I wonder why those were spared?"

"It could be that they were caught in the act before they had gotten around to destroying them," Gawain said, taking hold of her hand and giving it a light squeeze. "They'll feel ten times the hurt once I am through with them."

"Horrible people," Potter muttered. "Vile and vindictive."

Cherish tried to look on the brighter side. "We shall turn this place into something spectacular. Lovelier than ever before." She turned to Gawain. "The farms are very good income producers. I might need to borrow some funds from you at first. Merely an advance. But—"

"Cherish, everything I have is at your disposal," he said, cutting her off before she could finish her sentence. "Whatever you need, you shall have. It will be yours to do with as you wish. No loan. No advance. All of it freely given, along with my heart."

Potter smiled with such pride at Gawain's words. But the man had always been more of a protective grandfather than a butler to her, especially these past months since the death of her father and the arrival of her toad relatives.

As for Gawain, he was once more leaving no uncertainty as to the reason for their marriage. Honestly, was he going to shout his love from the rooftops next?

Cherish smiled up at him. Truly, she loved this man.

"You must stop gushing over me or everyone will believe you have turned soft as pudding," she teased once Potter had left them to attend to the task of supervising the staff.

"No, love. Soft is not the way I would describe myself whenever I am around you." He cast her a smoldering look that left no doubt about his meaning.

They climbed back in the rig and moved on for a quick inspection of two of the Northam farms. By this time, it was well into the afternoon and Cherish had developed a pounding headache. Although the farms had not been damaged last night, they had been neglected over the months and required some work to be put back in shape.

"Let's call it a day, love," Gawain said, once again helping her into the rig and noticing that she was rubbing her temples to ease the pounding in her head.

"I'm all right. Truly. We ought to make a stop in Brighton before returning to Fiona's home. It won't take us long to review the land registry records. If my head is still sore, there's a reliable apothecary near the registry office. I visited him regularly when my parents were in failing health. He'll give me something for this headache."

"As you wish," Gawain said, not entirely pleased by her decision. "But we can put off Brighton until tomorrow."

"No, I'd rather keep going."

He sighed. "Or I can drop you off at Fiona's and then ride to Brighton on my own."

She cast him a stubborn look.

He chuckled and kissed her. "Fine, Brighton it is."

Cherish insisted they stop first at the registry office, where they received their first good news of the day: it turned out that Northam Hall and its farms had quietly been deeded to her by her father several years ago. "He must have done this shortly after my mother died. Why did he not tell me? All of this misery could have been avoided."

"He must have wanted it to be a surprise for you, and never considered that his trusted solicitor would collude with his own brother to hide this asset from you. I would not be surprised if they were in the midst of forging a conveyance from you to your uncle and were just waiting for a suitable moment to have it recorded."

She pursed her lips as she contemplated the possibility. "Why do you think they waited?"

"Your father might have used a local solicitor instead of turning to his London man. They might not have realized your father had already transferred it to you. Or they knew and were just waiting for the right moment to record a forged deed. They had to be worried that news of this transfer would reach your ears. Perhaps the solicitor balked at actually forging a conveyance deed. Who knows? I'm just glad it is legally yours."

They drew the rig up next in front of the local apothecary, a place Cherish knew quite well from her time spent tending her parents during their illnesses. "I won't be a moment," she said, hopping down to run into the shop.

The proprietor, Mr. Drake, was a kindly older gentleman who greeted her warmly. "What brings you here today, Lady Cherish?"

"A terrible headache, Mr. Drake. Would you have something that might ease it?"

"Never you worry. I have a shop full of remedies. May I be so bold as to ask...are the rumors true?"

She arched an eyebrow. "Which rumors?"

He raked a hand through his thinning hair. "Well, I've heard several that seem quite unbelievable. The first is that Lord Northam and his wife have absconded."

She smiled. "Yes, they've run off to the north. I do not expect we shall ever see them in Brighton again."

He cast her a hopeful look. "And they've left you all on your own?"

Cherish laughed. "Yes, thank goodness."

"Indeed," he said with obvious relief. "Forgive me if I speak out of turn, but good riddance to them."

"I heartily agree," she said with an emphatic nod.

He removed a glass jar filled with a white powder from one

of the shelves and set it on the counter. "I've also heard... But it seems so unlikely... And yet I see the Duke of Bromleigh seated in the conveyance just outside my window. Have you... Are you..."

"Married to the Duke of Bromleigh?" She cast him a beaming smile. "Married to him and desperately in love with him. Yes, I am now the Duchess of Bromleigh. It is a love match, Mr. Drake. Isn't it wonderful?"

His broad smile matched hers. "I always knew you were someone special and deserving of the very best, Lady Cherish. Well, you are now a duchess, and I must address you as Your Grace. You shall become a legend in these parts, for you've caught yourself a Silver Duke."

She laughed again.

"Let me prepare this for you. I'll be right back," he said, skittering behind a curtain into his workroom.

Cherish had been standing beside the counter for perhaps a minute when a maidservant rushed in. The woman had a grim look on her face and was quite rude in ignoring Cherish when she politely moved aside and smiled in greeting. She received a dour huff in response.

"Where is that useless fellow?" the woman muttered when the apothecary did not immediately step out of his workroom. She rudely peered behind the counter and huffed again when she saw no package waiting for her on the counter.

Mr. Drake probably had it safely stowed in a drawer or on a shelf in his back room. He wasn't about to leave his medicinals out in the open for anyone to grab.

"Mr. Drake!" the maidservant shouted, frowning at him when he emerged from the back of his shop. "You assured me that the potion would be ready. My mistress needs it now."

The man obviously did not like her tone and was going to make her wait, but Cherish urged him to attend to the unpleasant woman first. "You are too kind," Mr. Drake grumbled, setting aside Cherish's powder in order to be rid of this rude patron.

The woman grabbed her package and walked out without so much as a nod of gratitude.

"An ugly business," the apothecary muttered.

Cherish had seen the markings in Mr. Drake's book and knew the woman had picked up an oleander potion. But Cherish made no comment, for it was none of her business. She should not have been looking over the dear man's shoulder.

There was a common use for such potions. She had read extensively about medicinals while taking care of her parents and come upon a particularly helpful book on the healing *and* poisonous properties of plants. Oleander was commonly used by women who were with child and no longer wanted that child.

It saddened her, but who was she to judge?

She had married a duke and her situation was secure. But what of that dour maid's mistress? Perhaps the lady in question was not married and would be thrown into the street if her family ever found out.

She took her own package, thanked Mr. Drake as she left his shop, and then climbed into the waiting rig.

Gawain was frowning. "What was Lady Albin's maidservant doing in the shop? Did Lady Albin send her in there to insult you?"

Cherish's heart lurched. That unpleasant woman was Lady Albin's maid?

"Not at all. In truth, I doubt she knew who I was." But this meant the oleander potion was for Gawain's former love. She gasped, for suddenly it all made sense. She now understood the reason Lady Albin had turned up at Fiona's party, and why she had been relentless in her pursuit of Gawain. The brazen woman had even stolen into his bed in an attempt to seduce him.

Gawain was studying her expression intently. "Cherish, what is going on? What are you not telling me?"

A *failed* attempt to seduce him.

The child was not Gawain's, of course. He had been so righteously indignant in finding her in his bedchamber that he had moved in with Reggie. But this explained why Lady Albin was so determined to get into his bed and have intimate relations with him.

He was to be her dupe.

This was her scheme to force his hand and have him marry her. All it took was one night of lovemaking, and then she would come to him a few months later, claim the child was his, and force him to marry her. Being honorable, Gawain would have agreed.

What Lady Albin had not counted on was his never touching her. Or his getting married.

Dear heaven. What horrible people. What a horrible day.

"Gawain, I will tell you once we have left Brighton."

He arched an eyebrow. "Why wait, Cherish?"

"Because you are going to fly into a rage when I explain what I think happened. Oh, not in a rage at me...but..." She sighed. "Let's just get back to Shoreham Manor."

CHAPTER EIGHTEEN

G AWAIN LISTENED WITH mounting anger as Cherish explained the purpose of the oleander potion. The horse leading the rig sensed his fury and grew agitated, but Gawain quickly calmed him down before both Cherish and the horse began to panic. "Sorry, love. But *bollocks*. Are you saying she used some churl to get her with child, and then came here to seduce me? All this in order to trap me into making her my duchess?" He shook his head and laughed with open bitterness. "Why am I not surprised she would stoop to such measures?"

"It would have worked had you bedded her," Cherish said.

"But I didn't. Thank the Graces I was already in love with you when she appeared with her cat claws out and ready to dig into me. But I am heartsick for that innocent life that will never be. I also feel sorry for the churl she used to get her with child. I hope he did not love her, for he would be yet another casualty of her plot. But this is the essence of who she is, someone who will not give a care for who she damages in order to get what she wants. I'm just surprised she waited this long to approach me. Shows how much she really thought of me…which is nothing at all."

Cherish took his hand and brought it to her lips. "I like you."

His laughter was a mix of frustration and genuine warmth. "I like you, too."

He seethed for a while longer, but soon his anger began to abate. Mostly, he was relieved to now be married to Cherish.

How was there any comparison between this jewel of a wife beside him and the manipulative schemer that Katie was?

"Gawain, are you all right?" Cherish asked him a few minutes later.

"Yes, love." He wrapped an arm around her shoulders and drew her closer to his side, needing to feel her softness against him. "You know," he said as Shoreham Manor came into view and his tension began to ease, "there's a time-proven method of getting rid of your headache."

At first, she thought he was serious and was about to tell her of a useful remedy, but then she noticed the heated look in his eyes. "Oh? Does it require my going up to our bedchamber with you?"

His lips twitched as he tried to suppress a smile. "Yes, that is part of it."

She laughed lightly. "And does it require removal of clothing?"

He chuckled. "It would be helpful."

"Yours and mine?"

"Well, I would not require you to do anything I would not do. So, yes. If your clothes come off, then mine will too. Fair is fair."

Her lilting laugh was sweet and mirthful, and he silently gave thanks that he was now married to Cherish. He had been quietly expressing his gratitude to the heavens above for avoiding disaster during this entire trip from Brighton to Fiona's home. It distressed him to think he might have been stupid enough to bed Katie had he not already met Cherish and fallen in love with her.

He hoped he would have had better sense than that.

"We do have some time before everyone is called to supper," Cherish said, regaining his attention. "I am eager to test out your home remedy."

He flicked the reins to urge their horse to a trot. "You won't be disappointed, love."

Fortunately, the house party guests and Fiona were all out on the back lawn having afternoon tea when they arrived. Gawain immediately led Cherish upstairs to their bedchamber and locked the door behind them. "Love, shall I pour you a glass of water to drink with your medicine?"

She sat on the bed and shook her head. "No, I am keen to try your method first."

He smiled at her. "To be honest, I have no idea whether coupling actually works to clear out a headache. That was a fabrication on my part."

She held out her arms to him. "I suspected as much, but let's give it a try. Truly, Gawain. I think being in your arms is the best possible medicine for me."

"The feeling is mutual, love." He set about undressing, and then undressed her, marveling at the perfection of her body. He unpinned her hair, running his hands through the lovely cascade of molten gold curls down her back.

He wasted no time in getting her under him and kissing her with scorching heat, for he wanted to leave no doubt how strongly he desired her. He kissed her lips and kissed her lower, preparing her so that she was hot and receptive by the time he entered her. At the same time, he took the peak of her breast into his mouth and suckled, aware of her heightened pleasure and wanting to give her a slow build because he did not want a fast coupling.

He needed to hold her and love her, needed to lose himself in all the sensations she aroused in him with the warm scent of her body and her kittenish purrs. She tasted like sweet cream and strawberries, incredibly satisfying. "I love you, Cherish," he said, watching her beautiful face in all its purity and all its sensuality as she reached her moment, and then he reached his.

He fell back against the mattress, his body in a divine sweat. She did not seem to mind at all and nestled beside him. He gave her a gentle kiss on the forehead. "How is your headache, love?"

She laughed. "Completely gone. Truly. A miracle cure."

He leaned over and kissed her on the lips. "You are the miracle. I hope you know that."

She grinned at him. "For someone who had closed himself off so completely, you certainly are showing a remarkable amount of affection."

"Only for you," he said with a light chuckle, and kissed her again. "Otherwise, I remain the surly Silver Duke of reputation."

In truth, he was more of a savage duke, because he was still enraged by what Northam and his wife had done to Cherish. He meant to bring this pair down and have them crawling on their knees begging for her forgiveness.

But she was a soft thing, and he had no intention of marring this moment with his angry thoughts, whether of the Northams or of Katie. There was nothing to be done about his former love, either. He expected she would end up punishing herself without need of his interference because she did not have it in her heart to love anyone but herself. She would end up in her waning days alone, blaming everyone else for her misery.

But he thought no more of the Northams or Katie while he now had Cherish in his arms. In due course, they readied themselves for supper.

Everyone had questions for them the moment they walked downstairs. Cherish made no secret of what her uncle had done to her, or of the fact Northam Hall and its farms were now securely in her ownership.

Gawain noted Lord Fellstone's expression as she related what they had discovered today, and knew the man would regret not having taken the risk on Cherish. Northam Hall alone was a substantial asset, and Gawain expected to learn she had a solid fortune. Not that he intended to touch any of it. He would leave the management of her assets to her, unless she asked for his advice.

As for Fellstone, he had to give the man a nod for his good taste in liking Cherish. Although Cherish was now out of his reach, perhaps Lady Eugenia's impressive wealth would ease his heart. She was a *ton* diamond and beautiful. Fellstone might grow to love her.

Not that Gawain should care about that lord and his problems. Perhaps Cherish was turning him soft.

Yes, she had definitely turned him soft, he realized when Fiona's parlor games began. His demonic cousin had saddled him with Lord Pershing, Lady Yvonne, and Margaret again. They came in dead last, as usual. This time, he took it in good spirits and did not mind that Lord Pershing snored on the settee the entire time, or that Lady Yvonne thought London and Paris were countries, or that Margaret cheered more heartily for Cherish's team than her own.

He could not blame Margaret for adoring Cherish. He adored her, too.

And he made this eminently clear to Cherish when they retired to bed later that evening.

EPILOGUE

Northam Hall
Brighton, England
August, 1818

G AWAIN STOOD ON the terrace of Northam Hall with Reggie on a particularly fine summer's day as they watched their wives engage in lawn games with the other house party guests. Reggie, much matured and proving to be of great help in managing the Bromleigh properties, had married Margaret three months ago, and appeared as besotted with the sweet peahen as Gawain was with Cherish.

The current game was archery, and teammates Margaret and Cherish were demolishing their competition. "You are a terrible influence on Cherish," Reggie jestingly remarked. "She is as ruthless as you and Fiona at these games, not to mention she is turning Margaret into a competitive beast with killer instincts. We should not have allowed them to team up. They are showing no mercy to the others."

Gawain laughed. "I shall be content so long as they beat Fiona's team. Stomp on them. Rout them. Annihilate them."

"Uncle Gawain!" Reggie tried to appear disapproving, but Gawain saw the twinkle in his eyes and knew he was just as eager to see Fiona defeated. They loved her, of course. But Gawain was out for sweet revenge for the team she had saddled him with during her own house party last year.

What misery!

And Fiona had yet to stop teasing him about it.

His friends, Camborne and Lynton, had admired her diabolical genius when told about the torment she had put him through. Those Silver Dukes would arrive soon, but Gawain was already exacting this harmless prank on Fiona. Why wait when the perfect opportunity had already presented itself?

And what could be sweeter revenge than to have Cherish and Margaret, the two sweetest and gentlest ladies at this party, defeat her?

"You invited Pershing just to stick him on Fiona's team, didn't you?" Reggie accused. "Lord, he's so drunk, I'm surprised he is still standing. I ought to go over and take his place. He is going to shoot someone through the eye with his arrow, probably himself. The man is utterly useless. His arrows have yet to hit a single target."

Gawain stopped him. "Fiona is about to strangle him with his own bow. I cannot wait to watch this."

Durham now joined them, laughing just as hard as he and Reggie were as they watched Fiona chasing Pershing around the lawn. "You are cruel, Bromleigh."

Gawain grinned. "Pershing is too drunk to keep running for long. He'll pass out soon. I'll rescue him before Fiona actually strangles him," he said. "Oh, hell," he added a moment later. "Cherish is going to rescue him. Botheration—I had better get down there before she ends up with a black eye."

He raced onto the lawn and caught his wife gently around her increasing waist. "Love, you are in no condition to be mixing it up with those two."

"Fiona knows my condition and will be careful around me," she assured him.

"But Pershing doesn't. You are only four months along and hardly showing yet. I will have to kill him if he hurts you, accident or no."

She cast him a loving look. "Gawain, you are being apishly

protective again. But very well. For the sake of saving Pershing's life, go ahead and separate those two before Fiona knocks out one of his teeth. You know how competitive she is, so why torment her? You are having far too much fun with this."

"It is nothing to the agony she put me through last year. Although she did find me my perfect match, so I suppose I ought to be grateful. All right, I'll put Durham on her team tonight. He's a very smart fellow. I'll even let her team win, if that will make you happy." He gave Cherish a lingering kiss, and then ran off to haul Fiona off Pershing, who was sprawled on the grass and not moving. "He looks dead," Gawain muttered. "You didn't kill him, did you?"

"No, but it isn't for lack of trying," Fiona grumbled. "I can hear him snoring. Just leave him there. He is in no one's way and will eventually wake up on his own. I hope it rains on him."

Gawain glanced up at the sky that was a deep, cloudless blue. "No rain today."

"Too bad." Fiona sighed and returned to the other guests to finish the archery game her team could not possibly win, since Pershing had just forfeited his turn.

Gawain returned to Cherish's side, amazed by how exquisite she looked. She grew lovelier by the day—quite a feat, because she had always been strikingly beautiful. There was a serene beauty about her, an ethereal glow that radiated from within.

She had wrapped herself around his soul.

He was shamelessly happy in this marriage. But it was easy to love Cherish because—these cutthroat house party games aside—she was the kindest, sweetest, and most caring wife a husband could have.

"Gawain, I see Potter setting out refreshments on the terrace. Would you care for some lemonade?"

"No thank you, love." He had gone hard after her uncle, the Earl of Northam, because she was such a genuinely good person and had not deserved any of that oaf's cruel treatment. His villainous accomplices were now disgraced and imprisoned.

Gawain, with the assistance of Reggie, Durham, and London's finest Bow Street runner, Homer Barrow, had recovered all she was due to inherit. At his behest, the Crown had imposed a heavy fine on Northam, burdening his entailed estate so that he and his wife were forced to live on the brink of penury, as they deserved.

"Are you sure I cannot pour you a lemonade?" Cherish asked. "It is getting warm out here."

"I'm fine, sweetheart. Reggie, Durham, and I shared a bottle of brandy earlier."

"Hmm, no wonder you have a naughty glint in your eye. You are forbidden to carry me off into a quiet corner and kiss me senseless. Understood?"

"Is it so bad? I am only ever naughty with you."

She blushed. "Well, perhaps later."

Cherish, who truly did have a soft heart, had been quietly assisting the tenant farmers and staff who worked on Northam's entailed properties. They could not possibly make ends meet because Northam did not have the means to pay them due to that crushing fine imposed on him.

Gawain had no quarrel with how she chose to spend her own funds now that she had put her own holdings, Northam Hall and its farms, back in good order. She was a capable estate manager and knew what she was doing. He did not interfere other than to insist she not give so much as a ha'penny to her uncle and his greedy wife.

He was not certain she had obeyed him. But he wasn't going to look into it or ever confront her about it. If she took mercy on them, then so be it. This was who she was, and he loved her for all of her qualities. With her farms back in shape, she could easily afford to be generous.

She had also spent the year putting the manor house back in order. New paint colors and wallpaper for the walls that were light and breezy, and reflected the countryside and sea close by. New drapes and decorative pieces for each room. The result was an elegant, yet inviting and warm, seaside manor.

This party was Cherish's way of showing off her newly refurbished home.

Here was where they would spend their summers, while the rest of the year would be spent between London and the Bromleigh estate. Gawain was glad Cherish and Fiona would have these summer months to enjoy each other's company, for they were true friends and cared for each other as sisters. They had also taken Margaret into the fold now that she had married Reggie.

Margaret was sweet and adorable, but still a peahen. Well, catching up on all the education she had been denied was a daunting task, and Gawain had to give her credit for her diligence and enthusiasm for it.

"My love? You are lost in your thoughts."

He shook out of them and escorted Cherish onto the terrace now that Potter had finished setting out refreshments for their thirsty guests. "Not at all. I am merely plotting my next revenge on Fiona."

"Gawain!"

"All right, no more irking Fiona. I'll behave." They settled with their guests to enjoy the light fare of cakes and lemonade. He tried to be an attentive host, engaging the various friends in conversation and keeping an eye on Pershing as he awoke and stumbled off in the wrong direction. He sent one of the footmen after him.

But mostly he watched Cherish smile and chatter with the ladies in her company. A gentle breeze blew off the water and rustled through the trees that provided shade. Cherish's hair shimmered gold as dapples of sunlight adorned her locks and the wind ruffled a few curls. She glanced over at him with her big brandy eyes and cast him a beaming smile.

This was what she was—gold to his silver. Sweetness to his bullheadedness.

"Excuse me a moment," he said, leaving his guests to make his way toward Cherish. "My dear, I have need of you for a moment."

"Oh, have we forgotten something?"

He led her back inside the house. "Only this," he said, and kissed her with all the love he felt in his heart.

She laughed and returned his kiss with equal fervor. "I love you, Gawain."

"Mutual, sweetheart." He had his hand now protectively placed on her stomach and was shocked to feel a light flutter.

"That's your son," she said with an improbable certainty. "A miniature Silver Duke."

"Or a sweet version of you," he insisted.

But five months later, Cherish delivered a howling and healthy boy.

This Silver Duke was well pleased.

And more in love than ever with his wife.

THE END

Also by Meara Platt

FARTHINGALE SERIES
My Fair Lily
The Duke I'm Going To Marry
Rules For Reforming A Rake
A Midsummer's Kiss
The Viscount's Rose
Earl of Hearts
The Viscount and the Vicar's Daughter
A Duke For Adela
Marigold and the Marquess
The Make-Believe Marriage
If You Wished For Me
Never Dare A Duke
Capturing The Heart Of A Cameron

BOOK OF LOVE SERIES
The Look of Love
The Touch of Love
The Taste of Love
The Song of Love
The Scent of Love
The Kiss of Love
The Chance of Love
The Gift of Love
The Heart of Love
The Promise of Love
The Wonder of Love
The Journey of Love
The Treasure of Love

The Dance of Love
The Miracle of Love
The Hope of Love (novella)
The Dream of Love (novella)
The Remembrance of Love (novella)
All I Want For Christmas (novella)

MOONSTONE LANDING SERIES
Moonstone Landing (novella)
Moonstone Angel (novella)
The Moonstone Duke
The Moonstone Marquess
The Moonstone Major
The Moonstone Governess
The Moonstone Hero
The Moonstone Pirate

DARK GARDENS SERIES
Garden of Shadows
Garden of Light
Garden of Dragons
Garden of Destiny
Garden of Angels

SILVER DUKES
Cherish and the Duke
Moonlight and the Duke
Two Nights with the Duke

LYON'S DEN
The Lyon's Surprise
Kiss of the Lyon
Lyon in the Rough

THE BRAYDENS
A Match Made In Duty

Earl of Westcliff
Fortune's Dragon
Earl of Kinross
Earl of Alnwick
Tempting Taffy
Aislin
Genalynn
Pearls of Fire*
A Rescued Heart
*also in Pirates of Britannia series

DeWOLFE PACK ANGELS SERIES
Nobody's Angel
Kiss An Angel
Bhrodi's Angel

About the Author

Meara Platt is a USA Today bestselling author and an award winning, Amazon UK All-star. Her favorite place in all the world is England's Lake District, which may not come as a surprise since many of her stories are set in that idyllic landscape, including her award winning, fantasy romance Dark Gardens series. If you'd like to learn more about the ancient Fae prophecy that is about to unfold in the Dark Gardens series, as well as Meara's lighthearted, international bestselling Regency romances in the Farthingale series and Book of Love series, or her more emotional Moonstone Landing series and Braydens series, please visit Meara's website at www.mearaplatt.com.